WHEN SHE FELL

Karen Cole travelled round the world teaching English before she began writing. She lived in Cyprus for nineteen years where she wrote four popular thrillers, including the bestseller, *Deliver Me*. Karen has recently returned to her roots in the Cotswolds, where she lives with her family. *When She Fell* is her fifth novel.

Also by Karen Cole

Deliver Me
Deceive Me
Deny Me
Destroy Me

KAREN COLE

WHEN SHE FELL

QUERCUS

First published in Great Britain in 2022 by

QUERCUS

Quercus Editions Ltd
Carmelite House
50 Victoria Embankment
London EC4Y 0DZ

An Hachette UK company

A CIP catalogue record for this book is available
from the British Library

PB ISBN 978 1 52941 596 4
EB ISBN 978 1 52941 597 1

10 9 8 7 6 5 4 3 2 1

Typeset by CC Book Production
Printed and bound in Great Britain by Clays Ltd, Elcograf S.p.A.

Papers used by Quercus are from well-managed forests and other responsible sources.

For Jill

One

The book is waiting on my doormat when I wake up.

A normal book. Nothing unusual.

I pick it up, tear off the brown cardboard wrapping and run my fingers over its smooth cover. On the surface it's just another run-of-the-mill thriller. Publishers send them to me all the time, hoping I'll provide publicity by writing a good review on my blog or in the *Post*. From the looks of it, this one is no different from the rest – a twisty, not-so-mysterious mystery. I've read so many of them I can usually guess what will happen in the end.

On the front there's a picture of a sheer rock face with a small, silhouetted figure perched on top like a bird about to take flight. The title, *Falling*, is splashed across the page in slightly raised, dark blue letters and the author's name, Avery Lewis, is written underneath in slightly smaller font.

The blurb at the back informs me that it's the fourth in the Inspector Hegarty mysteries and that I won't be able to put it down.

Under the book there's a postcard from Dad who's on a skiing holiday in France. Chris, the half-brother I've never met, has added his name in large, clumsy letters at the bottom with a row of kisses. I can just imagine Olena sitting them both down in their luxurious chalet and forcing them to write it. I can hear her tinkling laugh as she takes off her fur hat, tosses her golden, blonde hair and bats her false eyelashes.

'Really? Do I have to?' Dad says in my imagination.

'Oh, yes, for me, please, my darling boy' (that's what she calls him, *darling boy*). 'They are your daughters after all.'

I tear the postcard neatly into four pieces and chuck it in the bin. I haven't had anything to do with Dad since I moved to England from Cyprus and I'm not about to start now.

Then I weigh the paperback in my hands and thumb the pages, inhaling its potent, new-book smell. At this moment, I have no idea how much this seemingly innocent novel is going to change my life. If I did, I'd probably make a bonfire in the garden and burn it or toss it in the bin along with Dad's postcard.

But I don't throw it away. Instead, I carry it, like the Trojan Horse it is, into the kitchen where Athena's sitting, hunched over a bowl of cereal. She glances up at me with bloodshot, sleepy eyes.

'What's that?' she croaks.

'Nothing exciting.' I put the book on the table and pour myself a coffee, glancing critically at my younger sister.

She looks rough. Her thick, brown hair is a mess. Her mascara is smudged, and her silky, teal crop top is stained with wine.

'What time did you get home last night?' I ask, trying not to sound judgemental.

'Twenty minutes ago, if it's any of your business.' She takes a slow sip of coffee and eyes me coldly over the rim of her mug. Her voice is hoarse as if she's been smoking all her life.

At least she's speaking to me today.

The things we both said last night linger in the air, poisoning the atmosphere. It started as a disagreement over money: our landlord has recently put the rent up and we've been having problems paying. Athena thinks we should accept Dad's 'generous offer of help'. She thinks I should forgive him and move on. But for me that's out of the question.

The argument became heated and soon morphed into a full-blown fight – personal and ugly. The past was weaponised. I think at one point I called Athena selfish, and I know she called me a coward.

Coward – the one word she knew would hurt the most.

Still, she's my sister. We'll forgive each other eventually. We always do.

'Where did you go last night?' I ask carefully, slotting a slice of bread into the toaster, staring out at our small, bedraggled garden and the cold, grey sky beyond.

'We ended up at some guy's house.' She shrugs vaguely and picks at her nail varnish.

I sigh. 'Haven't you got lectures today?' My annoyance is mixed with guilt. I promised myself I would look after Athena while she's living with me in London and, so far, I haven't done such a great job.

'I've got a seminar, but I think I'll skip it this morning. I feel like crap.' She stands up abruptly. 'I'm off to bed. Goodnight, Alex.'

I watch as she shuffles out the door. I can't believe the change in her. Athena has always been the model sister in our half-English, half-Cypriot family. Head girl at school. Voted by her classmates as most likely to succeed. While I was skipping school and generally rebelling against everything, Athena always strove to be perfect. As a teen-ager any grade less than A star would result in months of soul searching and furious study. Lately though, I hardly recognise her. She doesn't seem to care about her degree, and she's been running wild, as if, for all those years, the bad behaviour had been bottled up inside her and now someone had shaken the bottle and unscrewed the lid.

Oh well, what can I do? I'm not her mother.

She hasn't got a mother.

I try to prevent my thoughts from running down dark and familiar paths by flicking idly through the book I've been sent.

Falling.

On the last page, there's a short bio.

Avery Lewis was born in Cornwall. For many years she worked in London as an accountant at a large financial services firm before giving up the rat race to move to Cornwall where she lives with her husband and two children, a dog, a goat and seven chickens.

It sounds cute and homey, I think, and doesn't quite square with the photograph at the back of a slightly haughty-looking woman with sleek ash-blonde hair and dark, impenetrable eyes.

To Joe – all my love to infinity and beyond, says the dedication on the second page.

I'm guessing that Joe is Avery's husband and that she's a fan of the *Toy Story* movies.

Absent-mindedly, I take a bite of toast and start reading the first chapter.

Chapter One

No one knew who the dead woman was.

A dog walker found the body on the beach below the cliffs at Bosigran and alerted the police.

Detective Harry Hegarty had checked the missing persons register and spent all morning talking to people in the nearby villages but had failed to come up with any leads. There was no one who even came close to matching the dead woman's description. Now he was sitting in the caravan – his home until the renovations to his cottage were completed – listening to Radio 2 and staring at photos of the victim spread across the small, pull-out table.

The case was strange and perplexing. For one thing she didn't look like the kind of person who wouldn't be missed. Her clothes were expensive, and she was wearing a gold band on her ring finger. In her pocket was a paper napkin with a five-digit number on it. But apart from that and the wedding ring there had been nothing about her person to identify her. She had no purse, no credit cards and no distinguishing marks. Also, the mauve silk shirt and tight skirt she'd been wearing weren't exactly suitable for a walk in the country.

It was almost as if she'd dropped from the sky and for one crazy moment it occurred to him that she could have fallen from a plane. It wasn't as ridiculous as it sounded. It had happened before. He remembered reading about it in the papers. A Kenyan stowaway, presumably an illegal immigrant, had fallen from the landing gear compartment as a plane was landing in London.

But Bosigran cliffs weren't under a flight path and the autopsy revealed that the woman's injuries were probably caused by a fall of about twenty-six metres, exactly the height of the cliffs. In Hegarty's view, the most likely explanation was suicide. But if that was the case, how had she got there? There was no vehicle in the small car

park near the site. Had she walked to the cliff edge and if so, from
where? The nearest houses were several miles away.

I reach the end of the page and close the book with a snap.
Then I yawn and glance at my watch.

7.10 am. Shit.

I'm going to be late for work unless I hurry. I can't afford
to be late. They're already talking about downsizing at the
paper, and I'm pretty sure there's a target on my back. Last
in, first out. I don't want to give them any excuse to get
rid of me. If I lost my job, then Athena and I really would
be in trouble. I drain my coffee, pull on my coat and scarf
and dash out the door, down the road to the tube station.

It's not my day. The train stops halfway along the line
and while we're stuck at the station, a bored voice on the
intercom announces something about a fault on the line.
I tut and raise my eyebrows along with all the other pas-
sengers and I follow the confused and disgruntled crowd
to the replacement bus that's been laid on.

Not only that, but the elevator in our building is broken
and I have to run up four flights of stairs to get to our office.
When I finally arrive, I'm dishevelled and short of breath
and the morning briefing has already started.

Everyone is sitting round the dark wood, oval table in
the meeting room.

'Nice of you to grace us with your presence, Alex,' Lou says sarcastically as I sidle in, trying my best to be invisible.

'I'm so sorry, the train was . . .'

She casts a withering look my way and raises her hand to shush me.

'Dan was just telling us this great idea he has for a feature on immigration,' she says. 'Please carry on, Dan.'

Dan smiles, a slight, smug lift of the lips, and begins to expound on his theme as I creep into a seat at the table, getting out my iPad as silently as possible.

'And so, I want to get away from the sense of immigrants as faceless numbers and look at the individual experience . . .' he's saying.

I drift off. I'm still brooding over my argument with Athena last night and our dire financial situation. She has a point. We're already barely scraping rent. But the thought of accepting money from Dad is repugnant. There must be another way. I need to work out how to get more advertising for my blog or maybe I can start working weekends. I noticed they were hiring at the Turkish café by the tube station. How hard could it be to get a job there? Athena could work weekends too. It'll be okay. We will manage.

'How about you, Alex?' Lou's question jolts me out of my thoughts, and I start and blush.

'Erm, sorry I didn't catch what you said.'

She purses her lips. 'What have you got for us? Did you manage to get that interview with Gemma K?'

Gemma K is a singer, who used to be part of a successful pop band in the nineties. She's just written an autobiography which is currently topping the bestseller charts. I've been trying to contact her for an interview for several days without any success.

'Not yet,' I mumble. 'I'm working on it.'

'That's a shame.' Lou frowns and taps her fingernails impatiently on the desk. 'Well, have you got anything else for us in the meantime?'

'Um . . . I was thinking about writing something about traditional children's books and how young girls are stereotyped,' I improvise.

Lou's frown deepens. 'Maybe, if you can find a new angle. But I think that topic has already been done to death.' She closes her file and stretches her mouth into a tight smile. 'Never mind, Alex, I'm sure you'll think of something fantastic.'

Those are the words she says. But her eyes say something else. Something that sounds to me very much like, 'Your days are numbered at this paper, Alex. You'd better start packing up your things and looking for another job.'

Trying to stay positive, I head to my desk and phone Gemma K's publicist again.

He sounds irritated and preoccupied. 'Gemma's out of the country until next week, I already told you that.'

'Well, maybe we could organise a video call or . . .'

'I don't think so,' he cuts me off. 'Look, we'll get back to you when she has time, okay?' he says and hangs up before I have time to reply.

I sigh and log into my computer, read and answer a few emails. Then I do some research on Gemma K just in case by some miracle I ever manage to get an interview with her. I read about her teenage struggles with drug addiction and her on/off relationship with the lead guitarist who apparently has been unfaithful to her several times.

Then, on impulse, I type Avery Lewis into the search engine.

She pops up on Goodreads as the author of *Little Nobody*, the first Harry Hegarty novel, and on a few other sites. There are a couple of photos: a black and white picture of her gazing dreamily into the distance, and another where she's resting her chin on her hands and smiling winsomely at the camera.

Underneath the images there's a news piece. From the *Cornish Gazette*, dated just over ten months ago.

Intrigued, I click on it and find myself looking at a photo of a bleak stretch of Cornish coast draped with police tape flapping in the wind. I scroll down and read the accompanying article.

Local Woman Believed Drowned

A local woman who went missing a week ago is believed to have lost her footing and been swept away to sea, police said yesterday after her belongings were found by a hiker on the cliffs at Bosigran.

Police are keeping all lines of enquiry open and have appealed to the local community for information after Avery Lewis, 41, disappeared in a lonely spot at the base of Bosigran cliffs.

'I'm not giving up on her yet,' her husband Joseph Lewis, 36, told the Gazette. *'She could still be alive.'*

Avery!

Is she dead? I hope not. But it seems pretty likely all things considered. I scroll down, curious to see if there's any more information. But there's nothing to suggest she turned up alive.

I scan the news story again.

Bosigran. My eye snags on the word and my breath hooks in my throat. Wasn't that the place . . .?

What a weird coincidence.

Avery Lewis fell off the cliffs at Bosigran – in exactly the same place as the character in her book.

Two

When I arrive home at the end of the day, Athena's bedroom door is firmly shut. In the kitchen the dishes are piled high by the sink, the counter is covered with crumbs and there's an open pot of peanut butter on the table with the knife still wedged inside. In the living room Athena's folders and books are scattered everywhere and the snake's cage is wide open. I sigh and look in the bedding at the bottom of its tank. Sometimes it buries itself in the straw. But it's not there, which only means one thing: it's loose somewhere in the flat.

Why did I agree to Athena getting a snake in the first place? The last time it disappeared it was missing for days, and we finally found it coiled on a ledge halfway up the chimney.

I bite back a wave of fear-fuelled anger. I can just about

cope with the creature when I know where it is. When I don't, I'm constantly on edge, wondering when it's going to slither up behind me and slide its way up my leg. I can't help feeling that on some level Athena's done this deliberately as a way of getting back at me for our argument last night.

I storm to her room and hammer on the door.

'Yeah?'

She's sitting on her bed looking at her laptop and the snake is winding itself around her shoulder, its flicking tongue probing the air.

I shudder. 'I've been at work all day,' I say. 'Do you think that maybe you could get out of bed and clean up the kitchen? And can you put that thing back in its cage please?'

Athena doesn't look up. 'She's not a thing. Her name's Ruby and she's not doing you any harm.'

'Yes, but I can't relax when she's out of her cage.'

'She needs her exercise,' she mumbles. Then she tips her head back and I see that her eyes are red from crying. My anger immediately dissolves. Athena rarely cries. Like me she learned to hide her feelings at a young age, so I know it must be something serious.

'What's up, Athie?' I ask more gently.

'It's nothing,' she says.

'It must be something. What is it? Your course? A boy? You know they're not worth it.'

Athena strokes Ruby's tail. 'I don't want to talk about it.'

'Okay. But you know I'm always here if you do.'

'I know.' She nods and stands up. 'I'll put Ruby in her cage, if you want.'

'It's okay. I'm going to go out for a run anyway. You can keep her out until I get back.'

I slip on a T-shirt, leggings and running shoes. Then I head across the road to the woods opposite our flat. It's a cold winter's day and the ground is hard and compacted with frost. My breath clouds in the air as I follow my usual route into Epping Forest, past a couple of dog walkers and another runner snorting like a bull. A weak sun breaks through the branches of the trees, creating small pools of light where the frost has melted and I settle into a steady rhythm, enjoying the feeling of power in my limbs and the clarity that physical effort brings.

I started running a few years ago. After I left university, I went through a rough patch. I was having trouble finding a job and my long-term boyfriend, Isaac, broke up with me because he wanted a commitment that I wasn't willing to give. After several lonely months of firing off applications and attending interviews with no response, I became depressed to the point where I found it hard to get out of bed in the morning. Eventually, worried that I was going to turn out like my mother and realising that I needed to do something, I went to the doctor, who, amongst other things, suggested that running might help.

I haven't stopped since. I love the way it makes me feel. When I run, all my worries slough off like Ruby shedding her skin and I know that I can tackle anything the world throws at me. More than once, I've come up with the solution to a difficult problem while on a run.

Today, as I skirt the edge of the lake, I think about Avery Lewis. How did she end up falling off a cliff in the same place as the character in her book? Was she inspired by her own writing to make some dramatic suicidal gesture? Instinctively I know that her death and the strange connection with her novel will make a good news feature. I'm badly in need of a story to impress Lou and I think this just might be the one.

I pass another jogger, who nods briskly at me. I smile back vaguely. I'm trying to think of a headline that sums up the mystery and is also pithy and engaging. 'A Case of Life imitating Art' maybe, or 'The Mysterious Death of the Thriller Writer'. Yes, I like the second one. Who doesn't love a mystery? But I need more information about Avery Lewis before I start writing and the obvious course of action is to speak to her publisher to see what I can find out.

Back home, I peel off my sweaty clothes and leap into the shower. After washing and dressing, I root around in the freezer and pry out some frozen chicken, chips and peas. That'll do, I think. I'm far too tired and preoccupied to cook anything more complicated.

Then I knock softly on Athena's door and open it carefully.

'Athie, do you want something to eat?'

No answer. She's fast asleep in bed. The covers have slipped off onto the floor. She's curled up on her side in a foetal position. Her cheeks are faintly flushed and her eye-lids flickering. She looks young and innocent, and I feel an unexpected surge of love. Our argument last night doesn't seem important anymore. I pick up her duvet, gently tuck it around her and kiss her on the nose. Whatever's been bothering her, sleep will probably help.

In the living room with Netflix on and Ruby safely back in her cage, I eat my dinner alone with the plate balanced on my lap. I'm reaching the end of the second season of *Peaky Blinders* and it's getting exciting, but this evening I'm finding it hard to focus, and after a while I pause the TV, realising I have no idea what's just happened.

I put my plate in the dishwasher and pace the kitchen. I can't stop thinking about Avery Lewis. My eye strays to the paperback, still lying on the kitchen table where I left it this morning. I pick it up and flick through the pages to the acknowledgements at the back.

Firstly, I want to thank my agent Olivia Brown for always having my back and I'd also like to express my gratitude to my brilliant editor, Lucy Rivers . . .

Olivia Brown.

I switch on my laptop and type in her name. It doesn't take long to find her. A photo of a cheerful-looking young woman pops up on the screen. According to Google, she works for a small literary agency called Peppercorn Books and on her profile it says that she's interested in representing young adult and psychological thrillers as well as literary fiction. There's a list of her more famous clients. And at the bottom of the page there's also a contact phone number and email address.

I don't waste any time. Once I've made up my mind, I can be laser-focused on the task in hand. Composing my message carefully, I explain that I work for the *Post* and would love to interview Avery Lewis for an article I'm writing about her new novel, *Falling*. I know that Avery's probably dead and that therefore the chances of actually getting an interview are very small, but it'll be interesting to see how Olivia answers. I add that I'm a huge fan and that I've read all her books. (A small white lie that can be soon remedied if I actually get any response.) When I'm done, I read my message through, checking for grammar and spelling mistakes. Then I press send.

Next, I fire off a message to the editor mentioned in the acknowledgements, thanking her for the copy of *Falling* she sent me and asking for more information about Avery.

Then, feeling tired, even though it's only ten o'clock, I switch off my laptop and head to bed.

Passing Athena's room, I can hear that she's awake and talking in a low voice to someone on the phone. One of her friends in Cyprus, I guess. Perhaps she's just homesick, after all. It's been such a long time since we've been back. I pop my head round the door and say goodnight. Then, shivering in our unheated bathroom, I brush my teeth, wriggle out of my clothes and dive under the duvet.

Snuggled under the covers, I open the book on my bedside table, a historical novel set in Tudor England.

This is my favourite part of the day when I finally curl up with a good book and immerse myself in another world, a world where my own worries and troubles aren't important. I don't remember a time when I didn't love books. Many of my happiest memories of my mother are of her reading to me. We would sit together on summer evenings on the swing seat in our garden watching the sun sink into the sea and she would read me anything and everything – from fairy tales to books about spiders and space. Somehow for me, stories became synonymous with that feeling of being close to her. The smell of her. The sense of complete safety and love.

But tonight, that feeling eludes me. I'm still on edge and my mind is crowded with questions. All I can think about is Avery Lewis and her mysterious death.

I put the book face down on the bedside table. Then, sighing and rubbing my eyes, I climb out of bed, wrap my dressing gown around me and wander into the living room.

Falling is still there on the coffee table, waiting for me as if it knows I'm coming. I snatch it up and scuttle back to my bed, hugging it to my chest.

Under the covers, in a pool of lamplight, I start to read the second chapter.

Initially, I'm confused and a little annoyed because there's nothing more about DI Hegarty, who I was starting to like. Instead, the narrative jumps backwards in time, and describes a young couple called Rebecca and John, who've just moved to the country to start a new life.

Rebecca's heart sank as they drove towards the village of Sancreed. The winding road became narrower and narrower, and she could no longer see the horizon. It felt like a metaphor for her life – as if her life was getting narrower, her choices more limited with every mile.

Things didn't improve when they arrived at their destination. The village was so tiny, barely more than a hamlet. There was nothing there, just a small church and village green and lots of smelly, old farm buildings. To someone like her who loved the hustle and bustle of city life it seemed dead. She was even more dismayed when John showed her their new home. The farmhouse they'd bought, sight unseen, was barely habitable and surrounded by miserable, scrubby fields.

As they climbed out of the Range Rover, it hit her with full force. This was a crazy, foolhardy venture. They'd given up everything for this dream; their friends, their jobs, their flat. But John had been so unhappy in London that in the end, she would have agreed to anything. Perhaps, she'd convinced herself, it was what they needed to mend their relationship. Perhaps this would be a fresh start.

She forced herself to smile at John, who was in the middle of telling her all his grandiose plans for the farmhouse. He had so many ideas and he was zipping from place to place and stumbling over his words in his eagerness to share them. She was glad that he seemed finally happy after those miserable months in London, but at the same time, she was worried that this mood wouldn't last. She'd seen him like this before and in her experience, this brittle period of frenzied energy and joy would inevitably be followed by a deep slump.

'Here, look at this,' he said, leading her round the side of the farmhouse and pointing at an old barn half hidden by overgrown hydrangea bushes. 'We'll convert this into a holiday cottage. We'll make a fortune in the summer renting it out to tourists.'

Rebecca inspected the building doubtfully. It was little better than a pile of rubble. How would they afford to do all the renovations necessary when they'd already sunk all their money into the mortgage?

There follows a description of Rebecca and John's life on the farm and all the trials and tribulations of trying to start life in a remote village in the far west of Cornwall.

On the face of it, they're a normal urban couple trying to make a go of it in the country. It could be a cosy and amusing memoir, but this is something very different. Gradually and subtly, it becomes clear that all is not well between Rebecca and John. And I find myself gripped, fascinated by their dysfunctional relationship. But it's not a comfortable read. John reminds me too much of my own father and I'm worried that things will not turn out well for Rebecca in the end.

I flick ahead. Rebecca and her husband John have been in their new home for six months and his behaviour is becoming increasingly erratic.

Rebecca had learned to read his mood the way a beaten dog reads its master's temper or the way a sailor learns to map the vagaries of the sea. It was a simple matter of survival. Today his mood was choppy and there was a squall on the horizon. When he was in this frame of mind, she knew she had to tread lightly and choose her words carefully.

She found him sitting at the kitchen table, his head in his hands, a row of empty beer bottles lined up next to him.

'The crop's ruined,' he said, lifting his beautiful, sea-green eyes to hers. She'd fallen in love with those eyes, and they still had the power to disarm her. But right now, they were bloodshot and dull with anger and resentment. This is all your fault, they seemed to say.

'There's always next year,' she said resting a hand on his shoulder. He brushed it off angrily.

'You don't understand,' he snapped. 'There won't be a next year. We've got no money. They're going to repossess the farm.'

Rebecca stared open-mouthed at him. She knew that they were in financial difficulty, but she hadn't realised how dire the situation was.

'Really? They're going to repossess?'

He nodded mutely, pulled a letter from his pocket and handed it to her.

It was from the bank. A final demand.

'Okay,' she said, breathing deeply. This was bad, but she wasn't about to give up without a fight. They could get through this. They just needed to think positively.

'It's okay, we can do this,' she said. 'We just need to tighten our belts that's all. Work out where we can make savings.' She took out a piece of paper, sat down at the kitchen table and started a list. In her experience there was almost no problem a checklist couldn't solve.

'We could sell the boat for a start,' she said. She had never understood why John had bought the boat in the first place. He didn't even know how to sail. John didn't answer and she looked at all the empty beer bottles on the table, feeling a sudden burst of frustration. 'And you know we'd save a lot of money if you cut down on your drinking.'

She knew as soon as the words were out of her mouth that she'd made a mistake. His face turned puce and there was that tell-tale vein in his neck bulging.

'That's rich coming from you,' he growled, slamming his fist down on the table. 'Remind me again, how much was it you spent on a train ticket to London last week?'

That was hardly fair. She'd sold her car to finance this venture. How else was she supposed to travel?

'I miss London. I miss all my friends. Are you suggesting I shouldn't see my friends anymore?'

That apparently was the last straw. 'Fucking hell,' he exploded. 'You're a miserable bitch, aren't you?'

'Please don't shout at me,' she said, trying to stay calm.

His voice got louder, and he stood up brandishing his beer bottle. 'I'll shout if I fucking want to . . .' He wasn't a powerfully built man, but he was bigger than her and for a moment Rebecca was scared that he would hit her with the bottle. But at the last minute he changed his mind and flung it at the wall. The bottle smashed and the glass shattered into thousands of tiny, glittering shards.

I close the book, feeling sick I haven't spoken to my father in years, but I suppose I'll never completely escape him. He's always there with me, a zombie memory, buried in a shallow grave.

'Leave me alone, Dad,' I say under my breath, and I turn off the lamp and close my eyes, trying to think of happier things, happier times when it was just me, Mum and Athena.

Three

In the dream I'm a child again and I'm in our old back garden in Cyprus. It's a scorching day and I've just come home from school. Bright pink bougainvillea trails along the wall and the dusty, silver-green olive trees in the field behind our garden droop in the hot, dry air. More than anything, I want to cool off in the swimming pool but when I dip my toe in the water, I see that it's full of dead and dying insects. I pick up the net and drag it listlessly through the water, scooping up all the cockroaches and ants the way my dad showed me, but every time I tip their carcasses into the field over the wall and return to the pool, I find they've multiplied. I clean faster, running to empty the net but to no avail. The numbers keep growing like a biblical plague and soon the water is a thick soup of twitching, drowning insects. Then there is no more room for them in the pool, and they teem out, crawling over the paving stones towards me.

I wake up gasping for breath and soaked with sweat.

It takes me several panicked seconds to realise where and when I am. I'm an adult and I'm in my small bedroom inside the flat I rent in Highams Park. Gradually my heart rate returns to normal. I sit up, breathing slowly. Everything's okay. I am safe.

In the kitchen Athena is clattering around making pancakes. The radio is playing a rap song and she's dancing to it as she whisks the eggs and milk. She seems much fresher and happier than yesterday.

'Do you want one?' she asks breezily.

'No thanks, I'm okay. You're in a good mood.'

'Nothing like a good night's sleep,' she says.

I make myself a hot chocolate and defrost a croissant in the microwave. My Saturday morning treat. Sitting by the window, I check my phone. There are a couple of messages from friends suggesting we meet up tonight. There's no response from Avery's editor but to my surprise, her agent, Olivia Brown, has already replied to my email.

Dear Alexandra,

I'm so thrilled to hear that you enjoyed Falling. *It's one of my favourites too. Avery Lewis was a fabulous author. Unfortunately, I'm sorry to inform you that an interview will not be possible as she passed away unexpectedly, ten months ago. We're all devastated here at Peppercorn Books. Avery Lewis was not only a valued client but also a friend. However, if you have any questions, please do not hesitate to contact me and I will try to answer them as best I can.*

Warm regards,

Olivia

I read it again, a wave of unexpected sadness washing over me. Avery Lewis is dead. I knew that she probably was, but there was a part of me that had hoped that she might still be alive.

I start drafting a list of questions to ask Olivia in my notebook, but halfway through I put down my pen and stare out of the window at our small, overgrown garden. I won't get the kind of answers I need from an agent, even if she was a friend of Avery's. To get to the heart of this mystery I need to understand who Avery was. I mean the real Avery, not her professional persona. And there's only one way to do that. Standing up, I scrunch up the list and chuck it into the wastepaper bin. Then I sit cross-legged on the sofa, my laptop balanced on my knees and log into Google Maps. I type Bosigran Cliffs into the search bar. And sure enough, it appears on my screen. The place is in the far west of Cornwall, right on the coast marked with an image of a hiker in an upside-down green teardrop. I shudder as I try not to picture that hiker plummeting over the edge and I drag the map inland with my cursor. A few seconds later I find what I'm looking for and the hairs on the back of my neck stand up.

A few miles from Bosigran: there it is: a place called Sancreed.

Sancreed. It's a real place! I zoom in and see that there is a Sancreed village hall and a Sancreed parish church. There are a couple of holiday cottages nearby, which gives me an idea. *'We'll convert this into a holiday cottage,'* John said.

It's a long shot, but worth a try. After all, I'd thought that Sancreed was fictional, and it has turned out to be real. What else in the story might be based on fact? Feeling a flutter of excitement, I open a new tab and type in Accommodation – holiday cottages – Sancreed. The first picture to appear on my screen is of a place called the Old Barn. I enlarge the photograph and peer at it closely. It's a small, grey, stone building next to a house called Foxton Farm, with a sloping, slate roof and a wonky, stone staircase leading up to a bright blue-painted door. It looks a bit ramshackle, but some obvious attempts have been made to prettify it. There are hanging baskets outside the door, an old carriage wheel propped up against the wall and a neatly trimmed hydrangea bush.

A hydrangea.

I pick up my copy of *Falling* and flick back to the pages I read last night. Yes, I remembered correctly: *an old barn half hidden by overgrown hydrangea bushes.* Of course, in the book the roof was broken and the building was a ruin but it's not inconceivable, in fact I think it's quite likely, that this was the place that Avery was describing. I feel a vibration, a kind of humming in the air – the feeling I get when I know I'm on to a great story. Perhaps if I do this right, it'll be enough to convince Lou that she can't afford to lose me. Holding my breath, I click on the bookings and see that the cottage is available next week.

Then I stand up and wander out into our tiny garden. Outside the sky is heavy and grey, pressing down on the city. The next-door neighbour's tabby cat is stalking along the fence and our damp washing hangs limply on the line in the cold, still air. Someone is using a leaf blower in a neighbouring garden. The sound bores into my head.

It would be good for us both to get away from London for a while, I think.

Four

On Monday morning I get to work early and pitch my idea about Avery Lewis to Lou in our small office kitchen.

'It's definitely got potential,' she says slowly, dipping her herbal teabag into the Badass Boss mug that Dan bought her for Christmas. 'But I still need your piece on Gemma K.'

'I'm working on it. I'll get it finished today. I promise.'

'Mm,' she says absent-mindedly. She's been distracted by something on her phone. She reads it, chuckling drily to herself. She's in a relatively good mood this morning. It's probably the best chance I'll have to persuade her to allow me to pursue this story. I take a deep breath and smile brightly. 'I was wondering if you could let me have a few days down in Cornwall for research.'

She looks up from her phone, her eyes narrowing. 'Why do you need to go all the way to Cornwall?'

'I don't know.' I struggle to put my thoughts into words. 'I feel I'm more likely to find out what really happened if I go to see the place where she lived and where she died, and I can add some local colour for the reader.'

She shrugs. 'Well, you've got some annual leave left, haven't you? Perhaps you could take a few days off next week, have a little break down in Cornwall.'

'Really? Thank you!'

Her face almost cracks into a smile. 'That's okay. But I still need the Gemma K copy ASAP.'

She takes a sip of tea and moves towards the door.

'I'll need to stay in a holiday cottage,' I blurt. 'Or a hotel. Is there any chance the paper could pay . . .?'

I break off as I see her expression.

'Absolutely not, Alex,' she says firmly. 'Now get that Gemma K piece finished. I want it by five today.' And she sweeps out of the room.

I watch her leave, sipping my black coffee. No one's remembered to bring milk as usual. I didn't really expect her to pay for the trip, but it was worth a shot.

I spend the rest of the morning typing up my piece on Gemma K. I'm not going to get an interview with her, but it'll have to do without. By lunchtime I've cobbled together something that's passable. I email it to Lou and then sit at my desk eating an egg mayo sandwich and checking my bank account. There's two thousand pounds in it. The last of the money Mum left me in her will.

It's an investment, I tell myself. Opening the holiday cottage website, I find the house in Sancreed that I've pinned, and make a booking for five nights. Three hundred and twelve pounds. Then I email the owner for directions.

When I get home Athena is at the kitchen table working on an essay.

'You've got reading week coming up next week, right?' I say.

She looks up curiously, tucking her hair behind her ears.

'Yeah. Why?'

'How do you fancy a trip to Cornwall?'

Five

As we approach Sancreed the sky grows overcast and the road becomes narrower until it's too tight for more than one vehicle to pass. The hedges on either side rear up like prison walls and it feels as though we are driving down a long, dark tunnel. I can't see anything except the thin ribbon of road ahead. I'm beginning to think that we are lost, and this drive might never end.

'Are you sure we're going the right way?' Athena says. She's just woken up and is blinking sleepily. 'I feel like we're in a fairy tale. What's the one where the forest grows up and the prince hacks it down to rescue the princess? Mum used to read it to us. Do you remember?'

'Sleeping Beauty.'

'That's the one.'

'Seriously, Alex, are we lost?' she says after a few minutes of silent driving.

'The Sat Nav said this way.'

'Yeah well. I read about a guy in Canada who drove into a lake following his GPS and there was a Belgian woman who drove all the way to Croatia on her way to pick up her friend from the railway station.' Athena goes on to list a long series of Sat Nav mishaps. 'This is just the sort of back of beyond place where global positioning doesn't work well,' she concludes gloomily.

I'm only half listening. I'm thinking about Avery and Joseph Lewis. What made them decide to move here? Were they lured by the dream of a self-sufficient life in the country like Rebecca and John in *Falling*? I wonder if Avery felt the same sense of foreboding as Rebecca as she drove down these same roads and I give a small involuntary shudder. *The winding road became narrower and narrower, and she could no longer see the horizon. It felt like a metaphor for her life.*

The words from the book have seeped into my consciousness and I feel inexplicably uneasy and tense. My shoulders hunch tightly over the steering wheel and it's only when we finally reach the village, the open green and the small, grey stone church that I breathe a sigh of relief.

Foxton Farm is tucked up a narrow, unpaved road on the far side of the village. We roll up over the gravel driveway and park outside the main farm building. Opposite is a small, grey stone cottage with a blue door which must be the Old Barn. Maybe it's the drizzle that has started drifting out of a blank, grey sky but my first impressions are of a dreary and unappealing place.

'Mm, it's not quite the bucolic paradise I was imagining,' Athena sighs.

'Come on, it's not that bad,' I say, trying to convince myself. Everything is damp and dripping. A couple of bedraggled-looking crows are pecking at the muddy field beyond the wooden fence and rusted-up farm machinery is lying around. The whole place has an abandoned air and there's nobody here to greet us. There's no sign of the goat mentioned in Avery's bio, but I can hear chickens squawking somewhere nearby.

'Where do you think the owner is?' Athena says. 'Should we knock on the door of the house?'

'No, he said the key would be under the flowerpot.'

Sure enough, we find the key hidden under an empty pot on the windowsill. I guess security isn't much of an issue in this isolated spot. I slide the key into the lock, let us in, and we dump our suitcases in the small, cosy living room.

'It's not so bad inside,' Athena says grudgingly, as we inspect the rest of the cottage. There's a small, recently refurbished bathroom and two clean and comfortable-looking bedrooms. Both bedrooms look as if they've been decorated by a teenaged girl. There are two small four-poster beds with floaty-looking, white curtains and fairy lights draped across the top and pictures of gold and pink butterflies on the wall.

I make us a cup of tea in the kitchen-cum-living room. From the window there's a view of the farmhouse, grey and dour in the late afternoon light, and a small digger abandoned in the mud.

Well, we're not here to have a good time, I think.

Athena flings herself down on the sofa and tries unsuccessfully to connect to the WiFi.

'Oh God, it's not working, where's the code?' she says. After a fruitless search, she eventually gives up and flicks through the various brochures left on the coffee table.

'Anything interesting?' I ask.

'There's an open-air theatre that looks quite nice though it could be a bit cold at this time of year and oh, my God – I don't know if I can stand the excitement – there are some tin mines we can visit.'

'What? I love tin mines. I've always been fascinated by tin,' I say and she laughs. She seems to have cheered up since yesterday and I am hopeful that this week will do her good. 'I'm here to work, anyway. You should too,' I add. 'That was the whole point of bringing you here, so you could get on with your course work away from distractions.'

'Yeah, I know.' She sighs.

On the walls there are prints of local beauty spots, and

on a shelf above the TV there are some board games and a few books: a couple of guides to Cornwall, a book about the archaeological sites nearby, a well-thumbed copy of *Wuthering Heights*, *Jamaica Inn* by Daphne du Maurier, and a murder mystery by Avery Lewis. Not *Falling* but the first DI Hegarty mystery, *Little Nobody*. I pull it out and examine the back cover.

Athena is still leafing through pamphlets and brochures.

'We could go to St Ives, I suppose. Or . . . Ooh, we can go on a boat trip to see dolphins. I've always wanted to see dolphins. Alex! Promise me we'll go to see the dolphins.'

'Um, maybe,' I say looking dubiously over her shoulder at the price list. I sit down next to her and read through the folder of instructions the owner has left. Then I open my bag and take out the copy of *Falling* I've brought with me.

'Which room do you want?' Athena stands up, picking up her suitcase.

'I don't mind. You chose,' I say distractedly. I've opened the book and have started reading chapter four. I'm already engrossed as John and Rebecca's relationship deteriorates.

John was standing in the doorway of the kitchen, eyeing Rebecca coldly as she mopped up the muddy footprints left by Brian.

'What the fuck do you think you look like in that top?' he said.

Rebecca stopped mopping and stared at him in surprise. Brian had been round to fix their leaking pipes and they'd just been having

36

a pleasant beer and chat with him. John had been joking and smiling then. But now that Brian had left the atmosphere had suddenly soured.

'What's wrong with it?' she asked, fiddling self-consciously with the buttons.

'You can see right through it. You look like a whore.'

Was he joking? She couldn't always tell. Sometimes he said hurtful things that he later claimed had been in jest. Or perhaps it was his weird way of coming on to her. He'd complained recently that their sex life needed spicing up. Perhaps this was a kind of role play.

'I saw the way that old perve was looking at you. And the way you were flirting with him.'

Rebecca was baffled. 'Who? You mean Brian?' Brian was a pleasant, jovial man with thinning white hair and a steady stream of funny anecdotes about his grandchildren. She wasn't sure what she'd said that could be construed as flirting or why John would be jealous of him.

'Don't be daft,' she laughed. 'Brian must be at least sixty-five.'

She expected him to laugh too. Sometimes she could coax him out of a bad mood with humour. But when she looked up, John certainly wasn't laughing. His face was red with anger, his fists clenched tightly by his sides.

'Shut the fuck up. I know what I fucking saw,' he spat. And without warning, he lurched forward and gripped her arm.

'Let go . . . you're hurting me . . .' she protested.

But he had that look in his eyes. The one that meant there was

37

no reaching him. And with a swift sudden movement he twisted her
arm behind her back and pushed her forward, ramming her head
into the kitchen counter.

A car door slams outside, and I start, nearly dropping the book. My hands are trembling as I turn over the corner of a page to keep my place and put it on the coffee table. The argument between John and Rebecca is painful to read. The jealousy and controlling behaviour is all too familiar.

Dragging myself out of the book and back to the present, I peer out of the window and see that a Range Rover has pulled up. A young woman is lifting shopping bags out of the boot, a man in a raincoat is gesticulating, and a young chocolate Labrador is scampering around barking manically. The man must be Avery's husband, Joseph Lewis, I think, with a thrill of excitement. But who is the young woman? Surely he hasn't replaced Avery already?

Fired up with curiosity, I pull on my boots and dash to the door.

As I approach the car, the dog bounds up to me, splashing through a puddle and jumping up, nearly knocking me over in his enthusiasm.

'Barney! Come here!' The man turns. He's wearing black wellies and his face is half hidden in the hood of his dark green raincoat.

'I'm so sorry,' he says, striding over and yanking the dog by the collar.

'It's okay. I like dogs,' I say, brushing muddy pawprints from my top.

He pushes back his hood, the ghost of a smile on his lips.

'I'm Joe. Joe Lewis,' he says, shaking my hand.

I am taken aback by his appearance and blood burns in my cheeks because I can't help thinking of what I've just been reading. I don't know what I was expecting. I suppose subconsciously I must have been thinking that Joe would look like John, the husband in Avery's book with beautiful green eyes glowering with resentment and thinly suppressed rage. The man in front of me is nothing like my image of John. He's ordinary-looking, maybe a little gaunt, with a well-trimmed beard and curly brown hair. He doesn't look sinister at all, just tired, and his eyes are circled with shadows as if he hasn't slept well in a while.

'You found us okay?' he enquires politely, looking from me to Athena, who has followed me out and is shivering in her thin top.

'Yes, thank you. Your instructions were good.'

'And is everything alright in the cottage? Have you got everything you need?'

'Um, I think so . . .'

'Er, is there any WiFi?' Athena interrupts. 'Have you got the code?'

He frowns. 'Yes, but the connection is bad in the cottage. We do mention that on the website. Anyway, if you need to use the WiFi you can always pop into the house. We keep the conservatory open for guests.'

Athena shoots me a horrified look that clearly says 'Where the hell have you brought me?' but is too polite to say anything out loud.

'Lily, why don't you show her where to go?' Joe says to the girl beside him, who glares at him scornfully. She's younger than I first thought. Maybe sixteen or seventeen. *Thanks to Lily and Gabe* it said in the acknowledgements at the back of *Falling*. Of course, I think, she must be Avery and Joe's daughter, not a new girlfriend. She's startlingly beautiful, with strange, haunted, grey eyes and thick dark eyebrows that right now are knitted tightly together in a sulky frown. She turns to Athena and sighs loudly.

'This way,' she says ungraciously, and she strides off towards the house. Athena shoots me a helpless look and then trails after her, trying to keep up.

Joseph Lewis frowns at her retreating back. 'Please excuse my daughter,' he says. 'She's not herself lately.'

'Oh?'

He takes a deep, ragged breath. 'Her mother died recently.'

For a moment he looks away at the sodden fields and when he turns back to me, I feel a chill in my bones because he's talking about Avery of course and his eyes are suddenly drained of all their warmth, lost in some bleak, empty world of their own.

'I'm so sorry,' I say at last. What else can I say in the face of such grief? Up until now I suppose I've been treating the death of Avery Lewis as if it were a puzzle to be solved – just another mystery like the ones in her books. But now, confronted by the obvious and terrible devastation she left behind, I'm ashamed of myself. Of course, Avery Lewis was a real person who died leaving behind real people who loved her and are clearly traumatised by her death.

'She'd been ill for some time,' Joe blurts into the silence. 'So, it wasn't a complete surprise, but it's still . . . hard . . .'

'Ill? Yes, of course,' I murmur. But I'm still trying to process what he's just said. I know that she wasn't ill. She fell from a cliff. It was in the newspaper.

There's a silence. A rook caws in a tree above our heads and then flies away up to the rooftop holding a berry in its beak. Joe Lewis gives himself a shake and assembles his features into a smile. It's not as warm as before but that terrible look of grief in his eyes I found so frightening is gone and he's a genial host again.

'Well let me know if there's anything I can help you with,' he says. 'There's a really nice pub in the village. They do great food, and we sell fresh eggs here on the farm if you need any.'

Six

Why did Joe say Avery was ill? My heart beats rapidly as I walk back to the cottage. It's a strange thing for him to say, especially given that her death was in the newspaper and so everyone must know how she died, but it occurs to me that maybe he means that she was suffering from a mental illness and that she committed suicide. As I reach the door I turn and look back to find him staring at me, a strange, hungry expression in his eyes. I smile uneasily and he raises his hand and then disappears into the house.

Back in the cottage, feeling slightly unsettled, I turn on the heating, unpack my clothes and plug in my phone to charge. There are a few sachets of Nescafé and sugar in a jar on the kitchen counter but no milk in the fridge, so I make myself a coffee with a spoonful of sugar, then turn on my laptop and start writing a few notes for my article.

Opening a new document, I record my first impressions of the farm:

A shabby, dreary place . . . listless in the winter drizzle.

And of Joseph Lewis:

Conventional appearance. Would look more at home in a bank than on a farm. Not much resemblance to Rebecca's husband in Falling. John's character seems unlikely to be based on him.

After a couple of minutes, I shut the laptop. I don't even know what happened to Rebecca and John in the story. There is no point in trying to start my article until I've finished *Falling* and found out how it ends.

The book is still where I left it on the coffee table next to a pile of pamphlets. I find my place. Then, while I'm reading the next chapter, I run myself a warm bath.

Chapter Five skips forward in time to DI Hegarty and his attempts to identify the dead woman on the beach. He has no luck with discovering what the number on the napkin is, but the napkin itself is more promising. It turns out to come from a café called the Lazy Cat which he locates in a nearby village.

Pausing to turn off the taps, I balance the book on the edge of the bath and stir the water, mixing the cold and hot. Then, after testing it with my toe, I step cautiously into the tub.

Warm water envelops me, and I continue reading, holding the book above the waterline with one hand and getting the edge of the paper wet as I skip a few pages, skimming over the details of policework and DI Harry Hegarty's private life. I pick up with him arriving at the Lazy Cat.

It was the kind of establishment Harry usually avoided like the plague. For a start it was vegan. And it had a new age, hipster vibe, or whatever the term was that people used nowadays. He ordered a plain cheese sandwich to the confusion of the young girl with piercings behind the counter and rejected the bewildering variety of herbal teas on offer.

'Builder's tea with two sugars please,' he said, flashing his badge and watching her eyes widen with surprise.

'Have you got a moment for a chat?' he asked pleasantly.

'Sure,' she said, pretty eyes wider still.

She brought out a hairy, tattooed young man to cover the counter and they sat opposite one another at a table in the corner.

'Recognise this woman?' Harry asked, sliding a photograph across the table to her. He had chosen the least graphic image he could find but she was still visibly shocked.

'Yes. Oh my God. What happened to her?' she exclaimed clapping her hand to her mouth.

Finally. Someone who knew the dead woman. Harry was getting somewhere. He leaned forward, trying not to appear too eager.

'I don't suppose you happen to know her name?' he asked casually.

She chewed her lip and flicked a crumb from the table. 'I can't remember, Rachel or Rebecca maybe – something like that. She moved here from London a while back. She lives up at Finchley Farm with her husband. They come in here sometimes. She always orders the same thing.'

'Which is?'

'Oh, avocado and falafel wrap and a fresh orange juice.'

Harry nodded. It probably wasn't important, but years of experience had taught him that the devil was in the detail.

'Actually,' the girl continued, 'I thought she'd left her husband. I thought maybe she'd moved back to London.'

'What made you think that?' Harry asked sharply.

She shrugged vaguely. 'Oh, just because I hadn't seen her around for a while.'

'And you say she lived at Finchley Farm.' Harry took out a notepad and pen and wrote down the name. A while ago he'd been issued with an iPad to use to take notes, which was supposedly more convenient, but he still preferred to use a pen and paper. 'Can you tell me where that is?'

'It's not far from here. Five minutes. Turn up the path just past the church. You can't miss it.'

'Thank you very much,' Harry said, draining his cup. 'You've been very helpful.'

He probably should have called his partner. Death notifications were meant to be done in pairs, but it was his day off and he wasn't really supposed to be here in the first place. He didn't fancy explaining what he was doing to Molly — who did everything by the book to the detriment of common sense.

Finchley Farm was run down and looked abandoned. Only the car parked outside and the dogs that ran up barking persuaded him that it was still inhabited. He half expected a wild man with unkempt hair and a shotgun to be living there, but the dark-haired young bloke who came to the door was well-groomed, polite and friendly. He didn't seem phased at all when Harry flashed his badge and there was only a slight frown of concern when he said gravely, 'I'm afraid I may have some bad news.'

'Perhaps we'd better go inside,' the man said calmly, and he ushered him into a large farmhouse kitchen where they sat opposite each other at a rustic, oak table. He was the kind of person women might find attractive, Harry supposed grudgingly. Handsome and well-built, in his thirties with curly, black hair and intense, greenish-grey eyes. He looked not unlike a younger version of Vicky's new partner, which didn't incline him to feel well disposed towards him. But he tried to put thoughts of his ex-wife to the back of his mind. There was no point in thinking about her. It only made him bitter and angry. Harry needed to keep an open mind.

'First of all,' he said taking out his notebook, 'can I ask your name?'

'Sure,' the young man said. 'It's John, John Baker.' He shifted a little in his seat and gave Harry a pleasant smile. 'What's this about, detective? Should I be worried?'

Harry cleared his throat. It was better to be direct in these

46

circumstances. Beating around the bush would only make it more painful in the long run.

'*We found the body of a woman at Bosigran below the cliffs . . .*'

'*A flicker of alarm appeared in John's eyes. 'Now, you're scaring me . . .' he said with a small, uneasy laugh.*

'*I have reason to believe that she might be your wife.*'

John stared at him. The shock on his face was real, Harry decided. And it was pure shock. There hadn't been time for grief. Not yet. That would come later.

'*Is this your wife?' he asked gently. He hated this. Telling someone about the death of a loved one never got any easier and he really needed a fag right now. He placed the photo from his bag on the table and John picked it up with trembling fingers. He made a strange noise in his throat. Then he stood up abruptly, turning his back to Harry.*

'*Yes, that's her,' he said in a shaky voice. 'But I don't understand . . . What was she doing there?*'

'*You didn't know?' Harry exclaimed in surprise.*

'*No, I've been away. I only just got back. This morning actually.*'

That's convenient, thought the cynical police officer's part of Harry's brain. It might explain why he hadn't reported her missing for three days. But then who doesn't speak to their wife for three days? Didn't he phone or text her during that time? But those questions could wait. He didn't want to let John Baker know he regarded him as a suspect. Not yet.

*

The door handle rattles loudly.

'Alex are you in there? I need a pee,' Athena calls through the door.

I stand up, water sliding off my body. I feel a little dizzy. The room is fogged with steam, and everything seems unreal. Avery's story is bleeding into my own life and it's difficult to shake off. I open the window, put the book down on the toilet seat and wrap a towel around myself. 'Okay, I'm just getting out of the bath. I won't be long.'

My skin is pink from the hot water as I rub myself dry and pull on a pair of jeans and an old T-shirt. There doesn't seem much point in wearing anything else here, where you're always only a stone's throw away from a cowpat or mud.

I'm still warm from the bath and DI Hegarty's conversation with John is reverberating in my head as I emerge from the bathroom.

Athena dashes in past me and sits on the loo without bothering to close the door, letting out a long sigh of relief.

'That's better, I was busting,' she says.

Later, in the kitchen area, Athena climbs up on a chair and rummages in the cupboards. 'I'm starving,' she says. 'What are we going to eat? Oh my God. There's nothing here! Why didn't we bring any food with us?'

'I thought there'd be a shop in the village,' I say.

'What kind of place doesn't have a shop or even a take-away?' she exclaims. In disgust she tosses a half-eaten packet of spaghetti, a bottle of ketchup and a few sachets of sugar and milk onto the counter. 'That's all there is,' she announces gloomily. 'We're going to starve.'

'Have you heard of a thing called a restaurant?' I laugh. 'How about we eat out tonight and tomorrow we can drive to the nearest town and get supplies.'

'Alright,' she nods. 'Good plan. I'll just check to see if there are any restaurants nearby.' She reaches for her phone then gives a groan of frustration as she remembers there's no WiFi in the cottage.

'Why don't we try the pub in the next village that John recommended? That way we won't have to drive,' I suggest.

'John?' Athena looks puzzled. 'I thought he was called Joe.'

'Did I say John? I meant Joe,' I say feeling flustered. I really am getting too immersed in that book, I think. I look at the map on the coffee table. A walk in the fresh air to the pub will do me good.

'Did you talk much to Lily?' I ask Athena as we leave the cottage and make our way along the road into the village. We're walking briskly to keep warm, our breath billowing in the cold air. It's already getting dark and it's quiet – so quiet I can hear our footsteps crunching on the gravel and the rustle of small creatures in the hedgerows.

'She wasn't all that talkative.' Athena hunches over, shivering, her hands thrust deep in her pockets.

'That could be because her mother has just died.'

Athena stops abruptly and gawps at me. 'Really? Oh my God. I wish you'd told me.'

We carry on in silence for a while. 'How did she die?' Athena asks quietly at last.

'I don't know,' I lie.

'I tell you one thing; she doesn't get on with her dad.'

I look at Athena sharply. There's a frown on her delicate features. 'What makes you say that?' I ask.

'Didn't you notice the way she looked at him?'

I shrug. 'Kids are often embarrassed by their parents,' I say.

We're silent again then. Because we both know it isn't always as simple as that. I think about our own father. And wonder when I first started to hate him. I can't remember ever feeling anything else towards him. But there must have been a time when I was a little girl before I fully understood what he was, when I loved him. I reach into my memory for happy times. He was sometimes a fun dad when we were small. He bought us ice cream at the beach. He used to play Marco Polo with us in the swimming pool and we used to dive for coins and swim underwater through his legs. That was when we had the big house near the sea, before the economic crash, before we lost all our money. Before Mum died.

Seven

It's a Monday evening and the Crown Inn is almost empty. There's just an elderly couple sitting by the fireplace and two young men drinking at the bar, talking to a barmaid with red hair and a frilly low-cut top.

'They've got WiFi! Thank God for that,' Athena exclaims, noticing a sign behind the bar. She taps the code into her phone and stands beside me at the bar, frowning as she scrolls through her messages.

'What's wrong?' I ask.

'It's Albert,' she says, screwing up her face. 'He keeps messaging me. He can't accept that it's over.'

'I thought you liked him,' I say, trying to picture him and conjuring up a vague image of a good-looking boy with sandy hair and a cheeky grin. There have been so many guys already since Athena's been in England but none of them seem to last longer than a couple of weeks. Like me she has trouble trusting men.

I check my messages while we're waiting to be served but there aren't many. A message from Lou asking how I'm getting on, one from a friend in London inviting me to her birthday party next week and another from Olena. I ignore Olena's, reply to Lou, saying the article is coming on nicely, and to the friend saying I'd love to come. Then I scroll through Instagram but immediately regret it. One of the first posts in my feed is a picture of Isaac and his girlfriend announcing that they're going to have a baby. In the photo they both look so wrapped up in each other and so sweet it's hard to begrudge them their happiness. But I can't help also feeling a pang of regret. I know in my heart that Isaac will make a great father and it's hard not to think about what might have been if I'd had the courage to make a commitment.

'What's that?' Athena asks, leaning over and trying to see my screen.

'Nothing,' I say, slotting my phone back in my pocket.

'You girls staying at Foxton?' the barmaid asks me as I look up at the chalkboard menu. She's bright and friendly with pale blue eyes and freckles that extend over her generous cleavage.

'Yes, how did you know?'

She shrugs. 'A lucky guess.'

'We just arrived last night,' I say conversationally. 'It's a lovely place.'

She nods. 'They've done it up nicely. It was a wreck when they bought it. The old guy that lived there before was able to keep it up but was too proud to accept help.'

'So, you know the owner?' I say, sensing an opportunity to steer the conversation towards Avery.

She finishes polishing a glass. 'Joe? Not very well. He's not been here long. Charlie knows him better than me. You helped them with fixing the roof last summer, right, Charlie?' She's speaking to one of the men sitting at the bar.

The man pushes messy, black hair out of his eyes and looks up from his phone as if he's only just realised we're there. He's not as young as I first thought – in his mid-thirties maybe. His eyes are a startling silvery green and for a moment I'm reminded of Rebecca's husband John, in *Falling*. I look down at his hands which are covered in paint and dirt which is ingrained deep in the fingernails.

'That's right.' He smiles briefly. Then he glances back at his phone as if he doesn't want to talk anymore.

'Poor guy. I heard his wife died recently,' I say casually.

Charlie raises his head and gives me a slow, assessing look.

'That's right.'

'Yes, it was a terrible accident. She fell off the cliffs at Bosigran and drowned,' the barmaid says, shaking her head and tutting, but her eyes are alight with relish for the drama of it all. She leans on the bar. 'Those cliffs are treacherous in the winter. They ought to put up a warning. My friend Gerry wrote to the council about it, but they haven't done anything so far. They don't care, useless buggers. Mind you, God knows what she was doing up there on a day like that.'

'A day like what?' Athena asks. She's stopped reading her phone and is listening to the conversation, her mouth hanging slightly open.

'Oh – didn't you know? There was a huge storm. Wind, hailstones, lightning, the lot. The roads were flooded in Penzance, there was so much rain. She must have been out of her mind to go out in that.'

I close my eyes, trying to blot out a sudden childhood memory that's bulldozed its way into my mind. In the memory, I'm in bed, listening to the driving rain and thunder outside and the dripping of the rainwater from the leak in the roof where the solar heating panel is attached. I remember hearing a scream so piercing that it was audible even over the sound of the storm and going downstairs to find my parents fighting. Dad was gripping Mum by the shoulders, and she was struggling to break free. As soon as Dad saw me, he stopped and ushered me back up to bed, but the next morning Mum had bruises on her arms and a bump on her head from where he'd bashed it against the wall.

I feel slightly dizzy and sick, and I hold on to the bar to steady myself.

'Was it definitely an accident?' I force myself to ask.

'You mean . . . you think . . . she might have topped herself?' The barmaid gives a dramatic shiver. 'Who knows? I wouldn't be all that surprised. She was a bit weird. Kept herself to herself. Joe's alright – quite friendly, but she was a bit stuck up. Thought she was better than us, I suppose.' A strangely bitter look flits across her face. Then she seems to recollect herself. 'Anyway, what'll you have? Have you decided?'

I order fish and chips for Athena and a veggie burger for me. Then we take our drinks back to the table.

'Why didn't you tell me that she drowned?' Athena says as soon as we sit down. Her expression is neutral, but I know all too well what she's thinking. All the pain that runs like a fault line through us. The zombie grief that's easily woken.

'I didn't think you'd want to know.'

She frowns. 'I'm a big girl. I can take it.'

I sigh. 'I know.'

'Is that why we're here, really?'

'What do you mean?'

Athena tips her head to one side and smiles sceptically. 'I know you, Alex. Why were you asking the barmaid all those questions?'

I haven't told Athena until now because I wanted to protect her and I wanted to avoid stirring up old trauma. But Athena's not stupid. She'll work it out sooner or later anyway. So, I briefly explain about the article I'm writing, about the book I received in the post and the news story online. Then I give her a summary of the beginning of *Falling*, leaving out the part about John's abuse of Rebecca. She listens intently, resting her elbows on the table, chewing the nail on her little finger.

'So, you think Avery was murdered like the character in her book?' she asks when I've finished.

'I don't know.' I shake my head. 'It's a strange coincidence though don't you think? That they both died in the same way.'

'Mm.' Athena nods and chips thoughtfully at her nail polish. 'Amazing coincidences do happen though. It's all part of the patterns created by the universe.'

'What do you mean?'

'Well, for example, in 1911 three men were hanged for murder on Greenberry Hill. Guess what their names were?'

'I don't know, what were their names?'

'Green, Berry and Hill. Isn't that amazing? Things like that happen all the time. It's called synchronicity. I read about it when we were studying Jung.'

'I'm not so sure. I don't know if I believe in all that stuff.' I tear absent-mindedly at the corner of a beer mat.

At that moment the barmaid brings us two plates of food and we stop talking for a while as we wolf our meals down hungrily. Only now do I realise that we've eaten nothing since breakfast, apart from a packet of crisps at the service station on the motorway.

'How does the book end? Who was the killer?' Athena asks as she finishes and wipes grease from her lips with a serviette.

'I don't know. I haven't got to that part yet.'

She puts down the napkin and stares at me round-eyed. 'Why not? If I were you, I'd skip straight to the end and find out. Don't you want to know?'

'I don't know. I just like to do things in the right order I suppose. Call me crazy.'

Athena rolls her eyes.

'Do you think her husband killed her? It's always the husband, isn't it?' She leans forward, her eyes wide. 'Or that she killed herself?'

'I don't know. Maybe. That's what I want to find out.' I look out of the window at the black, star-dotted sky and think about what the barmaid said. The article in the local paper didn't mention anything about bad weather. It puts a different slant on everything. On the one hand it explains why Avery might have fallen – a strong gust of wind, a stumble on slippery rocks. But, on the other, it raises questions about why she was there in the first place. What drove her out along a cliff path in the middle of a storm?

We watch as the two men at the bar head to the pool table. There's the clunk of the balls as they feed money into the slot and Charlie's friend ostentatiously chalks his cue. He glances over at Athena to see if she's noticed him, but Charlie's attention is squarely on the game.

Athena's gaze slides over them, uninterested. 'Why come all this way to write the article? Haven't you heard of the internet? What's your plan, Alex?'

'I think my writing will be better, more fleshed out, now that I've seen the place where Avery lived. I can get more of a feel for who she was,' I explain. 'But I don't really have much of a plan. I've tried contacting the local police, but I haven't heard back yet. I was thinking of taking a trip to the police station in Penzance tomorrow, see if they'll talk to me. Do you fancy coming?'

Athena frowns. 'Not really. I've got a couple of essays to write.'

We put on our coats and head to the bar to pay the bill.

'You girls leaving already?' asks the man with Charlie, leering at Athena. 'The night is young. Fancy a game?'

'No thanks,' she says icily.

'Ignore him. He's harmless really,' says the barmaid.

'Enjoy your holiday. And don't you go walking along no dangerous cliff paths.'

'Thanks, we won't,' says Athena. She wraps her scarf around her neck, shooting the man at the pool table a contemptuous look.

I smile at the barmaid, but I don't say anything because walking along the cliff path is exactly what I was planning to do. I want to see the spot where Avery died for myself.

It's late by the time we get back to the cottage and we're both exhausted. I tumble into bed without bothering to change out of my T-shirt and I pick up *Falling* to read. But I'm so tired the words merge in front of my eyes in a meaningless blur, and I drop off to sleep, the book still in my hand and the lamp still lit.

Eight

A sound.

I wake with a jolt in the middle of the night to a strange high-pitched scream. I sit bolt upright in bed, my heart hammering, and glance at the time on my phone. Three o'clock. It was just an animal, I think. A dog or a cat maybe? Turning off the lamp, I lie back down and pull the duvet over my head. Apart from the weird screech it's deathly silent, so quiet I can hear my own breath and my heartbeat drumming in my ears. I'm used to the comforting background hum of city life – the traffic, aeroplanes, the people in the flat next door. The quiet here is so deep and absolute, it's unnerving and I can't get back to sleep.

Throwing back the covers, I climb out of bed and open the curtains. It's not as dark as it should be. The sky is a sort of luminous aubergine colour and I soon realise why.

Snow has fallen during the night and it's gleaming softly in the moonlight, covering the digger and the cars in a layer of white. Next to the recycling bins something moves furtively. An animal. It freezes when it clocks me watching it and its neck dips, cringing in fear. I hold my breath. It looks so wild and strange standing in the swirling snowflakes, its yellow eyes glowing in the darkness. I exhale slowly as it slinks away out of sight.

Just a fox.

I'm about to head back to bed when I notice that there's a light on in an upstairs window of the farmhouse. A shadow flits past the window. I grip the windowsill. Of course, it's only Joe or Lily. There's nothing to be afraid of. But what are they doing up at this time of night? Perhaps they were woken by the fox, like me. The shadow slides back from the window out of sight.

I shut the curtains quickly, jump back into bed and fall into a restless sleep.

I wake again to a grey, otherworldly light. A layer of snow is coating the ground outside the window. I stare out at it gloomily. If it doesn't melt, I won't be able to drive to Penzance as I planned, and it'll be a waste of a day. Also, I realise as I head to the kitchen in search of breakfast, we've got no food and if the snow doesn't melt quickly, we won't be able to drive to a shop to get some. While I'm drinking a cup of coffee, Athena comes bounding out of her bedroom already fully dressed.

'Have you seen outside?' she exclaims. Snow is still a novelty to her. The only time we ever saw snow in Cyprus was up in the Troodos mountains. We used to drive up there as kids, a long, winding drive with our parents arguing in the front seat, and Athena and I would get out for half an hour and throw snowballs and slide down the hills in makeshift sleds. Then we would sit in the car, drying our socks on the car heater.

'We should build a snowman,' she says, 'before it melts.'

She's already pulling on her coat and boots.

'How old are you?' I ask, laughing.

'How old are *you*, Grandma?' she retorts. 'Come on, it'll be fun.'

Athena's enthusiasm is infectious, so I take another sip of coffee and then put on all the clothes I can find. We didn't really expect it to be this cold and I haven't brought anything really warm but multiple layers should be enough to keep out the worst of the chill. Outside, the temperature is actually fairly mild, and the snow is soft and slightly sticky, not deep, so we have to roll a lot of snow to make a small, misshapen, muddy snowman. While I'm admiring our handiwork, Athena rolls another couple of small balls and attaches them to the snowman's chest.

'It's a snowwoman,' she says defiantly when I laugh.

'Why does it always have to be a man? It's like the default gender is male even though women are fifty per cent of the world's population.'

I don't answer because I've just noticed the fox's pawprints in the snow over by the recycling bins and next to them, a line of human footprints. The footprints are too small to be Joe's. Lily must be up already, I think. She can't have got much sleep last night if she was still up at three in the morning and then got up before us.

'Great snowman.' Joe's cool voice breaks into my thoughts and I start with surprise. He seems to have appeared from nowhere. I certainly didn't hear the door open. He looks different from yesterday. More rested. More handsome. He's carrying a shovel and Barney is beside him, leaping and barking at the snow excitedly.

'It's a snowwoman,' Athena corrects him.

'Oh, yes I see.' His eyes glint with amusement and fall on me.

I smile back. Then I take a deep breath.

'I don't suppose you've got any food we can buy, have you? We can't get to a shop because of the snow.' It's embarrassing to have to ask, but I'm already really hungry and who knows when the snow will have melted. 'You said yesterday that you had some eggs for sale?'

'Sure.' He looks surprised. 'No problem.' He ducks into the house and emerges a few minutes later with a plastic bag full of food; bread, eggs, a couple of tins of baked beans and fruit.

'Will that do?' he asks.

'Yes. that's great. Thank you so much. I'll just get my purse. How much do we owe you?'

'No charge,' he says. 'I can't have you girls starving now, can I?'

'That was nice of him,' Athena says once we're back inside the cottage, warming our hands by the radiator.

'It was,' I agree. It's true that Joe Lewis seems like a nice, normal man. But I still can't get the image of John smashing Rebecca's head against the kitchen counter out of my head.

I spend the rest of the morning curled up on the sofa reading *Falling*. I've got to chapter five, and Rebecca and John's relationship has deteriorated even further. After a particularly vicious argument, Rebecca storms out of the house and wanders through the village until she stumbles upon an old Iron Age settlement, called Carn Euny.

Rebecca sat on the remains of what might once have been a round house wall. She lit a cigarette and stared at the rolling fields spread out under the indolent, evening sun.

She felt relaxed for the first time in ages. She was always on edge around John, worried about saying the wrong thing. But here she could finally breathe. It was so quiet she could hear the wind sifting through the grass and the sound of her heart beating against her ribs.

She should leave John, she thought. It would be so simple to get a train back to London. It was only a few hours away. He couldn't stop her. She could ask for her old job back. Simon would help her. But where would she live? They'd already sold their flat.

A bird trilled in the bushes. There was something other-worldly about this place and Rebecca couldn't help thinking about all the people who'd lived here before. Why had they abandoned this place? Had they all died of famine or illness, or had they just drifted away slowly, seeking a better life elsewhere? An irrational fear stirred in her and it occurred to her that perhaps they'd never really left. It was easy to imagine they were still all around, going about their daily business, hunting, working in the fields, recounting stories around the fire.

Telling herself she was being ridiculous, she stood up and began to explore the site. Hidden by grass and nettles at the far end of the field, she found a stone doorway and, peering into the darkness, she saw that it led to a narrow passageway. Inside, to the right, was a small round chamber and she ducked through the low entrance and stood in the centre of the room staring up at the small skylight.

'Magical place this, isn't it?'

She started and whipped round. For a crazy second, she thought she'd conjured up one of those ancient villagers from her imagination. He was a burly man, with an unkempt beard and wild, reddish-brown hair. It wasn't such a stretch to picture him with *a pitchfork in his hand or his face covered with soot and sweat, smelting iron at a forge. She blinked and clutched at her chest until her heart rate returned to normal and she noticed the blue jeans he was wearing, the tattoos snaking up his forearms and the twenty-first-century phone poking out of his back pocket.*

'Er yes,' she agreed when she had regained her composure.

'It's called a fogou.'

'What?'

'The passageway. It's known as a fogou. No one really knows what it was used for. Maybe it was for storage or for rituals of some kind.'

'I see,' she murmured, making her way past him into the open air.

'I didn't mean to startle you,' he said, following her. 'You looked really scared, just now.'

'Oh. It's just that I was thinking about the history of this place and the people that lived here and . . .'

'You thought I was a ghost.' He grinned.

'Well, yes, sort of,' she admitted with a small, embarrassed smile. He laughed heartily.

Even though he was a stranger, there was something about him, something about the way that he laughed that felt completely natural and disarming and she found herself laughing too.

'I'm pretty sure I'm real,' he said pinching himself and then wincing in pain. 'Ouch,' he exclaimed comically. 'Why did I do that?'

She laughed again and this time she found she couldn't stop. She laughed until there were tears running down her cheeks. And

when she finally stopped, she realised that it was the first time she'd
laughed properly since she'd arrived in Sancreed.

I reach the end of the chapter, mark my place and close the book. Then I rifle through the pamphlets on the coffee table. I can't find anything about Carn Euny but when I look in the guide to Cornish archaeological sites, it's mentioned near the beginning and, judging by the map, it's really close to Sancreed.

'Do you want to go for a walk this afternoon?' I ask Athena after we've had a lunch of scrambled eggs and toast. 'There's this Neolithic site near here that Avery mentions in her book. I'd like to take a look.'

'Old stones. Sounds exciting,' Athena says sarcastically. But then she nods glumly. 'Why not? There's nothing else to do.'

Shoving the guidebook into my small backpack and pulling on my trainers, I head out into the snow and slush with Athena through the village until we reach a couple of signposts both pointing to Carn Euny.

We take the shorter route down a narrow pathway overhung with frosted vegetation and bare branches coated with snow until we emerge onto the edge of a field. Then we tramp across the field to a wooden kissing gate.

'I wish we'd brought boots,' Athena grumbles. 'My feet are already wet.'

My trainers are soaked through, and my feet are cold too but I'm not thinking about that. I'm transfixed by the scene in front of me. It's a winter wonderland. Glistening white snow blankets a strange landscape of ridges and mounds. Here and there the snow has melted, and the remains of old stone walls and patches of green grass are visible.

'It's pretty much as she described it in her book,' I say, 'except it was summer when she came here.'

'Cool,' says Athena blowing on her hands and hopping up and down. 'Can we go now? I'm freezing.'

I ignore her and read the notice board. On it there's an artist's impression of what Carn Euny might have looked like in the Iron Age and a couple of paragraphs about the history of the village. But I'm more interested in the very recent past. This is the place Rebecca met Dom in *Falling*. It must have been an important place to Avery. I guess she came here quite often, and I wonder if the fogou she described actually exists.

'I just want to see if I can find the fogou,' I say.

'The what?'

I circle round to the far end of the site and am excited and a little unsettled to find a stone doorway, exactly as she described, half hidden by dead bracken and ferns. Stooping to enter, I can see that it leads into a dark, dank passageway with a small circular chamber off to one side.

'You've got to admit this is pretty cool,' I say, standing

inside and looking up at the skylight. 'Just think how old this place must be.'

We circle back to the village, taking the alternative route, and on a small track we come across a spring and an old well hidden amongst the trees. Next to the well is a gnarled, old tree covered in lichen. Hanging on its bare branches are a lot of colourful ribbons and rags, which the guidebook informs me are cloughties.

'People tie them to the branches as a sort of offering. It's a Celtic tradition which has survived to this day,' I tell Athena. As I get closer, I see that it's not just ribbons that have been tied to the tree. There are all kinds of objects: a Celtic cross, shells, jewellery. There's even a photograph of a middle-aged man.

Athena shivers. 'It's a pretty spooky place don't you think? Let's get out of here.'

I agree. In the still, cold air and the silence it makes me think of witchcraft and druid sacrifices.

'Okay. You're right. It's giving me the creeps,' I say, and we carry on as quickly as we can in the snow and slush back to Foxton Farm.

Nine

Most of the snow melts overnight and the next morning it's raining, a thin, dreary drizzle drifting out of a leaden sky.

I decide to drive to Penzance as I originally planned. The roads are mostly clear and salted but I drive slowly and carefully along the narrow, winding roads in case there's any remaining black ice.

The police station in Penzance is just a few streets back from the sea front. It's a squat, grey building and it looks grim and uninviting in the rain. I hesitate outside, fighting an instinctive shyness. They'll think I'm wasting their time and will probably just tell me to get lost. It will be embarrassing.

What does that matter? I tell myself to grow a pair and then reflect that Athena would probably say that was sexist. Why should males have a monopoly on bravery? Why shouldn't we say, 'grow a pair of breasts or grow a uterus?' That's what she would say, I think, smiling at our imaginary conversation and feeling more confident as I push my way through the heavy doors into the ridiculously overheated police station.

'Hello? Can I help you?' asks the officer on duty, a bored-looking young woman shuffling papers behind the Perspex screen.

'Er, yes.' I try to sound casual and self-assured like I've got every right to be here. 'I'd like to speak to someone about Avery Lewis.'

She blinks at me, confused. Clearly, she hasn't a clue what I'm talking about. 'Avery . . .?' she repeats with a puzzled frown.

'Yes, Avery Lewis, she died nearly a year ago in an accident at Bosigran cliffs.'

'Ah yes,' she says slowly. 'What's your name? Are you a relative?'

'My name's Alexandra Georgiou and no I'm not related,' I admit. 'But I think I might have some information that's relevant to her death.'

'I see,' she says, her eyes widening. Then she shuffles around in a drawer. 'Well, fill in this form and I'll see if I can get hold of Sergeant Metcalfe for you.' She slides a paper through a slot in the Perspex screen.

'When will he be back?'

She shrugs. 'I'm not sure. I can take your name and number if you like, and he'll get back to you.'

I swallow my frustration. 'I'm only here for the day. I really need to talk to him today. Please.'

She gives me a long, hard look and sighs but then she picks up the phone and, moving away from me to the back of the room, she talks to someone in a low voice.

'You're in luck. He'll be here in about half an hour,' she says grudgingly, coming back to the desk. 'If you don't mind waiting.'

'Thank you. I'll wait.' I look at my watch. It's two o'clock and I'm hungry. But I don't want to risk missing Sergeant Metcalfe, so I sit down on a hard, grey bench, fill in the form and read the notices pinned to the noticeboard on the wall. There's a poster that says, 'Free ride in a police car for all thieves,' an information leaflet about how to secure your home against burglaries and a couple of missing persons fliers; a middle-aged woman who is without her necessary medication and a heartbreakingly young boy who has been missing since April last year. I make a note of the number to ring and then take out my copy of *Falling* to read. But I've only read a few pages when a large silverback of a man with thinning grey hair and muscles running to fat, shambles out from a side door.

'Alexandra Georgiou?' he says, glancing down at the piece of paper in his hand and then up at me.

'Yes.'

'Nice to meet you. I'm Sergeant Metcalfe.' He gives me a kindly smile and holds out a large, paw-like hand for me to shake.

'Come on through.' He leads me down a grey-carpeted corridor to a small untidy office, full of half empty boxes. 'Sorry about the mess, I'm moving out of here in a couple of days. I'm retiring at the end of the week.'

He plonks himself down behind the desk, folds his arms and smiles benignly at me like a friendly uncle. 'So, Dawn tells me you've got some information about Avery Lewis?' he says.

'That's right,' I begin nervously. I need to get this right. I don't want him to think I'm a nutter, a rubbernecker or that I'm criticising his policework in any way.

'About a week ago I received this in the post.' I take the copy of *Falling* out of my shoulder bag and hand it to him. 'Avery Lewis wrote it.'

'Oh yes, the Inspector Hegarty mysteries. I haven't read them, but my wife likes them.' He turns the book over in his large meaty hands and reads the back cover out loud. '"*If you can't trust those closest to you, who can you trust?*" Sounds interesting, though they always make the police seem unbelievably stupid in these types of books, don't they?'

'And then I read this.' I show him a printout of the newspaper article I found online.

He picks it up, puts his reading glasses on and peruses it ponderously. 'That's odd,' he says slowly. 'But I don't see . . .'

'In the book the main character is pushed off a cliff at Bosigran, which is the same place as Avery Lewis disappeared,' I explain.

His eyes spark with interest. 'Hmm. That *is* a strange coincidence.' He looks back down at the article again and then glances up at me sharply. 'What's your connection to Avery Lewis?'

I don't want to reveal my real reasons, but I can't think of any other plausible way to explain why I'm here.

'I don't really have a connection. I'm a journalist,' I tell him reluctantly. 'I write book reviews, amongst other things. The publisher sent the book to me.'

As I feared it would, his manner shifts subtly. His grey eyes become slightly more wary, slightly less avuncular.

'Oh, so you're writing a piece about Avery Lewis,' he says.

'Yes, but that's not the only reason I'm here,' I add hastily. 'I thought you needed to know about this. I mean, it suggests that there's something suspicious about her death.' I flush a little. 'Are you certain her fall was accidental?'

To my relief he doesn't seem to be offended by the question. He just sits back, chewing the nail on his middle finger. Then he leans forward with a sigh and taps something into the computer keyboard. 'There was no reason for us to think otherwise.'

'There was a storm the day she died.'

He nods slowly. 'Yes, that's right.'

'Don't you think it's strange that she went out walking along the cliffs in such bad weather?'

He lifts his broad shoulders. 'No, not really. She could have gone out before it started raining and been caught out. If I remember rightly, the day started quite bright and clear. The storm came on suddenly.'

'What about suicide?' I ask tentatively.

He sighs heavily and taps a pen against the desk. 'It's possible, I suppose. But there was no history of depression and no real reason to think she'd killed herself. We found her rucksack at the top of the cliff and her phone on a ledge just below. We think she was trying to retrieve it when she fell.'

I absorb this new piece of information. The phone could have been there for many reasons, I think. She could have dropped it as she fell, or in a struggle . . .

'What happened to her phone? Do you still have it?'

'No, we checked it out and then returned it to her husband.'

'Do you think another person could have been involved?'

He raises an eyebrow and gives a small, wry smile. 'You mean you think that someone killed her?'

'Not really. I'm just exploring all the possibilities.'

To my surprise he doesn't dismiss the idea out of hand

but appears to consider it seriously. 'It's impossible to say with a hundred per cent certainty,' he says at last. 'But it's very unlikely.' He gives me a whimsical smile. 'I'm sorry to disappoint you. I know the alternative would make for a better story.'

'What makes you say it was very unlikely?'

'Well.' He presses his fingers together. 'There were no signs of a scuffle at the top of the cliff and no other footprints. And her car was parked in the car park. There were no other cars there. We have a reliable witness who saw her arrive on her own and didn't see anyone else in the area.'

'A witness? Can you tell me who?'

He smiles and wags his finger at me as if I'm a naughty child.

'I'm afraid I can't give out that kind of information.'

I feel frustrated. 'So, you think that the similarity between what happened in the book and in real life is just coincidental?'

'Most likely yes, but I agree it's interesting.' He sits back, chewing his thumbnail. 'If you don't mind, Alexandra, I'd like to keep this book and the article for my records.'

I can't very well refuse. 'Um, well, I only have one copy. Can I have a photocopy of the article?'

'Sure.' He stands up and lifts a pile of papers off the top of the photocopier, pushing a few buttons. The machine whirrs and beeps.

'There you go,' he says, handing me a couple of sheets of paper. 'I'll let you know if anything further comes to light.' He fidgets and moves the objects on his desk around. 'Is there anything else I can help you with?' he asks.

I take a deep breath. 'There's just one other thing. Can you tell me where she died?'

'She fell into the sea just below the cliffs at Bosigran. But you already know that.'

'Yes, but where exactly? I want to go there,' I explain. 'I want to describe the scene, you know, to add a bit of atmosphere for my readers.'

'I see.' He appears undecided for a moment. Then, with a single swift action, he tears a piece of paper from the pad on his desk and on it he draws a few squiggles and a square. 'This is the car park,' he says, tapping the square with the nib of his pen. 'You can't miss it. It's next to an old, ruined mine. We think she fell roughly a mile along the cliff path from there. About here.' He marks the spot with a big x. 'You will recognise it because there's a distinctive rock there. We call it the Old Man of Bosigran. It looks like an old man's face.'

'Thank you so much,' I say as he hands over the paper and I stuff it in my pocket.

'Be careful mind,' he says as I'm leaving. 'We don't want another accident on our hands.'

Ten

I know Metcalfe meant to be careful on the cliff path, but his words ring in my ears as I step out of the police station into the cold damp air, and I'm filled with sudden self-doubt.

What if my instincts are wrong and Avery's death was nothing but a tragic accident? What if there's no story and I'm meddling in something that is none of my business? But I can't stop now. All I know is that I need to see the place where she disappeared with my own eyes.

Before returning to the car, I wander through Penzance town centre and trawl the bookstores until I eventually find another copy of *Falling* in a charity shop. Then from Penzance I drive along the winding roads towards St Just and Bosigran and find the car park marked on the map by Sergeant Metcalfe. It's not hard to locate. The ruined mine chimney is quite distinctive. There are no other cars.

I suppose not many people are crazy enough to go walking on a cold, miserable day like this.

At least the drizzle has stopped, I think, as I follow Metcalfe's map down a path overhung with small, lichen-covered trees and across the heath until I reach the coastal path. But it's still bitterly cold and the wind bites through my coat in vicious little gusts, whipping up the waves down below into small white peaks. As I pick my way along the slippery stone trail, I keep far away from the edge and try not to look down too much at the dizzying drop to the sea.

The path ascends, clinging on to the cliff. The ground underfoot is uneven, and the protruding rocks remind me of little jagged teeth. It would be so easy to trip, and I'm all too aware a misstep could be fatal or at the very least land me in hospital. Now I'm here it doesn't seem at all unlikely that Avery fell accidentally, especially if it was a stormy day.

The path is getting narrower and I'm seriously considering turning back, when I round a corner and spot a distinctively shaped rock jutting out into the sea just ahead of me. I'm guessing it's the rock Metcalfe mentioned. With a stretch of the imagination, it could just be a face in profile. That protruding part could be the nose and below it could be the chin. I walk towards it and come to a spot where there's a sheer drop to the sea churning below. This is it. This is the place where Avery fell, I think, with a sick lurch of certainty.

Pulling my camera out from my backpack, I take a few photos of the rock and of the sea. Perhaps I will want to describe the place in my article, you never know. But, as I step towards the edge to get a better view, I suddenly lose my footing. Loose stones scatter and tumble over the edge. I watch them plummet, horrified, clinging on to the rock behind me, my heart hammering a million beats a minute.

Stupid. Stupid girl.

Slow down, Alex. That could have been bad.

I sink down with my back against the rock, fighting a wave of vertigo. But I've come all this way, so I force myself to shuffle closer to the edge and look down. There's just one small ledge a few feet below. Is that where her phone landed? What was she doing when she dropped it? Taking a photo or answering a call? Apart from the ledge the rock is sheer. Her fall would have been unbroken. I try to work out how high it is, but I am not much good at judging distance – maybe thirty feet I estimate, shuddering. Did she die as soon as she hit the water? Or did she struggle for her life as she was swept away? I wonder if she remembered Rebecca's death in *Falling* and if she did, whether she appreciated the irony of her own situation.

I try to stand up, but my knees are trembling so much that I can't, so I stay sitting for a while with my weight firmly pressed on the rock behind me, listening to the sea slapping the rocks below and waiting for my heartbeat to steady. Apart from the sound of the sea, it's deathly quiet.

I'm not sure how long I've been sitting there when I hear the crunch of footsteps nearby heading in my direction. A hiker perhaps. I wait for them to round the corner, wondering how they will pass me at such a narrow spot. But I must have imagined it because no one appears. And for a moment I have the strong sense of a presence, someone up above, watching me. My heart is in my throat but I'm too scared to turn and look up. After what seems like a long time but is probably only a couple of minutes, a seagull above me shrieks and jolts me to my senses. I stand up shakily and make my way back towards the car. What was Avery doing here in the first place? I wonder. Perhaps she was researching her novel? But she had already finished *Falling* by the time she came here so what would have been the point?

Eleven

When I arrive back at Foxton Farm the cottage is empty and cold. There's no sign of Athena. Just her laptop and files open on the kitchen table.

Shivering, I turn on the heating and find a message pinned under a salt cellar on the kitchen counter.

Gone out. Back soon. Ax

I put on another jumper, make myself a warm cup of coffee and collapse on the sofa, tired out by the physical and mental strain of the morning. Then, lazily, I reach for the copy of *Falling* I bought in Penzance and scrutinise the photograph of Avery on the back, running my fingers over her sleek, ashen hair and trying to guess what lies behind that enigmatic smile.

'What happened to you, Avery?' I ask aloud.

She doesn't reply, of course.

I open the book. I'm convinced that the answers to all my questions must lie somewhere tangled up in the threads of her story.

But maybe I've been taking it too literally. I doubt that in real life Joe was the violent bully depicted in *Falling* or that everything that happened to John and Rebecca also happened to Joe and Avery. But there could be an element of truth in it. Authors must get their ideas from somewhere, and maybe if I read them carefully Avery's words will reveal clues about her state of mind and the people around her in the months before she died.

I turn to chapter six. We are back in the past and Rebecca has become friends with Dominic, the man she met at Carn Euny. While John is away staying with family, she visits his studio.

He offered her a beer and they sat in his garden in the evening sunshine as the shadows lengthened.

'I don't see you around in the village much,' Dominic said.

'No, we've been busy with all the renovations.'

She thought about last night – the argument about the cost of everything. She'd wanted to delay the building work in the barn until the house was finished and they had more money. But John didn't agree, and he didn't like being given advice. Advice was the same as criticism to him. And criticism dented his fragile ego.

He'd flown into a rage suddenly, catching her off guard. And after that there'd been no reasoning with him. She thought about the unreachable anger in his eyes as he'd grabbed her and, instinctively, she touched the tender, bruised skin on her arm. When she looked up, she saw that Dom was watching her intently and she flushed.

'We're hoping it will be all finished by next spring,' she said brightly.

He wasn't really listening. He had closed one eye and was holding up his finger and thumb as if he was measuring her.

'What are you doing?' she asked, feeling warmth flood her throat.

'I'd like to paint you,' he said. 'You've got an interesting face.'

It was a strange suggestion from someone she'd only just met. Maybe it should have been a warning, but it came so naturally she didn't feel threatened or insulted.

'Are you serious?' she asked.

'Deadly,' he said. His eyes held hers for a fraction too long. 'I'll pay you for your time of course.'

'I don't think so,' she said looking down, avoiding his gaze. It wasn't a good idea. John would be furious if he found out. He already flew into a jealous rage if she so much as looked at another man. The other day he'd accused her of flirting with the electrician, a man of nearly seventy who'd come to do the rewiring.

'Come here tomorrow,' said Dom, 'if you change your mind. I'll be here all morning.'

'I won't change my mind.'

*

Nevertheless, the next day she found herself outside his house at eleven o'clock. He'd said he would pay her, and God knew they could use the money. That's what she told herself anyway.

'You came,' was all he said when he opened the door, and his smile was so warm and purely happy that she felt herself melting a little.

'I can only stay for an hour or so. John will be back at lunchtime.'

'No problem. That should be long enough. Sit there,' he told her as he set up his easel.

She sat on the sofa near the window, one side of her face warmed by the sunlight. 'I'm not very good at keeping still, I'm sorry,' she said crossing and uncrossing her legs. She felt self-conscious under his scrutiny.

'Just move your head a little this way.' He stepped towards her and tilted her chin upwards. Then he stepped back and regarded her gravely. 'And take off your jacket.'

It was hot in the studio, which had big glass windows that trapped all the heat inside. And she couldn't think of a reason why she shouldn't, so, reluctantly she peeled off the old brown jacket she was wearing.

Underneath she had on a sleeveless white top and Dominic's eyes flickered over the bruises on her arm, but he didn't comment, just kept on painting her with smooth confident strokes, a frown of concentration on his face. His eyes traced her jawline and the curve of her shoulders and heat rose in her cheeks because it felt almost as if he was touching her.

After about half an hour of silent sketching and painting, he moved back and regarded his work, pinching his lower lip thought-fully. Then he smiled at her, a sweet, vague smile as if he was coming out of a dream.

'Not bad,' he said.

'Can I see?' she asked.

'Not yet.' He opened a cupboard and pulled out a bottle of wine and two glasses. 'I think we deserve a drink, don't you?' he said. And without waiting for her to answer he poured out two glasses and handed her one.

Then he sat next to her on the sofa. He was close, close enough that their thighs were nearly touching, but she didn't move away. Instead, she took a cautious sip of wine. What the hell? she thought defiantly. Will it hurt if I flirt a little? John already thinks I'm sleeping with half the village. I might as well give him something real to complain about. She felt strangely light and reckless, as if she was floating above herself and anything she did, didn't really matter.

'What happened here?' Dom said touching the livid bruises on her arm lightly with his thumb, bringing her right back down to her body with a jolt, as if an electric current had passed through her.

'Nothing,' she said, barely daring to breathe. She sat rigid as his hand rested on her skin. He rubbed her arm absent-mindedly as if he wasn't aware of what he was doing. Then their eyes locked, and her breath gathered inside her as if there was too much for her chest.

'Come here,' he said softly, pulling her close, and he kissed her hard on the lips.

There's a loud rap on the door and I'm dragged rudely out of Avery's world back into the grey winter's day.

'Athena . . .' I start, opening the door.

But I break off because it's not Athena. It's Joe.

'Hope I'm not interrupting,' he says, unsmiling.

'Not at all.' I flush a little, thinking about what I've just been reading.

'Good.' He clears his throat. 'I'm just checking that everything's okay. Have you got all you need?'

He's really aiming for that five-star rating on Tripadvisor, I think wryly. What else could account for this scrupulous attention to our welfare?

'Yes, everything's . . .' I start, then stop short, realising that this is the perfect opportunity to get to know him and discover more about Avery. 'Actually, I'm not sure how to work the DVD player.'

The truth is I haven't even tried to get it to work but the longer I can keep him here, the more I can potentially find out about Avery.

'Oh . . .' Joe frowns. 'I'm sorry. I thought we left instructions.' He steps past me into the living room and picks up the blue folder from the coffee table, flicking through the laminated pages. 'Ah, yes, TV-CD player. Here it is.' He taps at a page, and smiles at me. 'You're so young, you've probably never even seen a DVD player before.'

I shrug. 'We had one when I was a kid. We used to go to

the video store. I think we rented *Monsters, Inc.* a thousand times.'

'Mm,' he says absent-mindedly, fiddling with the remotes. 'You just press this red button, here on this one. And then turn it to AV 1. See?'

He aims the remote at the TV, but nothing happens. 'That's strange.' He kneels and peers round the back of the TV. 'Oh, it's not connected at the back. Here you go. It should be fine now.'

He fiddles around with the buttons and sifts through the box of DVDs. 'What do you fancy? We've got a whole boxset of *Friends*, *Fatal Attraction*, *The Godfather* . . . Now that's a good film.'

'Er . . . maybe *Friends*.'

He slides the disc out of its cover, slots it into the player and presses play. 'There you go,' he says triumphantly.

The theme tune starts up and the opening sequence of the show appears on the screen, the six friends capering about, splashing in a fountain and twirling umbrellas.

'Wow. It's a long time since I've seen this,' Joe says. 'They all look so young. And, my God, what are they wearing?' He chuckles. 'I can't believe we used to think that looked good. Of course, you're too young to remember. You weren't even born.'

Why does he keep bringing up my age? I find it annoying

for some reason. 'I'm not that young. I must have been about three or four when the first show aired.'

'Really?' He looks at my face as if he's trying to assemble the pieces of a jigsaw puzzle. 'That makes you what? Twenty-four?'

'Twenty-five.'

'An old lady.' His eyes glint with a hint of mockery. 'You'll be collecting your pension soon.' He looks around the room and his gaze lands on the copy of *Falling* on the coffee table. He stiffens, all traces of amusement wiped suddenly from his face.

'You're reading this?' He picks it up and flicks through.

'Yes.' I draw in my breath, my heart quickening. 'It's really good. It's hard to put down.' I watch him carefully. I wonder if he's read it. If he has, what does he make of the unflattering portrait of John and the passionate affair between Rebecca and Dom that seems about to begin?

His lips twist as if he's tasted something bitter. 'I think it's good too, but I may be biased. My wife wrote it.'

I aim for an expression of starstruck surprise but I'm not sure if I get it right. 'Really? Your wife was Avery Lewis?' I exclaim. 'I love her books.'

He looks at me sideways with a slight, wry smile, as if he can read my thoughts. He probably can. I was always terrible at lying. Then he glances back at the book in his hands. The smile disappears and an angry, wounded expression flashes in his eyes. I'm torn between instinctive sympathy and nagging doubt. I step back slightly. My fear is irrational, I tell myself. Even if he was violent towards his wife, it doesn't mean he's a danger to me.

'You must miss her a lot,' I say carefully.

There's a sharp intake of breath, and he turns away and gazes out of the window at the pale, silver sun, now sinking behind the trees at the far edge of the field. 'You could say that,' he murmurs. 'She died so suddenly. There was no time to adjust.'

'I thought you said she was ill,' I blurt before I have time to think.

He looks startled. Then he shrugs. 'Did I say that? I tell people that sometimes. It's simpler.'

I nod, feeling a sudden affinity with him. I understand why he lied. I used to tell people my mother died in a car accident. It was less complicated than the truth and people were less likely to ask painful questions.

'I'm so sorry,' I murmur. 'How . . .? I mean if you don't mind talking about it.'

He shakes his head vigorously and turns back to me. 'It's okay. I don't mind talking. It helps actually.' He swallows and then gives a deep, juddering sigh. 'She was walking by the cliffs. There was a storm, and they think she was swept away into the sea and drowned.'

'My God. That's terrible,' I say, feeling like a fraud.

His eyes are dark, unreachable. 'I just wish I knew what she was doing there in the first place. She hated hiking. She was a city girl through and through.' He smiles faintly. 'She complained so much when we moved here. She said she was allergic to the country air.'

So that part in the book was true, I think. Like Rebecca, Avery hated the countryside.

'Didn't she tell you where she was going?' I ask.

He's quiet for a moment. Then he sighs. 'No, I wasn't here. I was at a sailing event for a week in Southampton.'

I think about the boat that John bought in *Falling*. 'You've got a sailing boat?' I ask.

He nods. 'Avery didn't like sailing. She stayed here to do some writing.' He smiles ruefully. 'She had a deadline looming, anyway. I spoke to her on the phone from the hotel the evening before she died, but she didn't mention going to the coast. If she had, I would have told her not to. I knew there was a storm coming. All the sailing events had been cancelled for that day.'

'When did you find out that she . . .?'

'The police phoned me the day after . . . They told me a tourist had found her phone and rucksack on the cliff edge and handed them in to the police. At first, I thought nothing much of it. I just assumed she'd lost them. She could be quite absent-minded sometimes, especially when she was in the middle of writing. I called the landline a few times, but I wasn't really worried . . .'

There's a short silence. Joe's expression is bleak and lost and I feel a strange and inappropriate desire to reach out and touch him, to comfort him.

'Then when I arrived home at the end of the weekend and saw her car was missing, I knew something was wrong. I called the police and they started searching for her and a few hours later they found her car abandoned in the car park by the cliffs. That's when I knew something was very wrong.' He looks broodingly out of the window. 'I know what you're thinking,' he adds bitterly. 'You think she killed herself, don't you?'

I shake my head mutely.

'But she didn't. I'm sure.' He looks straight into my eyes. 'I knew her. She just wasn't the kind of person to give up. And she had no reason to.' He looks at me fiercely as if he's daring me to disagree with him. 'She booked a holiday in Malaysia for the two of us that afternoon. Why would you do that if you were planning to kill yourself?'

'You wouldn't,' I agree.

'There's something else.' He taps the front cover of *Falling*. 'You may think I'm crazy, but you must have read how Rebecca dies in the story?'

I nod, holding my breath.

'What did you make of it?'

'You mean . . .' I pretend to think. 'She falls from a cliff . . . just like your wife,' I say, as if the idea had only just occurred to me.

He nods. 'Don't you think that's strange?'

'You think she . . .'

'I don't know,' he interrupts, rubbing his eyes viciously. 'I've had odd thoughts lately. Crazy thoughts. There was a reader harassing her on social media. He was sending her weird messages. She complained about it at the time, but I didn't think anything of it. Now I wish I'd listened to her.'

I sit on the window seat, absorbing this new information, my mind racing. 'What kind of messages? Were they threatening?'

'Not exactly. It was more as if he thought he knew her. He wrote questions and then answered his own questions as if he was her. He carried on a whole conversation by himself.'

I hold my breath. 'Do you think he could have had something to do with her death?'

'Maybe. But the police said there was no indication that it was anything but an accident.' He sighs. 'I don't know, maybe I just need to find someone to blame. It's one of the stages of grief apparently, blaming others.' He turns and smiles at me as if he's just remembered where he is and who I am. 'Listen to me. You must think I'm completely nuts.'

'I don't think that at all,' I say gently. 'It's only natural to want to know what happened.'

He puts his head to one side and gives me a slow, measuring look. 'I've no idea why I'm telling you all this. Do people usually tell you all their secrets?'

My cheeks feel warm. 'Not usually. Maybe it's because I know what it's like to lose someone you love. My mother died when I was fourteen.'

I take out the photo I always keep in my wallet. It's just a passport photo and in it my mother's staring blankly at the camera, startled by the flash, but it's one of my most prized possessions.

'I'm sorry to hear that,' he says. His eyes on me are soft and flecked with amber. 'She looks a lot like your sister.'

It's true she does look like Athena. The same curly brown hair, the same intelligent brown eyes.

He hands me back the photo. 'You were even younger than Lily. That must have been tough.'

'It was.'

'Well.' He clears his throat and gives himself a shake as if he's just realised this conversation has become too intimate too quickly. 'I'll leave you to it. Let me know if you need any help with anything else.'

'I will, thank you.'

He heads for the door and hesitates on the threshold as if he's about to say something. Then he smiles briefly and steps outside. I watch him amble across to the main house, his limbs loose, his shoulders surprisingly broad. I

94

hadn't considered the possibility that Avery was killed by a stalker until now. I turn over the idea in my head. Some crazed fan who decided to make fiction reality. It's not completely unfeasible. It makes more sense than Joe killing her. He wasn't even here when she went missing. He was in Southampton, over a hundred miles away. Of course, he could be lying about that, but it would be easy enough to verify. Besides, I'm starting to like him. I don't want to believe that he is capable of murder.

Twelve

It's dark by the time Athena comes back, breezing in with a couple of shopping bags, looking wind-blown and rosy-cheeked.

'Where were you?' I say. 'I was starting to get worried.'

She unpacks a pile of food, enough to last at least a week, onto the table.

'Lily gave me a lift to the shop in St Buryan. I needed some tampons and I thought I'd buy something to eat while I was there in case you didn't get time. Then I went over to the house to use the WiFi.'

'I didn't think Lily was old enough to drive,' I say, starting to put the food she's bought into the fridge.

'She's seventeen. Apparently, she just passed her test. Her driving was a bit hairy. She forgot to put the handbrake on when we parked outside the shop. The car nearly rolled away down the hill.' She laughs. 'But we survived. Anyway, I thought it'd be good to get to know her. I thought I'd help you out with your article, find out more about her mother.'

'And?'

'She didn't tell me much we don't already know about Avery.' Athena turns on the oven. 'Shall we have pizza? I found out quite a bit about Lily though. She's not Joe's birth daughter, for a start.'

'Oh?'

'Yep. Her real dad left when she was ten and her mother met Joe. They were working together at some swanky financial services firm in London. Apparently, her family didn't like it when they married. They blamed him for the break-up of Avery's first marriage. And they still don't speak to him.'

Poor Joe, I think. It makes me warm to him, knowing that he had to deal with Avery's relatives. I imagine a tribe of people with Avery's cold eyes, looking down their long, supercilious noses at him.

'How about Lily?' I say aloud. 'Doesn't she blame Joe? Why didn't she go back to live with her real dad after Avery died?'

Athena rips the plastic wrapping off the pizza and places it on a baking tray. 'I don't know. Maybe she didn't want to live abroad. Her biological father lives in Germany. I think she didn't want to leave her boyfriend. There's this guy called Josh, who she's been seeing for a while.'

'Wow. You really got her life story, didn't you? You should be a detective.'

She chuckles and gives a little bow. 'That's not all. I asked her about the night her mother died.'

'You did? And?' I hope Athena wasn't too obvious in her questions.

'Apparently, Joe wasn't here the day she died. He was at some kind of sailing event in Southampton. So, I don't think he could have murdered her.' She grins.

So, Lily's account of what happened matches his. I feel strangely relieved.

'And Lily?' I ask. 'Wasn't she alarmed when her mother didn't come home? Joe says they didn't know until the police contacted him the next morning.'

'Lily was at a music festival with Josh and then she stayed over at his house. But Joe doesn't know that she stayed over. So don't tell him, okay?'

'Why would I?'

'I don't know. I suppose you wouldn't.'

Athena stands up and heads to her room. 'Anyway, I'm going to have a quick shower before tea. Can you keep an eye on the pizza?'

'What did you find out from the police?' she asks ten minutes later, when we sit down to eat.

'Not a lot. They're convinced it was an accident.'

98

She takes a bite of pizza, chews for a while, observing me thoughtfully. 'And? You don't believe them?'

'I don't know. I don't know what to think.'

Athena presses her lips together. 'I guess they know what they're doing, Alex.'

I shake my head stubbornly. 'Maybe. But I can't help feeling that there's more to it.'

She rests her chin on her hands and gazes at me pensively. 'You've got that look again. Remember? After Mum died? Don't you think you're becoming a bit obsessed? I'm not sure all this is healthy for you.'

I stop eating. The pizza suddenly tastes bitter.

'This is nothing like that,' I say defensively. 'It has nothing to do with Mum.'

Athena raises her eyebrows. 'Doesn't it? The fact that Avery Lewis drowned is not significant at all?'

I stand up and push the rest of my pizza into the bin with my fork. Then I hold on to the kitchen counter steadying myself, because I'm suddenly back there – at the edge of our swimming pool, looking down at the deep water, frozen in fear.

'Breathe, Alex.' Athena is standing next to me. She puts her arm around my shoulder.

I inhale slowly, trying to steady my racing heart.

'I'm sorry, I shouldn't have brought it up,' she says.

'It has nothing to do with the past,' I insist. 'There's something else going on here. I just know it.'

After Athena has gone to bed, I stay up for a long time, sitting in the window seat and staring out at the main house, watching the small pool of yellow light downstairs and the shadows moving inside. What are Joe and Lily doing now? I wonder. And what secrets are hiding in that house, behind its old, stone façade?

Thirteen

The turquoise water wobbles like jelly in a tiny breeze and the sun bounces off the windows of our house, dazzlingly bright and harsh.

The tiles around the swimming pool burn my bare feet and I hop into a shady spot under the bougainvillea. Every pore in my body is oozing sweat and even my thin school shirt feels too warm. In a minute I'll change into my swimsuit. For now, I pick up the net and drag it behind me, collecting the usual haul of dead ants, flies and beetles. I'm about to tip it out when I spot something under the water. Something large. Something slimy and disgusting, writhing like a snake. I drop the net in horror.

I wake up. My heart is hammering and tears are streaming down my cheeks.

After stumbling out of bed and splashing cold water on

my face, I stare at my reflection. 'It's not your fault,' I say out loud and the red-eyed, sallow-faced girl in the mirror breathes deeply and tries to smile.

After brushing my teeth, I pull on a tracksuit and trainers and head out of the house before Athena wakes up. I turn onto the driveway, feet pounding on the gravel, trying to outrun the ghosts of the past. I'm lost in thought, haunted by the images in my dream and I don't notice Joe heading towards the chicken coop, lugging a large sack of chicken feed with Barney at his heels.

'Whoa,' he says as I barrel into him. 'Where are you off to in such a hurry?' He drops the bag of feed and holds me by the shoulders, steadying me. Then he takes a step back and smiles broadly, his head tipped to one side. The smile transforms his face.

I gaze up at him, feeling dazed. 'I'm just going for a run,' I say.

'Hey. What's up? Are you okay?' His expression is full of concern, and I realise with embarrassment that it's probably obvious that I've been crying.

'Yeah, I'm alright.' I try to smile. 'I'm going to run to Carn Euny and back.'

'It's an interesting place,' he says. 'Well worth a visit.'

There's an awkward silence.

'Are you sure you're okay?'

'Yes, I'm fine.'

'Oh, well then.'

'See you later,' I say, heading towards the gate with Barney running up beside me, his tail wagging enthusiastically.

'Hey, boy, where are you going?' I reach down and pat him. 'Go on back now.'

'He'll probably follow you,' Joe tells me. 'The last few guests have taken him for walks, and he's got into the habit of going along. I hope you don't mind.'

'That's not a problem,' I say. 'But don't I need a lead? What if he runs off?'

'He won't. Don't worry about it. He knows his way home and there's no traffic to worry about round here.'

'Alright.' I continue towards the gate, feeling strangely self-conscious, aware that Joe is still watching me.

Don't be ridiculous. He isn't interested in you, I tell myself firmly. He's too old for you and isn't over the death of his wife yet. But something has changed since our conversation yesterday. There's a new intimacy between us and as I jog through the village, I find myself thinking about him. I think about the way the small scar under his right eye disappears when he smiles and how warm his hands felt on my shoulders. I'm so absorbed in these thoughts that I almost miss the signpost and the track to Carn Euny. But Barney heads up there automatically as if he knows where I want to go.

I follow him. A cold fog has descended, creating a sort of

fairy-tale atmosphere. Not a modern, light-hearted Disney fairy tale. More of an old-fashioned Brothers Grimm-type fairy tale – the kind where people die, and children get eaten. Thoughts of Joe recede, and I'm gripped by superstitious fear. I'm glad Barney is with me I think as he trots obediently by my side, a tennis ball in his mouth. Every so often, he cocks his leg to pee or drops his ball and gazes at me expectantly until I pick it up and lob it up the pathway for him to chase.

We emerge into a damp, misty landscape on the edge of the muddy field and run up to the wooden kissing gate that leads to the site. But as I open the gate Barney suddenly bounds off, ignoring my calls.

I look around, pausing for breath. The whole area is swathed in fog, as if the world is a computer game that's slowly deleting itself. There's no one else here and no sign of the dog.

'Barney!' I call, without much conviction and my voice sounds small and lost in the silence. It's eerily quiet. All I can hear is the sigh of the wind in the long grass.

Perhaps Barney has already made his way back to the farmhouse. There's no need to worry. Joe said that he could find his way home.

Before heading back, I peer inside the fogou, just in case the dog's inside. It's too dark to see clearly and it takes a few seconds for my eyes to adjust.

'Barney?' I call and I step inside, then duck into the small side chamber.

I'm just about to turn around and leave when I sense something – a vibration in the ground perhaps – a tiny, almost imperceptible darkening of the light. It makes my spine tingle and the breath catch in my throat. All my senses are suddenly on high alert.

'Avery?' I'm not sure if I say it aloud.

I blunder towards the exit. And for a second, I think I can see her, blocking the entrance, her dark eyes burning into me.

'Avery?' I whisper. I feel so much dread I think I might be about to pass out. Then the light shifts, and I realise that of course it's not Avery. It's a man, and as I get closer and emerge from the tunnel into the grey light, I recognise the guy we met in the pub the other night. I must have made an exclamation of some kind because he says cheerily, 'I'm sorry, I didn't mean to scare you. Are you okay?'

'Yes, I'm fine,' I say, feeling flushed and stupid. 'You just took me by surprise that's all. I didn't think there was anyone else here.'

He blinks at me and smiles. 'Oh, it's you,' he says. 'I'm Charlie. We met the other day, in the Crown, do you remember? You were with your friend.'

'My sister. Yes, I remember.'

'You on your own today?' He looks over my shoulder. I

wonder if he realises how threatening that question could sound to a woman in a lonely spot like this. Probably not, I think. He's a young, strong male. How could he know what it feels like to be at a physical disadvantage, to constantly have the background feeling that whoever you meet could be a threat? I edge my way past him cautiously.

I'm still nervous and I'm ridiculously relieved when Barney appears from nowhere, bounding up out of the mist looking like the Hound of the Baskervilles. He appears large and fierce. An attacker would think twice with Barney around.

'Where have you been, boy?' I say, crouching down and extending my hand. But, to my surprise, he ignores me completely and lollops over to Charlie, jumping up at him, tail wagging furiously.

'Get down, Barney,' I order ineffectually. 'I'm sorry,' I say to Charlie. 'He's not actually my dog. I'm just walking him for someone.'

'No worries.' He smiles down at Barney and pats his head. 'We're old pals, aren't we, boy?'

I absorb this. 'Oh, I forgot you know Joe.'

'Yeah, well I know him a bit. I knew Avery better.'

'You did some work at their house . . .'

'Yep, that and I gave Avery painting lessons. She wanted to learn to do oil paintings. I've got a studio in the village.'

'An art studio?' I say stupidly. My mind is working overtime.

'Yeah, that's right.'

My skin prickles. I think about the passage I read in which Dominic sketches Avery. It can't be a coincidence, can it?

'You gave Avery lessons?' I repeat.

'Yes.' He gives me a weird look.

I'm saved from embarrassing myself further because at that moment another dog, a small terrier, runs up and begins yapping and growling at Barney.

'Play nice now,' Charlie laughs as Barney backs away from the much smaller dog. 'This is Marshall. I'm afraid he's got a superiority complex. He thinks he's much bigger than he is, don't you, mate? I don't think you'd have a chance in a fight,' he says, pulling Marshall back by the collar. Marshall bares his teeth and growls softly as Charlie attaches a lead.

'What's your name, by the way?' Charlie asks straightening up. 'I didn't catch it the other night.'

'I'm Alexandra, Alex Georgiou.'

He stares at me. 'Georgiou, that sounds Greek.'

'I'm half Cypriot. I grew up there.'

'No kidding? Lucky you. Whereabouts?' He grins. 'I love Cyprus. I've been there many times. Ayia Napa. Protoras.'

We talk about Cyprus for a while and the conversation flows naturally, as if we've known each other a long time. Then he stands up and we head together to the exit. As we're walking, I glance sideways at him and observe that he walks with a limp, slightly favouring the left leg over the other.

He sees me looking and winces very faintly. He doesn't like me noticing I think, and I look away quickly, feeling a wave of sympathy.

'Well, it was nice to meet you, Alex,' he says pleasantly as we part ways. He rummages in his pocket and produces a business card with a flourish. 'My studio is just down the road. You're welcome to visit if you're passing. Just to take a look around. No pressure to buy.'

Fourteen

Joe is still outside, checking the oil in his engine when I return.

'Good run?' he asks, smiling. 'What did you think of Carn Euny?'

'Very interesting.' I pause to catch my breath and clutch my side because I've got a stitch. 'Actually, I met a friend of yours there.'

'Oh yeah?' He closes the bonnet and wipes his hands on his jeans.

'Someone called Charlie. He helped fix your roof, I think.'

I watch him carefully for a reaction and I think I detect a tiny flicker of anger or anxiety. But whatever it is, it's quickly disguised.

'Oh?' he says neutrally.

'He told me about his art studio in town. I was wondering if it was worth a visit.'

'I don't know. Never been there.' He frowns. 'I don't think . . .' He breaks off, biting his lip.

'You don't think what?'

'Oh, never mind.'

I decide it's best not to mention Avery's art lessons. I wonder if he even knew about them. Rebecca kept the fact that Dom was painting her a secret from John in *Falling*. Maybe Avery did the same.

'By the way, Alex . . .' he adds as I turn towards the cottage.

'Yes?'

He digs his toe into the gravel. 'Lily mentioned that your sister wanted to go and see dolphins. Lily and I are going out in my yacht today. I could take you both if you want? There's plenty of marine life even in the winter. We're certain to spot dolphins and we might even see a whale.'

I'm taken aback. 'Um . . . I'm not sure. How much would it cost?' I ask.

'No charge,' he says brusquely as if he's embarrassed by his own generosity.

I feel the ground lurch as if I'm already out at sea. I close my eyes and when I open them again, he's looking at me with a faint gleam of amusement.

'Well?'

'That's really kind . . .' I say. 'But I'm not so good on boats.'

'The weather's great today. I know it's cold but it's sunny and the water will be very calm. It'll be fun, I promise you.'

He fixes his dark eyes on me, and I find it hard to say no. Besides Athena will kill me if I pass up this opportunity.

'Alright then. Thank you.'

'Great.' He smiles broadly. 'It's a date then. We can get going at about nine-thirty. How does that sound?'

And he strides away and disappears into the house before I have time to change my mind.

Back in the cottage Athena is already up, sipping coffee and scrolling through her phone.

'Look,' she says showing me a photo she took in the snow yesterday. It's of me standing with my arm around the snowwoman we built, and Joe is standing in the background leaning on his shovel.

'Joe's offered to take us out on his boat to see dolphins,' I tell her. 'He said to be ready in about an hour if we want to go. What do you think?' I take off my trainers and fling myself down on the couch.

'What? Really? This morning? How much does he want?'

'For free.'

Athena's eyes narrow. 'What's the catch?'

'What do you mean, what's the catch? There's no catch. He's just a nice guy, that's all.'

111

She tucks her hair behind her ears and gives me a knowing look.

'He wants to have sex with you,' she says.

'What?' I redden. 'No, he doesn't. What are you talking about?'

'I've seen the way he looks at you.' She taps her phone, showing me the photo again. 'Look at the way he's eyeing you in the picture.' I glance at it and feel a flush of heat and confusion because she's right. He is staring at me with that strangely hungry look I've seen before.

'You're high,' I say. 'He's not interested in me at all. Anyway, he's too old.'

Athena shrugs. 'I'm just saying . . .'

She's wrong, I decide. If he wanted me in that way, he would have invited just me and not both of us.

But as I dive into a hot shower, the water stinging my skin, I feel unsettled. What if he is into me? When I finish my shower, I change into a pair of jeans and a long-sleeved top. I've got about forty-five minutes until we're due to go so I sit in the living room with my copy of *Falling*.

As a rule, I like to do things in order. Skipping to the end of a book feels wrong somehow, like eating your dessert before your main meal or cheating in an exam, but Athena's right. More than ever, I need to know how the book ends. Who killed Rebecca? Even though Avery's fate is unlikely to be the same as Rebecca's, it might give me a clue to her mental state and to the way she felt about the people in her life. So, I break the habit of a lifetime and turn to the last few chapters.

In chapter thirty-two, Harry Hegarty is in London and he's visiting an art gallery with Mona, a woman he met through an online dating app.

Harry would have rather been in the pub. His feet were killing him, and he was desperate for a ciggie. But Mona liked art and what she called 'culture'. She'd already dragged him around the V&A that morning and this afternoon they'd spent two hours at the Tate. Harry was bored and tired. He didn't think much of paintings in general, especially modern art, which was a load of hogwash in his view. Halfway round the Turner gallery he'd had enough, and he'd parked himself on a bench in front of a large painting of a boat in a storm, which at least looked like the thing it was supposed to represent.

'You go on ahead,' he said to Mona. 'I'm beat.'

'If you're sure.' Mona hesitated. 'I'll just have a quick look upstairs. I'll only be a few minutes.'

Needless to say, Mona was gone more than a few minutes and Harry soon got bored of sitting doing nothing, so he stood up and read the information panel next to the painting. He was interested to learn that, according to the blurb, Turner had tied himself to the mast of a ship during a storm so that he could recreate the power of the waves and the sea with more accuracy and realism.

Now that's commitment to your art, reflected Harry. It reminded him of those actors who spent days or even weeks in character so that their performance was more believable. What were they called? Method actors, that was it. So, Turner was like a method artist. His thoughts turned to Dom and how he'd said he liked to be present at the lambing so that he could paint the start of life with all the 'sound and fury' as he put it. It was arty farty claptrap, of course. How could you paint a sound? But it was interesting all the same. And something that had been nagging at the back of Harry's mind for a while suddenly came to the forefront.

Until now Harry hadn't been able to come up with a motive. Now he had one – or at least he thought he had one. But it was so twisted and for want of a better phrase, plain evil, that he wasn't sure it was possible.

I skim-read chapter thirty-three, which seems to be all about Harry's relationship with Mona and his grown-up daughter, who visits him and falls out with both him and Mona. Then I start chapter thirty-four in which he turns up unannounced at Dominic's art studio.

Harry had to admit the painting was very good. The sea itself was an almost motionless, shining grey. At the horizon the sea and the sky merged, and everything was shrouded in fog so that the central subject – a woman lying spreadeagled on the shingle – stood out in stark contrast. She was painted in exquisite but awful detail. Blood pooled at her head and her eyes were glassy and frighteningly empty. Harry gave a small, involuntary shiver. Although the woman in the picture's hair was red and Rebecca's was dark brown, Harry was almost certain that this was a portrait of Rebecca in her final moments.

What kind of monster, he wondered, could kill someone in cold blood and then calmly paint them as they lay dying?

'Can I help you?' Dominic appeared behind him as if in answer to his question. Harry swung round sharply, his fists clenched by his sides.

Cocky bastard, he thought with righteous fury. Dominic hadn't even bothered to hide the painting. He knew that it wouldn't be much use as evidence. After all, what did it prove? He'd painted a picture of Rebecca in her dying moments. So what? he would say to a jury. He hadn't actually been there. He had used his imagination. It proved nothing.

'This painting. It's interesting,' Harry said carefully.

'I'm glad you like it. It's part of my life and death series.' As Dom spoke his lips twisted into a slight but unmistakable smirk. He actually smirked and Harry couldn't escape the feeling that Dom knew that he knew and was revelling in it. Taunting him. With difficulty he managed to keep his voice steady.

'Do you use a model, or do you paint from your imagination?' he asked.

Dom laughed. He knew what Harry was driving at. 'Like most artists, it's a bit of both, I suppose,' he said. 'Sometimes I use my art to help me work through difficult emotions, like grief.'

So that was his angle. That's what he would argue in court – that he'd painted this as a way of dealing with his grief at Rebecca's death. Bullshit, thought Harry angrily. But how could he prove it?

I've reached the end of the chapter. Turning over the corner of the page, I place the book on the coffee table and go and make myself a cup of tea. So, Dominic was the killer, not John after all I think, feeling inexplicably relieved. Clutching my mug of tea in one hand, I skim-read the next few pages just to make sure there isn't another unexpected development right at the end. But there's no final twist, just the obligatory showdown that seems to come at the climax of all murder mysteries – the part when the detective decides to go and confront the murderer all alone for no obvious reason and the reader is left shouting at the page in frustration, 'Don't go there by yourself! Wait for backup, you idiot!' Then there is, of course, a struggle during which Dominic delivers a monologue about his motives for murdering Rebecca.

'Why?' Harry asked.

But was there really any point in asking why? he thought. Could there be any justification for killing someone in cold blood? Dominic enjoyed killing, that was all. It was as simple and banal as it was horrific.

Dominic's eyes were black and blank as a shark's. 'I had a near-death experience in a car accident a few years ago and since then I've been fascinated by death and the moment when consciousness leaves the body. I wanted to capture it truthfully.'

It's an interesting but macabre concept – how far would you go for your art? But I feel it hasn't been fully explored in the story and it doesn't really make sense. If Dom supposedly pushed Rebecca off a cliff top, how could he have been close enough to her to observe her dying moments in detail? He would have been at the top of the cliff, and she would have been at the bottom.

The writing in the penultimate chapters is not as good as the rest of the book. Sometimes it verges on cliché, and it seems rushed, as if Avery was in a hurry to get the book finished. To be frank, it's a bit of a disappointment.

In the final chapter, though, Avery is back on form. She describes the denouement in sensitive detail, and everything is wrapped up in a satisfying way. Dominic is arrested, Harry breaks things off with Mona and tries but fails to reconcile with his wife and daughter. In the last few pages, he's back in his caravan watching a video of his daughter and regretting past mistakes. I don't get time to read the very last page because I look up from the book and realise that it's nearly half past nine and it's time to go.

Fifteen

I didn't expect this.

I thought I'd be afraid of the waves but I'm not. Instead, I feel a rush of freedom, the long-forgotten joy of being on the water.

The boat speeds out of the harbour and I sit at the stern opposite Athena and Lily, the rush of cold air biting my cheeks. I pull my scarf up over my chin and look out over the wide expanse of sea. The mist has lifted and it's a clear, still day. The small, silver waves glitter in the winter sun and the horizon shimmers in the distance.

I glance at Joe who's at the helm, looking at me with an expression I can't quite read. He catches my eye and smiles, his eyes lit by the sun, and I feel an unexpected rush of happiness.

'Look!' Lily exclaims suddenly, breaking the spell. She's

pointing over the edge of the boat at something. I stand up unsteadily and lurch to their side of the boat, gripping the railing for balance and look down at a pod of dolphins, right by the hull.

'Aren't they amazing!' Athena shouts over the rush of the wind and she takes out her phone and snaps away.

I nod, trying to ignore the sudden wave of nausea that has washed over me. The last time I was out on a boat was with my father more than fifteen years ago. But I remember it clearly. It was one of his good days. He was in a sunny mood, laughing and joking. He taught me patiently how to raise the mainsail and to tack and jib and didn't get cross when I made mistakes. But all the same my hands wouldn't stop shaking as he watched me winding the rope round the winch, because I knew how suddenly and randomly his mood could alter.

Impatiently, I banish thoughts of Dad from my mind. What's the point in brooding on the past? Am I going to let him ruin this lovely day? Instead, I try to live in the moment, focussing on the sunlight dancing on the waves and on the dolphins, their sleek, black bodies slipping in and out of the water. They follow us for a while, leaping and diving in the wake and then after about ten minutes they vanish as suddenly as they appeared, swallowed up by the ocean. I peer at the shining black water rushing by, trying to catch sight of them again. But they've disappeared into the depths.

The sea is opaque. God only knows what else is down there under us, I think, and I find myself wondering about Avery's body. Shuddering, I glance over at Joe. Has the same thought occurred to him? It's impossible to tell what he's thinking but there's a grim expression on his face. He's staring straight ahead as if he can see something on the horizon I can't.

Suddenly he veers to the left, steering us sharply towards the cliffs.

'What the hell?' Athena shouts and her eyes widen with alarm. I clutch the rail tightly. We're going very fast and heading straight for the rocks. For a heart-stopping moment, I think we're going to crash into them.

'It's okay,' Lily laughs, patting Athena's arm. 'Look.'

To my relief, I see that we're rounding a headland. We arrive in a small bay with a tiny sandy beach, encircled by cliffs. There's a large cave cut into the rocks. Joe fixes the sail and drops the anchor a few metres from the shore. Then he fetches a Thermos of tea from the cabin and comes and sits with us at the stern.

'Great spot this, isn't it?' he says, pouring the tea into plastic mugs and handing them to us. 'Smugglers used to use this place. They used to transport contraband brandy and gin in the seventeenth and eighteenth centuries and store it here in that cave.'

'Really?' I look around, imagining a boat full of smugglers unloading barrels, rolling them up the beach.

We listen, sipping the tea, as Joe warms to his theme, telling us tales of smugglers and shipwrecks. He's a good storyteller and as he talks, the West Country burr in his voice becomes stronger. It's undeniably appealing – the deep, sea-washed sound of his voice and the way his eyes catch mine every now and then, as if we share a secret.

'There are so many legends about this cave,' he says. 'There's one about a mermaid, the Maid of Zennor, who used to hang out here. Apparently, she was so beautiful a local lad fell in love with her, followed her out to sea and was never seen again.' As he tells us this, he looks directly at me, and I feel the heat rise in my cheeks.

I'm attracted to him, I realise with a jolt of surprise and alarm. That's not part of the plan. And it's certainly not a good idea. I'm writing an article about his deceased wife and until very recently I thought he might have had something to do with her death.

It's okay, I tell myself, as we make our way back to shore. Everything's under control. Just because I'm attracted to him doesn't mean anything's going to happen between us.

Back on dry land the ground still seems to sway, and we stagger up the pier, laughing like drunks. Even Lily seems to be in a good mood and, as we walk into Penzance town centre, she's surprisingly talkative, chatting and laughing with Athena as they trail behind Joe and me.

'I've arranged to meet a friend of mine. I hope you don't mind,' Joe tells me, as we stop outside a quaint old pub called the Admiral Benbow. Inside the pub is painted in bright primary colours and crammed full of nautical memorabilia like a large brass cannon and a red and yellow painted ship's wheel.

Joe's friend is waiting for us at a table in the dining room that has been decorated to resemble a ship's galley.

'This is Steve,' Joe introduces him. 'Steve, this is Alex and Athena, and you know Lily, of course.'

'Lovely to meet you,' Steve beams, grasping my hand firmly and raising it to his lips. He fits in well in this place, I think, with his shock of white hair, weather-beaten brown skin and bright blue eyes. If you wanted to have a generic sailor in a movie, you'd probably cast him. All that's missing is an eye patch or a hook for a hand.

'Did you enjoy your boat trip, now girls?' he asks as we sit down to eat.

'It was great,' I say.

'Yeah, it was cool. That cave was amazing,' Athena agrees. She turns to Lily and Joe. 'Have you been there before?'

'Lots of times.' Lily shrugs. 'I swam to there once in the summer.'

'No! Really?' Athena smiles sceptically. 'It's too far.'

But Joe nods. 'It's true. Lily's a very strong swimmer. She

could swim before she could walk. Avery and I used to call her our little mermaid.'

Lily's face pinches at the mention of Avery's name and Joe's eyes cloud over. He still loves her, I think with a pang. Of course he does. It's only natural.

After that, Lily clams up and becomes her usual taciturn, surly self. But even if she wanted to speak, she probably would have difficulty getting a word in, because Steve can spin a yarn along with the best of them and keeps up a steady stream of anecdotes and jokes, laughing jovially and waving his fork around so that sometimes food flies off. Joe, Athena and I listen and laugh along politely, but Lily has retreated into her shell and spends most of the time fiddling with her phone. When we've finished eating, she stands up abruptly, stares defiantly at Joe and announces that she's going to meet Josh in town.

I watch Joe tense up. His eyes narrow and I think he's about to tell her that she can't. Instead, he just shrugs and says, 'Okay. But don't be late back. No later than twelve.'

'Sure,' she says airily, snatching up her bag. 'Bye.'

'And keep your phone on so I can contact you,' Joe shouts after her as she makes her exit.

Joe is silent for a moment after she leaves then he seems to collect himself and smiles at us both. 'I don't like her going out like this, especially with that guy. But what can I do? She's nearly eighteen.'

'Mm, she'll give you a few grey hairs that one, before she's finished with you,' Steve chuckles and claps him on the back. 'Girls eh? What can you do? Can't live with 'em. Can't live without them.'

On our way back to the car park, Joe and Athena walk on ahead. Athena is talking animatedly about something, waving her arms around, and I fall into step with Steve who continues to chatter away amiably.

'How do you know Joe?' I ask when he pauses for breath.

'Well now, we're sailing buddies. I met him at the sailing meet last year.'

'The same week his wife died?' I say, surprised.

'Yes, that's right.' Steve stops smiling and looks about as sad as it's possible for someone as naturally cheerful as him to look. 'I was with him when he found out. You've never seen a man so devastated. It nearly destroyed him.'

I look ahead at Joe and feel bad I ever doubted him.

'That's why it's so nice to see him looking so happy today,' Steve continues, winking at me. 'I think you might have something to do with that, young lady. You're obviously just what the doctor ordered.'

'Oh, Joe and I aren't . . .' I feel embarrassed. 'We're just staying in his holiday cottage. He offered to take us out on his boat, that's all.'

Steve stares at me. 'Oh really? I thought – Oh well, my

mistake. He's a good man though.' He nudges me and laughs. 'You could do a lot worse.'

We say goodbye to Steve at the car park and pile into Joe's SUV. In the car on the way back to Sancreed nobody says much. Athena and Joe seem lost in their own thoughts and I'm still thinking about the sail meet. There must have been a lot of people there. Steve's story ties in with what Joe told me and proves that he wasn't in Bosigran when Avery died. I look at his face in profile, the slight, worried frown on his forehead, and feel relieved. At least it confirms that he couldn't have been involved in her death.

Sixteen

'Would you girls like to come in for a drink?' Joe asks when we arrive back at Foxton Farm. He kills the engine and glances at Athena sitting in the back seat.

'I'm knackered,' she says, opening the door. 'But thanks, and thanks for the boat trip. That was really cool.'

'How about you, Alex?' Joe fixes his gaze on me as we climb out of the car.

'Well, I'm quite tired too . . .'

'Go on, just a quick one.' He gives me that same intimate smile as on the boat, and I find myself saying, 'Okay, why not?' Spending more time with Joe is an opportunity to discover more about Avery and get more information for my article. That's what I tell myself anyway. But I know in my heart that it's not the only reason.

Athena flashes me a look of surprise. Then shrugs. 'See you later then.'

What am I doing? I ask myself as I walk with Joe towards the house. I know what I'm walking towards and I'm pretty sure it's a bad idea. But it feels inevitable somehow. It's like I'm following a powerful, irresistible instinct, like a salmon swimming upstream to spawn or a bird migrating to a warmer climate.

Barney greets us at the door, jumping up at Joe and whimpering with joy.

'Hello, boy, did you miss me?' Joe stoops and scratches him behind the ears. 'Come in, Alex. Sorry about the mess.'

The house is dark and cold but doesn't look particularly untidy. I hesitate just for a moment on the threshold. Then I follow him in. Athena knows where I am. I finger the phone in my pocket for reassurance.

The living room is a strange mishmash of furniture. There's a large bookcase along one wall and an old stone fireplace. It's even colder in here and it smells of damp and woodsmoke. Perching on the sofa, I watch as Joe piles logs on the fire and then crouches down, twisting some newspaper and lighting it with a match. The flame flares and one side of his face is tinged with gold. I shiver and draw close to the fire, holding my hands to the warmth.

'Cold?' he asks, placing his hand on mine. He only touches

me for a second, but it sends an electric jolt through me, and I snatch my hand away.

'You're cold as ice,' he says calmly, as if he hasn't noticed how on edge I am. 'Hold on. I'll get you a jacket.' He disappears and returns a moment later with a soft, grey shawl. I wrap it round my shoulders, trying not to think about the fact that it must have been Avery's.

Once the fire is established, Joe offers me a drink. 'We've got wine or beer,' he says. 'But my homemade apple cider comes highly recommended.'

'Well, I guess I'll have to try the cider then.'

'Good choice,' he grins.

While he's in the kitchen fetching the drinks, I look around the room. There are pictures of sailing boats and seascapes on the walls. On the mantlepiece there are a couple of photos, one of Lily aged about ten in a blue school uniform, standing next to a slightly taller boy that I assume is her brother Gabe. Next to that is a photo of Avery and Joe standing on top of a mountain somewhere. Joe is beaming at the camera, his arm around Avery. But Avery, wrapped up in a red coat, her face half obscured by a fur-lined hood, looks cold and cross.

Drawn inevitably to the bookcase, I run my hands along the spines of the books, trying to figure out which belonged to Avery and which to Joe. On one shelf there's a neat row of Inspector Hegarty mysteries that look as if they haven't been touched. I pick out one called *A Normal Person with a Heart*.

I'm intrigued by the title and I'm reading the first page when Joe returns.

'Avery's third book,' he says close behind me. 'I think it's probably my favourite.'

I start guiltily as if I've been caught looking at something I shouldn't.

'What's it about?'

'Haven't you read it? I thought you said you were a fan,' he says, eyes narrowing slightly.

I kick myself and flush. 'Oh I am. I've read her other books. Just not this one.'

He shrugs. 'You can borrow it and see for yourself, if you like.'

'Thanks,' I say, slipping it into my bag.

He hands me the cider and sits on the sofa leaving space for me next to him. I waver for a moment then perch opposite him, on the edge of the armchair as if we're conducting an interview. I mustn't get distracted. I need to remember why I'm here. Focus on Avery.

'What was it like being married to a writer?' I ask.

He frowns. 'Just the same as being married to anyone else, I suppose.'

'It must be difficult being well known. You said that she was getting weird messages from a fan before she died?'

He nods. 'She wasn't exactly famous, but she had a few fans and yes, some of the messages she received were a bit stalkerish. There were a couple of strange phone calls in the week before she died as well.'

I lean forward. 'What kind of calls?' I ask.

'You know the kind of thing, heavy breathing mostly, I think. One time he asked her what she was wearing.'

'Did you tell the police?'

He nods. 'Yeah, I mentioned it after Avery died but they thought most likely it was just kids mucking around. I think they'd already decided her death was an accident.' He stares darkly into his glass. 'Do you mind if we don't talk about Avery this evening?'

'Sure. Okay, not if you don't want to,' I say, feeling bad for stirring up painful memories but also frustrated because I have so many more questions and I was about to ask him if he still has the messages saved on Avery's phone.

'I'd much rather talk about you,' he says, leaning forward.

'Like what?' I shift uncomfortably. This conversation isn't going the way I want it to.

'Like anything.' He smiles. 'What makes Alex Georgiou tick? What do you do for a living? Your family. What are you passionate about?'

'There's nothing much to know. I was born and brought up in Cyprus. I'm half Cypriot, half English. I'm a journalist.'

I watch him to see if me telling him I'm a journalist rings any alarm bells, but he doesn't seem all that interested.

'You said you didn't like the sea, but you were a natural out there on the boat today.'

'My dad used to take me sailing sometimes. One summer we all went sailing round the Greek islands.'

'That sounds like an idyllic childhood.'

I wince a little at that, but out loud I just say lightly, 'I suppose in some ways it was. What about you? Where did you grow up?'

'Born and bred in Cornwall, can't you tell, my lover?' His accent thickens again, and I smile.

He smiles back. 'I was a bit wild as a kid. I think I gave my poor old mum loads of trouble. I was always skiving off school. I couldn't stand being cooped up. In the old days I'd have gone to sea and become a pirate.'

I smile. I can picture him as a pirate. And I think I understand him. That urge to be free is something we share.

'I was a delinquent kid too,' I say. 'I could never see the point of school. I mean you hardly ever learn anything useful. Algebra for example. What's that about?'

Joe laughs. 'You're right. I don't think I've used much algebra since I left school.'

'After my mum died,' I continue, 'I used to skip school all the time. There was this old, deserted house near where we lived, and I would go there and sit in the overgrown garden on the edge of the empty swimming pool and just read all day.'

'I bet you learned more from those books than you would have done in school.'

'Maybe.'

We sit watching the fire flicker and the logs crackle. It feels surprisingly easy and natural talking to Joe. We drink more and the time passes quickly. I'm shocked when I look at my watch and realise it's already half past one.

'I'd better go,' I say standing up, feeling a little unsteady. The cider must have been stronger than I realised.

'Do you have to?' he asks softly.

For a moment, I hesitate. 'I think I'd better. Athena will be wondering where I am.'

He shrugs and his mouth lifts at the corner.

'I'll walk you across to the cottage,' he says as he helps me on with my coat.

'There's no need, really.'

'But I want to. Besides it's dark and badly lit. There's a lot of junk out there. You'll trip over something. Least I can do is light your path.' He fetches a torch from a drawer in the living room and holds my arm, steadying me and guiding me across the yard. Everything looks unfamiliar in the dark and strange shapes loom out of the shadows as the torchlight falls on them.

'Well, thank you.' I lean against the cottage door and

blink. The light from Joe's torch is shining in my face and I am momentarily blinded.

'Goodnight,' he says gruffly.

And suddenly without warning he leans over and kisses me on the lips. 'See you tomorrow, Alex,' he says and steps away into the night before I have time to process what has just happened.

Seventeen

A sound like a scream pierces the night.

I wake up, heart hammering.

It's nothing, I tell myself, just that fox again. I turn over and try to go back to sleep. But then there it is again, slicing through the silence like an alarm. I shiver under the duvet. The sounds of the night are so different from the London soundscape. I suddenly long for the familiar hum of traffic and the chatter of drunken people. There's something eerie about the silence here, as if the night were holding its breath. Waiting.

Then there's another noise. Something different. Right under my window. I open my eyes in the dark and sit up in bed, listening, my heart hammering.

There is something moving just outside the cottage.

Yes, there it is again, quiet but distinct, a sort of soft

scraping. It's not my mind playing tricks. I climb out of bed, pull the curtains open and look into the night, but the darkness is so thick I can hardly see anything. The only light comes from a smattering of pale stars in the black sky and a small square of yellow from the window downstairs in the main house. Is Joe still up? Or has he forgotten to turn off the light? Perhaps he can't sleep, like me.

I glance at the clock on my bedside table. It's three o'clock in the morning. Maybe it's Lily only just arrived back.

I'm about to go back to bed when a pulse of fear shoots up my spine.

From the darkness a hooded figure emerges, and heads towards the farmhouse. They move furtively in the shadows, and I watch, frozen, my heart in my throat. A burglar? Or worse?

I reach for my phone to call the police. My finger hovers, trembling over the buttons. But as the person reaches the house, the porch light flicks on and I see them clearly slipping a key into the lock. The figure is a woman and she's wearing Avery's red coat, the coat I saw in the photo in Joe's living room. For a second, I think it's Avery and I'm gripped by a kind of superstitious horror. But then I breathe a slow sigh of relief. Of course, it's only Lily. She must have borrowed her mother's old coat. I watch her let herself in and the door close behind her. Then I head back to bed, feeling foolish, vaguely wondering what she was doing outside our cottage and why I didn't hear Josh's car drive up.

Eighteen

'You were a long time last night.' Athena eyes me suspiciously as I shuffle into the living room the next morning.

I take a couple of Paracetamol from my handbag and wash them down with tap water.

'We got to talking.' I drain the glass and fill it again. I feel dehydrated and my head is throbbing after that cider last night.

'Oh yeah?' Athena looks at me sharply. 'Are you sure that's all?'

The kiss.

It doesn't count, I think. It didn't mean anything. 'Yes, of course that's all,' I say. 'Joe's just a really interesting guy.'

I'm putting two slices of bread in the toaster, trying to ignore Athena's sceptical smile, when I notice a white envelope on the counter. It has ALEX written on it in jagged capital letters.

'What's this?' I ask picking it up.

'Someone put it through the letter box last night.' Athena shrugs. 'I'm guessing that it was Joe.'

In spite of myself, I feel a pulse of excitement in my throat as I tear open the envelope. What could Joe want to say? Another invitation? An apology?

The message inside is simple and stark and definitely not from Joe.

I read it twice, my breath hitching in my throat.

STAY THE FUCK AWAY FROM JOE LEWIS.

I stare at the words, feeling nauseous. 'Oh my God,' I say.

'What is it?' Athena peers over my shoulder.

The toast pops up. I stare at it blankly. I'm finding it hard to speak. I hand the paper silently to Athena.

She reads it quickly, shaking her head and tutting.

'Nice,' she says sarcastically. 'Who the hell wrote this?'

I place the toast on a plate and hack at the butter which has gone hard in the fridge, trying unsuccessfully to spread it.

'I don't know.'

My head is buzzing. I suppose anyone could have seen us out yesterday. A jealous ex maybe? A friend of Avery's? Then, I remember seeing Lily letting herself into the farmhouse last night. Of course. 'It must have been Lily. She must have seen us . . .'

'Lily? No way!' Athena looks at the letter again. And shakes her head in disbelief. 'Seen what?'

'Nothing.' I'm thinking rapidly. Maybe Lily came home earlier than I realised and saw us kissing. But wouldn't we have heard the car? Maybe not if Josh had dropped her at the end of the driveway.

'It must have been her,' I say half to myself. 'I saw her last night. She was just outside our cottage.'

Athena stares at me. 'Are you sure?'

'Yeah, she was wearing her mother's red coat.' I sigh. 'I suppose it's only natural for her to be upset. I mean, remember how we felt when Dad first got together with Olena?'

'Upset about what, Alex? What would she have to be upset about?' She gives me a direct, quizzical look and I blush.

'Well, maybe we kissed a bit.'

She claps her hand to her mouth. 'I knew it! Oh my God, Alex. Are you sure you know what you're doing?'

'It didn't mean anything. We'd just drunk too much cider, that's all.'

'So, Lily saw you?'

'I suppose she must have.'

'Mm, I guess that would be upsetting,' Athena muses. 'Even so –' she taps the paper in her hand – 'this is pretty unhinged if you ask me. Maybe you should take it to the police.'

I shake my head. Lily's been through enough as it is. 'There's no need. We'll be leaving soon.'

I sit down at the small table and take a bite of toast but I don't feel hungry. No matter how much I tell myself that note is just from a mixed-up teenaged girl who's grieving her mother, it's still upsetting.

'Maybe you should confront her,' Athena suggests.

'What would I say though?' I sigh. 'I don't understand it. There's nothing between me and Joe anyway.'

'Isn't there?' Athena arches her eyebrows.

'No, there isn't,' I say firmly.

I don't want to talk about Joe and last night. It makes me feel all kinds of unsettling and confusing emotions. I haven't had a boyfriend since Isaac and there are so many reasons why getting involved with Joe would be a bad idea, not least the fact that I'm writing about the death of his wife. So, I change the subject abruptly to something I know will distract Athena.

'By the way,' I say casually, 'I read the end of *Falling* yesterday.'

'You did?' She leans forward, a gleam of interest in her eyes. 'What happened in the end? Who killed Rebecca?'

I shake my head. 'In the book Rebecca was having an affair with an artist that lives in the village and, in the last few chapters, he kills her.'

'Why?'

'Because he wants to create an accurate painting of the moment of death.'

Athena's mouth hangs open. 'That's sick.' She puts her bowl in the dishwasher. 'I'm not sure it's a very believable motive either.'

I shrug. 'Stranger things have happened.'

'I suppose.' She frowns thoughtfully.

'Anyway, do you remember that guy we met in the pub the other day? He was called Charlie,' I say.

'The fit one or his creepy friend that kept staring at me?'

'The fit one, I suppose. Well, I forgot to tell you I bumped into him the other day. We got chatting and guess what? He told me that he used to give Avery art lessons.'

Athena claps her hand to her mouth. Her eyes are round. 'Do you think they were having an affair like the characters in the book?'

'I don't know, probably not. But he might know something useful. He gave me his card. I was thinking of paying a visit to his studio this morning.'

Athena chews her lip. 'Are you sure that's a good idea?'

'Why not?'

'I don't know. What if he's a crazy killer?' She smiles but she's only half joking. 'Do you want me to come with you?'

'No,' I say firmly. 'He'll be more likely to talk if I'm by myself.'

'Suit yourself,' she says. 'But I'll keep my phone near in case there's any trouble.'

Nineteen

After breakfast, I stash the note in the inside pocket of my handbag along with my tampons and Paracetamol. Then I put on my coat and head into the village.

As I walk past the squat, silent, dark-windowed buildings, I try to shake the sensation that I'm being watched. That note has set me on edge and although I'm pretty sure it's from Lily, I can't help feeling that everyone in this tiny hamlet is aware of my actions and judging me. Let them judge, I think defiantly. I've done nothing wrong. Joe's wife is dead.

Charlie lives at the far end of the village in a quaint, whitewashed stone cottage with a slate roof. The sound of the doorbell is drowned out by a loud, mechanical droning coming from the back of the house. I follow a sign to Charlie's art shop pointing down a side path and find myself in a small, untidy back garden dominated by a large piece of driftwood, which Charlie is attacking with a chainsaw. His clothes and his hair are covered in a light dusting of sawdust and in spite of the cold, sweat is running down his face. He's so completely absorbed in his work that he doesn't notice me until I eventually manage to catch his attention by waving and shouting.

He glances up and kills the power, removing his protective goggles.

'Alex!' he greets me as if we're old friends.

'I hope I'm not interrupting,' I say. 'I was in the village, and I thought I'd take you up on your offer to look around your studio.'

'No, not at all. I'm always glad of an excuse to stop work.' He grins. To my relief he puts down the saw and gestures for me to follow him. 'Come with me.'

He leads me through to his studio, which is in a sort of conservatory with grimy windows and plants lined along the sills. The room is filled with such a jumble of objects that at first it's hard to make sense of what I'm seeing, and I feel slightly dizzy trying to take it all in. Paintings, canvases, easels, an eclectic collection of ornaments and random objects from the beach are crammed onto shelves and any available space. But at least half the room is taken over by strange and beautiful, twisted wooden sculptures. Pieces of uncarved driftwood are lying around like the bones of some huge, ancient creature.

I pick out a seahorse that has been cleverly carved to follow the natural grain of the wood and run my fingers along its smooth surface, wincing at the eye-watering price tag. I had intended to buy something just to make my visit seem more natural, but I can't afford this.

'I found that piece of wood on the beach near here,' he says behind my shoulder. 'It's one of my favourites.'

'It's beautiful,' I murmur, putting it back and looking around for something less expensive. 'This place is amazing. How long have you lived here?'

'About five years. I moved here from London. It was my escape from the rat race. I worked as a teacher for ten years, would you believe?'

I pick up a smaller piece, a crudely carved fish on a stone plinth and turn it over in my hands. 'Really? So, what made you decide to move here and set up this studio?'

He leans against the window seat. 'Well, I went to art college, and I always wanted to sculpt. But life takes over, doesn't it? It's too easy to get caught up in the daily grind.' He stares out at the garden and the block of wood lying like the corpse of a giant washed up on his lawn. 'Then one day, on my way to work some fucker in a Mercedes knocked me off my bike. I nearly died.'

I inhale sharply. The accident. The near-death experience. Dominic nearly died in *Falling* and that was the reason he became obsessed with painting death. It can't be a coincidence.

'I was in hospital for months,' he continues. 'It took a whole year of physical therapy before I could walk again.'

It explains the slight limp I noticed at Carn Euny. 'That must have been traumatic,' I say quietly.

He nods, his lips pressed firmly together. 'Yes, it totally changes your perspective on life, nearly dying like that. It makes you reassess everything. I decided that I couldn't waste any more time in a job that I hated. So, I quit, moved here, set up this studio and the rest, as they say, is history.'

'You were brave to give up your job,' I say thoughtfully. 'It can't be easy to make a living from your art. Do you ever regret it?'

He shrugs. 'Never. This place gets under your skin. It's so incredibly peaceful here. Besides, I get by. I had some savings and I sell a few pieces in a gallery in St Ives. Sometimes I give private lessons.'

'Like to Avery Lewis?'

He gives me a quick, sharp look, which I pretend not to notice.

'Yes,' he says quietly. 'She was quite good, actually.' He opens a side door to a large cupboard and pulls out a canvas. 'She painted this in her last lesson.'

It's an oil painting of the moon shining on dark blue water. The brush strokes are clumsy, and the subject matter is clichéd, but he's right. There's something about it, an energy that's undeniable.

I glance into the cupboard and just catch a glimpse of a stack of canvases covered by a sheet of plastic before he closes it. I think of the paintings in Dominic's studio and wonder why they are covered.

'You paint as well?' I ask.

'Yes. I dabble,' he says tersely. 'But sculpture is my thing.'

I look back at Avery's painting. 'She was a talented person,' I say. 'Did you ever read any of her books?'

He shakes his head. 'Not yet. Funny thing, I didn't even know she was a writer until I read about her death in the paper.'

'She didn't ever mention it?'

'No. We weren't that close.'

I find that hard to believe. I take a deep breath. 'That's strange,' I say, 'because I think there's a character based on you in her fourth book.'

He scratches his head and a cloud of sawdust scatters. Then he puts down the painting and stares at me.

'What do you mean?'

I open my shoulder bag and extract the copy of *Falling* I bought in Penzance. 'Listen to this,' I say, finding the page I've marked and reading out loud.

It was spring when Dominic Brown first came to Finchley Farm. He appeared on the doorstep, a monument of a man, standing

*square in the doorway. His hair was a mass of curls and his brown
eyes glowed with a strange light that Rebecca found fascinating.*

*'What did he want?' John asked, peering suspiciously out of the
window at Dominic striding away across the fields.*

*'He wants to paint our sheep giving birth,' Rebecca answered. 'I
told him we'd let him know.'*

*John shrugged. 'Bloody weird if you ask me but I don't see why
not.'*

I close the book and look up at Charlie, who is listening
intently.

'See? He's an artist like you.'

Charlie makes a dismissive sound in his throat. 'It's not
me. I don't have brown eyes, for a start. They're green. And
I'm not that tall.'

'You're quite tall.'

'Six foot. I'm hardly a giant. And I certainly never painted
Joe and Avery's sheep. They don't have any sheep.'

'Yes, but Dominic's an artist like you. And listen to
this . . .'

*Dominic's studio was in the centre of Sancreed at the back of the
house in a sort of conservatory. It was full of strange but brilliant
paintings, which he said depicted a near-death experience. He'd had
an obsession with death ever since he nearly died in a car accident
several years before . . .*

'That can't be a coincidence. You must have told Avery
about your bike accident?'

146

He shakes his head, looking genuinely mystified.

'I suppose I must have. I can tell I'm going to have to read this.' He takes the book from me and flicks through, a faint frown on his face. 'So, what happens to this Dominic character? He sounds like a great guy.' He smiles wryly.

I decide it's best not to mention the fact that Dominic turns out to be a psychopathic killer who ends up murdering Rebecca in cold blood. 'I haven't read it all,' I say. 'But Rebecca and Dom become lovers later in the book.'

'What? No kidding!' he exclaims, laughing heartily. 'Now I'm *definitely* going to have to read it.' He turns a couple of pages and is silent for a moment, his eyes flicking over the page, his mouth lightly open. 'Oh my God,' he says and reads aloud. '*Dominic kissed her neck and began to unbutton her blouse. His hand snaked down over the curve of her breast.*' He twinkles at me. 'She had a good imagination, I'll give her that.'

'So, it wasn't based on real life?' I ask.

He barks with laughter. 'You mean, you think . . .? No. Like I said, I barely knew her, not to mention the fact that she was married.'

'But she was an attractive woman.'

He shrugs. 'I suppose so, if you're into that kind of thing.' He hands the book back to me. 'If it is based on me, I don't know what to think,' he says. 'Whether to be flattered or insulted.'

147

'Maybe it's not meant to be you,' I say. 'I was just struck by the similarity between your studio and the art studio in Avery's book and the story about the accident.'

I pause, wondering how much he really knows and how far to probe for information.

'There are a lot of other weird similarities between the book and real life,' I say at last. 'For example, her character, Rebecca, falls off a cliff at Bosigran and dies just like Avery did.'

He stares at me with what looks like genuine astonishment. 'You're not serious!' he exclaims. 'Jesus.' He rakes a hand through his hair. 'This is all too weird. Would you like a drink, Alex? I think I need one.'

'A cup of tea would be nice. Thank you.'

He disappears into the house and returns with a tray of tea and biscuits, and he draws up a chair for me. As he hands me the cup, I notice that his hand is shaking slightly.

'It's almost as if she had a premonition of her own death,' he says.

'Yes. Or copied her own writing. What do you think really happened to her? Do you think she killed herself?'

His eyebrows knit together. 'I don't know . . . I mean, I assumed it was just a terrible accident, but this sheds a new light on things.'

'It does, doesn't it?' I'm glad he sees it too. I'm not crazy.

'Did she ever mention anything about strange messages and phone calls?' I ask.

Charlie frowns. 'Now that does ring a bell. I can't remember the details though. Why, do you think . . .?'

'I don't know. How was she when you last saw her? Did she seem frightened or upset?'

Charlie appears to consider this idea. Then he shakes his head. 'No, not really. She was a little concerned about her daughter acting up and getting in trouble at school. But the last time I saw her, about a week before she died, she was in good spirits. She was planning to go to London for the week to visit her son at uni. She was excited about that.'

I take a sip of tea, thinking about the acknowledgements in *Falling*. '*Thank you to my son Gabriel and my daughter Lily.*'

'You mean Gabriel?'

He shrugs. 'I guess. I don't know his name.'

'How long was she in London?'

He doesn't answer. Instead, he chews his nail, giving me a long, direct look. Then he smiles slowly. 'Why are you really here, Alexandra? Why are you asking all these questions about Avery Lewis? You're not just here on holiday, are you?'

I open my mouth. I'm about to protest that I don't know what he's talking about but there's something about the conspiratorial way he's smiling that invites honesty.

'No, you're right,' I admit. 'I'm a journalist. I'm researching a story about her.'

'You're writing an article about Avery?' He stares at me. 'Why? Was she that famous?'

'Not really. I'm looking into her death. It's strange that she died the same way as the character in her book. I mean, it can't be a coincidence, can it?'

'Mm, it's an enigma,' he says, giving me a mischievous smile. 'I like mysteries.'

I try to ignore the way he's looking at me. As if I'm a particularly interesting mystery to be solved.

'By the way, you mustn't tell Joseph Lewis what I told you,' I say hastily. 'He doesn't know. I mean I . . .' I flush. 'I'll tell him eventually. He just doesn't know yet.'

Charlie shrugs and smiles. 'Your secret's safe with me.'

Twenty

Why do I feel like Charlie wasn't telling me the whole truth? I have an inkling that he knew Avery better than he's letting on.

As I leave his studio and make my way back through the village, I start to regret confiding in him. I barely know him, after all, and I wonder why I told him so much. It's not like me to be so trusting. But there's something about his open, carefree manner that invites familiarity. I find myself wondering if Avery felt the same way. Did she confide in him too?

I head up the narrow track to Foxton Farm, turning over our conversation in my head. It's interesting that Avery went to visit her son in London just before her death. Perhaps something happened to her there, something that led to her death either directly or indirectly. I decide I need to speak to Gabriel. But how to get hold of him? I can't very well ask Joe for his contact details. How would I explain why I needed them? No, I need to get Gabriel's telephone number somehow without Joe knowing. But how? As I reach the farm a plan forms in my mind. It's a bit risky but it just might work.

'Alex!' Joe answers the door. 'What can I do for you?'

I try not to get distracted by the warmth of his smile and the way his eyes light up when he sees me.

'I'm sorry to bother you, I was just wondering if I could use your phone,' I tell him glibly. 'I need to ring Athena and I can't find my mobile.'

'Sure. It's no bother. Come in.' He ushers me through into the kitchen. 'Now where did I put it? I'm always losing the bloody thing.'

He finds it charging on the kitchen counter and hands it to me.

'Are you sure she's not in the cottage?' he says. 'I thought I saw her not long ago.'

'Well, she's not there now,' I say, blushing a little at the lie.

'Do you want something to drink?'

'Er yes, thanks, a coffee please.'

I figure if he's busy making a drink he'll be less likely to notice what I'm doing. While he's filling the kettle, I move away to the far corner of the room and scroll through his contacts. As I hoped, Gabriel's number is near the top. I repeat it a couple of times under my breath. Then I glance at Joe who is spooning out coffee into mugs and I call Athena.

'Hello? Alex?' She sounds sleepy. 'Are you okay?'

'Oh, thank God, Athena,' I say loudly so that Joe will hear me. 'It's me, Alex.'

'Yes, I know. Where are you? Are you still at the art studio?'

'I'm at the farmhouse with Joe. Where you are? I've been worried about you.'

'What do you mean, where am I?' she mutters irritably. 'I'm right here, in the cottage. How was the art studio? What was Charlie like?'

'Well, you could have told me. See you in a bit,' I say and press end call, cutting off Athena's baffled protest.

'Everything okay?' Joe asks, when I give back his phone.

'Yes, she's alright. Thank God. She just went for a walk. She'll be back soon.'

I turn to go, repeating Gabriel's number in my head.

'Thank you,' I say. 'For letting me use your phone.'

'You're welcome. Hey, what about the coffee?'

'Oh yeah, I nearly forgot.' He hands me a steaming mug and I perch on a bar stool and gulp it down as quickly as possible, scalding the roof of my mouth in the process.

'I enjoyed our chat last night,' he says, smiling mischievously, his eyes crinkling.

'Mm, yes.' I try to avoid his gaze. Looking at him makes me feel giddy and breathless.

'You're due to leave tomorrow, aren't you?' he says softly.

'My God, are we really? I'm losing track of the days,' I blurt. I'd almost forgotten that our visit is nearly over. The past couple of days have gone so quickly. I'm not ready to go. Not yet. Not now I feel like I'm just starting to get somewhere.

'It's flown by, hasn't it?' he says. 'At least it has for me. I would have liked to get to know you better. Last night . . .'

'Well, I'd better go,' I interrupt him, standing up abruptly and ignoring the sudden flash of hurt I see in his eyes.

'Actually, I was wondering if you might want to stay a bit longer?' he says in a rush as I head for the door. 'The cottage isn't booked next week, and you could stay, free of charge.'

'Um . . .' I feel a lurch of panicky indecision. What should I do? I need to get back for work, but I feel I haven't got to the bottom of what happened to Avery yet. And there's an uncertainty, a lost-little-boy look in his eyes that I haven't seen before, and it makes me want to hug him.

So, I find myself saying, 'Sure. Why not?'

His face lights up. 'Great,' he says, 'I'll book you in for another week then.'

'Okay. Thank you.'

'I'm really glad you've decided to stay,' he says at the door. He places his hand on my arm and, for a second, I think he's going to lean in for another kiss. For a second, I want him to, really badly. But then he changes his mind and pulls away at the last moment.

This isn't good. What am I doing? Cold, damp air wraps itself around me as I cross the courtyard to the cottage. Joe obviously thinks I'm staying because of him and because of that kiss last night. Am I? It's true that I'm attracted to him. But getting involved with him is out of the question for so many reasons. For one thing, there's Avery. He's not over her death yet. For another, he's at least ten years older than me. Not to mention the article I'm writing. If he finds out that I've been lying to him all this time, I doubt he'll forgive me.

I let myself into the cottage and safely out of view of the main house, I save Gabriel's number to my contacts before I forget it. I'm not sure what I'm going to do with it. He's not likely to agree to meet and talk to a strange woman, after all. But it's a start. I'll think of a way to persuade him to talk to me later.

Athena is in her bedroom folding T-shirts and stacking them in her suitcase, which is open on the bed.

'What the hell was that phone call all about?' she asks, looking at me curiously.

'It's complicated.'

She raises her eyebrows but doesn't push for an answer.

'Thank God we're going home tomorrow,' she says, shoving her trainers into a plastic bag. 'I can't wait to get back to civilisation and WiFi. I think we're both starting to lose it in this place.'

I sink down on the bed and pick at some imaginary fluff on the bedspread. 'About that,' I say gingerly. 'I've booked the cottage for another week.'

She stops packing and gawps at me.

'What? Why? Haven't you got enough material for your article by now?' She frowns crossly and rams her hair-dryer into the suitcase. 'I can't believe you decided that without consulting me. There's no way I can stay. I've got lectures and there's Ruby to think about. Someone's got to feed her.'

'You don't have to stay with me. I'll drive you back to London. I've got some things I need to do there anyway and then I'll come back by myself.'

She presses down on her suitcase and zips it closed. I can see the thoughts whirring through her head. 'How can you afford it?'

'Joe offered to let me stay for free. The cottage is empty anyway.'

'Ooh.' A long drawn-out Oh. 'This is about Joe, isn't it? What's going on between you two?'

'Nothing,' I say hurriedly, my cheeks burning. 'It's about Avery and this article I'm writing.'

It's true, I tell myself. I do want to know what happened to her. No, it's more than that. I *need* to know. It's almost become a compulsion. I feel connected to her in some mysterious way I can't explain. I only know that if I don't find out the truth, I'll feel that I've let her down somehow.

Athena smiles sceptically. 'What about your job?'

'I'm going to call in sick.'

'That's crazy, Alex.' Athena's smile vanishes. 'You've already had one week off. They'll fire you if you're not careful and you worked so hard to get that job. It's your dream job and besides, what about money?'

I don't answer. I can't explain it to her. I know it's a risk but I'm counting on this article being so impressive that firing me wouldn't cross Lou's mind. If I do it right, it could be the making of my career.

Not that I've actually written anything yet. I guess I should get started, so I have something to show Lou.

In the evening, while Athena is watching an episode of *Friends*, I sit on my bed with my back propped up against the headboard, my laptop balanced at an angle on my knees and open a word document.

The Mysterious Death of the Thriller Writer.

I type. Sometimes if you leave something for long enough

the subconscious has time to percolate, and the words just pour out, fully formed.

No one knew who the dead woman was.

A dog walker found the body on the beach below the cliffs at Bosigran and alerted the police.

This is the compelling start to Falling, the new murder mystery by Avery Lewis.

Less than two months after she wrote those words the forty-one-year-old author of the Inspector Hegarty mysteries was herself dead, drowned in the sea in shockingly similar circumstances.

A strange coincidence? Or something more sinister?

It's not unknown for fiction to be eerily prophetic. A book called Futility written by Morgan Robertson fourteen years before the Titanic sank describes a massive ocean liner called the Titan that crashed into an iceberg. There weren't enough lifeboats, and many people died. And in 1994, Tom Clancy wrote about a hijacked aeroplane that hit the Capitol building a full seven years before 9/11. There are many other examples of literature foreshadowing reality. But, to my knowledge, authors don't usually predict their own futures and yet, in Falling, Avery Lewis did just that, with an accuracy that could give even the least superstitious person pause for thought. Because both Avery and her main character, Rebecca, died by falling from the Bosigran cliffs, a remote place on the far west coast of Cornwall.

There are many other similarities between Avery's life and the book she wrote, from the renovated farmhouse where she lived to the . . .

To the . . . what? I chew my thumbnail trying to think of a suitable ending to that sentence. But I'm temporarily out of ideas and am beginning to feel tired, so I stop typing, save the document and snap the laptop shut. How is Joe going to feel when he reads this? How will Lily feel? Most likely they'll be hurt and angry and they'll have every right to be. I don't like the idea of upsetting them but at the same time I can't let this story go. It's just too good.

Twenty-one

'I think you're making a mistake.'

We're driving back to London along the A30. A thick fog has descended, and it feels like driving through a cloud. I'm blindly following the red rear lights of the car ahead. Wind turbines loom out of the mist, rotating slowly like huge alien creatures. Athena is staring out of the window. Her thick eyebrows are knitted together, and her expression is grim.

'What if you lose your job? What if they fire you?'

I grip the wheel as the car ahead drives through a puddle, kicking up spray. 'Once Lou reads the article I've written about Avery, she'll be begging me to stay,' I say with more confidence than I actually feel.

Athena glares at me. 'I just don't understand. You can always stay in contact with Joe on WhatsApp or whatever. You don't need to go back there.'

'I told you, it's not about Joe.'

She sighs. She clearly doesn't believe me. 'What do you see in him anyway? He's old enough to be your father and he's not even that good-looking.'

Irritation bubbles up inside me. I can't understand why this bothers her so much. It's my business what I do. It has nothing to do with her.

'It's not all about looks or age. Some of us aren't as shallow as you,' I retort.

'That's nice,' Athena responds tartly. 'Thank you.'

We spend most of the rest of the six-hour journey in stony silence broken only by a stop at a motorway service station on the M5 where Athena flounces off ahead of me towards the rest rooms and we eat greasy burgers sitting at different tables in the fast-food restaurant.

When we finally arrive home, tired and grumpy, Athena dumps her suitcase in the hallway, snatches up her coat and heads out of the house without a word. By the time she gets back, I've already eaten my supper and am sitting with my feet up drinking a glass of wine and watching the news on TV.

'There's some ravioli in the microwave,' I say coolly as she slinks by.

'Thanks.' She hovers in the doorway, looking contrite. 'I'm sorry, Alex,' she says. 'Whatever you do, it's up to you. I only said what I said because I care about you. I don't want you to get hurt.'

I turn down the volume on the TV and smile at her. Her face is pink with cold air, and she looks sweet and forlorn. I know that what she's saying is true and I can never stay angry with her for long. Besides we've only got each other, and we need to look out for one another.

'I know. I'm sorry too. I didn't mean to call you shallow. I know you're not.'

'Friends?'

'Friends.' We hug tightly and I feel her shoulder blades poking through her T-shirt and feel a familiar urge to protect her. What I'm protecting her from, I'm not sure. But underneath the bravado I've always felt there's something fragile about Athena. Invisible fault lines that need to be handled gently.

Twenty-two

Maybe Athena's right. Maybe I am making a mistake and blindly blundering down a path that leads nowhere.

But I can't stop thinking about Foxton Farm and Avery's death. I can't believe it was just a senseless accident. That there was no meaning to it.

I keep replaying the conversation I had with Charlie in my head and returning to Avery's last week alive, those few days that Charlie told me she spent in London. If I knew what happened to her during that time, it might answer some of my questions or at least point me in the right direction. I need to speak to her son and find out what he knows.

After Athena's gone to bed, I finally drum up the courage to call Gabriel's number, the number I stole from Joe's phone.

'Hello?' a sleepy, gruff voice answers.

I clear my throat. 'Er, yes, hello. Is that Gabriel Lewis?'

'Speaking.'

I fight the panicked urge to hang up. I really should've thought through what to say before calling. 'Er . . . yes . . . hello. My name is Alex . . . Blake and I write for the *Post*,' I rattle off quickly. 'I'm writing a book about thriller authors, including your mother, Avery Lewis, and I was wondering if we could meet to talk.'

He sounds taken aback. 'My mother? Why do you want to talk to me? How did you get my number?'

'I'd like to include some biographical detail,' I say, answering the easiest question.

'I don't think so. I'm kind of busy.'

'I'll pay you,' I say quickly before he hangs up. 'Fifty pounds for an hour of your time.' I'm betting that as a student he'd welcome the cash. I can't really afford to throw the little money I have left around, but I need to speak to him, and it seems like it might be the only way to persuade him to meet me.

There's a silence on the other end of the phone, an exhalation of breath. 'Um, yes okay,' he says at last. 'When?'

'Tomorrow if possible.'

'I'm busy tomorrow. I've got lectures in the morning and in the afternoon.'

'It won't take long. I could meet you at midday and buy you lunch. Where would be convenient for you?'

He hesitates. 'Okay. There's a nice restaurant near the university, called The Plate.'

'Okay? Great. I'll see you at twelve then, outside The Plate.'

'Sure.'

Twenty-three

I recognise Gabriel straight away from the photo in Joe's living room. He's lounging against the wall outside the café – a tall, lanky lad with dark, greasy hair, pale skin and Avery's beautiful, liquid, black eyes. A couple of students are with him, rucksacks slung on their backs, self-conscious smiles on their faces. One of them says something in a low voice as I approach, and they laugh loudly and clap Gabe on the back before dispersing.

'Gabriel Lewis?' I say.

'Yes. Well, it's Monroe actually. Gabe Monroe.' He takes my proffered hand in his cold, clammy palm, and I wipe my hand on my jeans as I follow him into the café.

Monroe must be Avery's first husband's surname, I think. It would have been natural for Gabe to have kept his original name after Avery's second marriage.

Inside the café, we sit at a table in the corner next to a large replica of a Chinese terracotta warrior. Gabe examines the laminated menu, poring over every item and eventually orders chicken strips and rice with a Fanta. I skim the vegetarian options and choose a falafel wrap and a glass of wine. I might need the wine to boost my confidence, even though I think Gabe is probably even more nervous than me, a fact that helps to put me at my ease.

'Thank you so much for agreeing to meet me,' I say, while we're waiting for the food to arrive.

'S'okay.' He shrugs, not meeting my eyes and fumbling awkwardly with the paper wrapping on a straw.

'I'm a big fan of your mother's work,' I continue.

'Thank you.' Blood creeps up his cheeks and there is a wrecked look in his eyes. I remember how young he is, not so much older than I was when my mother died, and my heart reaches out to him.

'I'm so sorry about what happened,' I say quietly.

A bleak lift of the shoulders. 'Yeah.'

There's not much that can be said in the face of such loss.

The drinks arrive, and he bends his head over his Fanta, his hair falling over his face so I can no longer see his expression.

I realise I'm going to have to work hard to get him to open up and I start with what I hope is a fairly safe, inoffensive topic. 'Was Monroe your mother's maiden name?'

'No, it was my father's.'

'Your father is . . . John, right?' I hazard.

'Tom.'

'Yes, that's right. Tom Monroe. Can you tell me about him?'

He frowns. 'What do you want to know?'

'Anything and everything. The more detail I have for my book the better. I might not use it all, but anything could be useful. What does he do for example? How did he meet your mother? How long were they together?'

'He's an architect. I'm not sure how they met. They were together about fifteen years. They divorced about five years ago. He lives in Germany now.'

He breaks off as the food arrives and we eat in silence for a moment.

'They separated when she met her second husband, Joseph Lewis. That's right, isn't it?' I say between mouthfuls.

'Yeah.'

'Did they stay on good terms – your mum and dad?'

Gabe looks uncomfortable. He stabs a strip of chicken with his fork. 'Not really. They didn't meet or speak to each other after she left.'

If this were an Inspector Hegarty mystery, I reflect, Tom Monroe would certainly be a suspect in Avery's death. He had an obvious motive.

'Your father was angry when she left him, I suppose, it would only be natural,' I murmur.

'Not really. I mean, he was upset of course but he was willing to stay friends. It was Mum who stopped talking to him. She wanted to make a clean break from her past life.'

He sounds strangely bitter, and I glance at him curiously.

'He didn't break off all contact with you though?'

'No, we speak on the phone occasionally and two summers ago my sister and I stayed with him in Germany.'

'But he hasn't been here to visit you in the UK?'

'No.' He shakes his head. 'He hasn't been a big part of our lives since Mum remarried.'

There's no emotion in his voice as he says this, and I wonder if he really isn't bothered by his father's apparent lack of interest or if he's just putting on a brave face. Sometimes an absent father is better than the alternative, I reflect, and then before my thoughts get darker, I change the subject.

'Your mother came to visit you at university, right, about a week before she died?' I say.

His face leaches of colour. He looks more lost than ever. His pale skin is pinched and creases around his eyes like someone much older. 'Yeah. She brought my keyboard. I hadn't been able to fit it in the car the first-time round.'

I put down my knife and fork and wipe some sauce from my chin with a napkin. 'How was she?' I ask gently.

'What do you mean?'

'Did she seem normal, or was she upset about anything?'

He gives me a strange look. But he appears to consider the question. 'No, I don't think so. She was concerned about the book she was writing. But otherwise, she seemed okay.' He tears at a small packet and salt spills onto the table. 'We didn't talk for long. She had to go and meet her agent.'

'Her agent? You mean Olivia Brown?' I lean towards him, my elbows resting on the table.

He puts a forkful of food in his mouth and tips his chair back. When he's finished chewing, he says, 'Yeah. That's what she said.'

'Do you know why she wanted to talk to her?'

'Nope.'

I have the strong feeling that Gabe is holding something back.

'Are you sure your mother didn't tell you anything important, Gabe?' I ask softly.

He puts down his fork and gives me a searching look as if he's trying to decide if he can trust me. For a second, I think he's going to tell me something. But then he hunches over like a hermit crab retreating into its shell. 'No,' he says not meeting my eyes. 'Why would she?'

'Did you read her last book?'

He shakes his head. 'I haven't read any of her books. Before she died, I never seemed to have the time and then after she died . . . it was too . . .'

'Painful?'

He nods.

'The victim in the last book she wrote dies in the same place and in the same way as your mother.'

His eyes widen in what looks like genuine shock. 'That's weird,' he says. His fingers drum nervously on the table.

'I was wondering if it's possible that her death wasn't an accident . . .' I begin.

'Her death was an accident,' he interrupts firmly, pressing his lips together. And I guess I've gone too far because he looks pointedly at his phone and says coldly, 'I'm sorry I need to go now.'

Then he stands up abruptly and walks towards the door. As he passes me, I grab his arm.

'Wait.'

He stares down at my hand, and I drop it, realising I probably seem overly intense.

'What?' His eyes are defiant and sullen.

'I'm sorry,' I say lamely, sliding a fifty-pound-note into his palm. 'It must have been difficult for you talking about your mother. Thank you for your time.'

'Sure,' he mutters, and he slips out of the café before I can say anything else.

Shit, I think. That didn't go as well as I'd hoped. I pray to God he doesn't mention this to Joe.

There's a stale, rubbery smell on the underground. A pungent whiff of machinery lubricant mixed with unwashed bodies and leftover food. I grip the metal handrail tightly and plant my feet firmly, steadying myself against the swaying of the train and the other bodies jostling into me. I'm only half aware of the press of people around me as I replay my conversation with Gabe in my mind. I'm sure he was keeping something from me. His expression gave him away.

Avery was worried about something, something more than her book and a bolshy, teenaged daughter. Did she tell Gabe what it was? And if she did, why won't he tell me? Who is he protecting?

The crowd of commuters thins as we near the end of the line and I breathe a sigh of relief as the train emerges into the open air and pulls into Highams Park Station. As I cross the road and walk up the tree-lined avenue to my house, I plan my next steps. I need to talk to Avery's agent, Olivia Brown. Maybe she'll be more forthcoming.

As soon as I get home, I fire off a message, attaching a copy of the beginning of my article.

Hi Olivia, I type breezily. *I hope you're well. Here is the start of a piece I'm writing about Avery Lewis. I'd like to meet and discuss a few points. Would tomorrow be possible?*

I'm not optimistic that Olivia will agree to meet at such short notice, but even so, I check my inbox obsessively all afternoon. There's no message from Olivia but just after five o'clock my phone beeps and an unfamiliar number flashes up on my screen. Thinking it might be her, I swipe upwards to answer.

'Alexandra *mou!*'

I clutch the phone tightly. Only one person calls me Alexandra. I should hang up straight away, but I don't. I'm not sure why. Maybe it's curiosity.

'How did you get my number?' I demand.

'How are you, sweetheart?' he says in the Greek accent he's never quite lost.

'Don't call me sweetheart.'

'Okay. *Endaksi.* Sorry. Listen, I know you don't want to talk to me, but I spoke with Athena . . . and she told me you're short of money. If you give me your bank details, I can pay in some cash. How does ten thousand euros sound?'

Pretty damn good is how it sounds. For a second, I'm sorely tempted. But it's only a second.

'No thank you, Dad.'

'It's no problem. Business has been booming lately. We've had a lot of tourists visiting the hotel this past year. Russians, Israelis, Germans. All Olena's contacts have certainly helped. We're even thinking of expanding.'

I picture Dad's hotel, The Olive Grove, a large sprawling complex built in what used to be a quiet, unspoilt bay near Ayia Napa. I've never actually visited but I've seen photos online. I dread to think where he got the money to build

173

it in the first place and how he persuaded the government to give him planning permission.

'I really don't want your money,' I say through gritted teeth.

'But Alexandra . . .'

'Bye.' I hang up before he has the chance to say anything else.

My hands are shaking as I switch off the phone. I know he'll try to ring again. Bloody Athena. How dare she give him my number? I'll have to change it again now.

I don't have the courage to switch on my phone again until late in the evening and, when I do, a short message flashes up on the screen. It's from Olivia. 'Great to hear from you Alex, I could meet at four o'clock tomorrow at Hyde Park – the lido café. Does that suit you?'

Twenty-four

The temperature has dropped several degrees overnight and the air is icy. I'm at Hyde Park Lido, shivering in my thin coat and looking out at the boating lake gleaming in the winter sun. Olivia is late, so I buy myself a hot chocolate in the café, then wander outside and sit at a wooden table looking at the ducks sleeping by the lakeside, their beaks tucked into their chests, feathers fluffed against the cold.

A grey squirrel scampers along the path in front of me and up a tree and I'm blindsided by a sudden memory:

Christmas 2004. I was ten years old. We were in St James's Park feeding the squirrels, which were so tame that they came and ate right out of our hands. It was just me, Mum and Athena. Dad had stayed in Cyprus, and I'd never seen my mother so relaxed or happy. When one of the boldest squirrels climbed up onto her shoulder, we fell about laughing and my mother laughed most of all. And the sound of her laughter was pure joy.

Sometime later during that holiday there were long, tearful late-night phone calls with my father while Athena and I were in bed, supposedly asleep. At the time I had no idea what they were discussing. It was only when I was much older, I realised that the trip to England had been an escape attempt. Mum had planned to leave my father permanently but, somehow, he'd persuaded her to return.

And I think, with a stab of intense pain, what if we had stayed? What if we hadn't returned? Would she still be alive now?

'Hi! You must be Alex,' says Olivia, interrupting my thoughts and making me jump. She's standing over me, holding out a gloved hand and smiling. She's a few years older than her picture but still attractive. Her curly, black hair is tucked under a woollen hat, a few strands escaping. 'It's great to meet you,' she says, all bubbly professionalism.

'Thanks for seeing me at such short notice,' I say, shaking off thoughts of my mother and pulling back a chair for her to sit. 'Can I get you a drink?'

'No thanks. I can't stay long.' She perches opposite me with her back to the boating lake. I take the lid off my hot chocolate and the steam rises in the chill air.

She tips her head to one side and gives me a friendly,

appraising look. 'I read the start of your article and I'm intrigued. It could be great publicity for the Inspector Hegarty series.'

I feel a rush of relief. I hadn't really expected such a positive response. 'I'm glad you like it,' I say. 'But I want to make sure I do Avery justice and not treat her death as something sensational. I mean, I'd like to get to the heart of who she really was as a person and a writer, not just focus on the way she died. That's why I wanted to talk to you.'

Olivia nods her approval. 'Okay. What do you want to know?'

'What was she like? Did you know her well?'

'Not all that well. But I was at college with her years ago. I knew her a bit from then. We went on a skiing holiday together with a crowd of other students.'

'Really?' Olivia doesn't look old enough to have been at college with Avery. I take a sip of chocolate, reassessing her age and wincing as the hot liquid burns my lips.

'We kind of lost touch until she contacted me a few years ago about publishing her first book.' Olivia smiles. 'I was worried that it would be bad, and I'd have to let her down gently, but I was very pleasantly surprised.'

I remember what Athena said about Avery meeting Joe when they worked at an accounts firm.

'She worked at a financial company before she became a writer, didn't she?'

Olivia nods. 'That's right. At a place called Holden and Pierce.'

I make a mental note of the name. 'And she left because she wanted to write full-time?'

She frowns. 'Not really.' She leans in. 'Actually, I heard a rumour that she'd been fired, which was one of the reasons she started writing.'

'Fired?' I say, nonplussed. 'Why?'

'I believe there was some money that went missing,' she says vaguely. 'Apparently, cheques were forged. She over-charged customers, that kind of thing.'

I'm astonished. It doesn't fit with the picture of Avery I've been building at all. 'Why wasn't she arrested?'

Olivia shrugs. 'They hushed it up. I think the owner of the company knew her parents and they didn't want any scandal attached to the company.'

'What was she like at college?' I ask. 'Was there any sign that she was dishonest?'

'No, nothing like that.' Olivia shakes her head and stares pensively out at the lake. 'But she was a rule breaker. I suppose you could say she was someone who lived life to the full,' she says. 'The first time we went skiing she went off-piste just for the hell of it, dragging me along with her. We were nearly caught in an avalanche.' She laughs. 'That was the kind of person she was.'

I think about what Sergeant Metcalfe told me about

finding her phone on the ledge and his theory that she had been trying to retrieve it when she fell. 'So, it wouldn't have been out of character for her to take risks?'

'I wouldn't have thought so,' she smiles.

'For example, she might have tried to climb down a sheer cliff face to get something she'd dropped?'

Olivia's eyes widen. 'Why? Is that what happened?'

'Maybe. They found her phone halfway down the cliff. They think she was trying to get it when she fell.'

Olivia bites her lip, and her eyes fill with tears. 'Sorry,' she says brushing at her eyes.

We sit in silence for a while. On the lake a swan glides past and a Canada goose tucks its head under its wing.

'Did you know her first husband, Tom Monroe?' I ask finally.

'Sure. I knew him vaguely at university. They got married in their final year. Avery was already pregnant with Gabriel then.'

'He must have been devastated when she left him for Joe?'

'I imagine so, but I don't really know. I wasn't in contact with them at the time they broke up and she never talked about him.'

'What did you talk about? Did she talk about her personal life much?'

'She talked about her kids, how Gabe was in university and how she was worried about Lily.'

'Lily. Why?'

'Oh, I don't know, she was acting up. Generally being a teenaged girl. I told her she'd grow out of it.'

'Did she mention Joe at all?'

Olivia shrugs. 'Not much. But I got the impression they were very much in love. He was very romantic. But then again Avery had that effect on men.'

'She was very beautiful,' I murmur.

'Yes, but it wasn't that. It was a quality she had.'

Of course. I can't compare to someone like that, I think. Then I angrily brush the petty thought away. It's so stupid to be jealous of someone who's dead.

'She came to see you the week before she died, didn't she?' I ask.

Olivia seems taken aback. She starts and flushes, then smiles. 'You certainly do your research, don't you? Yes, we met for lunch to celebrate the publication of her last book and to discuss *Falling*. I thought we were both happy with it as it was, so I was surprised when she emailed me later with revisions to the ending.'

'She changed the ending?' I blow on my hot chocolate and take a sip, thinking about how the last chapters had seemed rushed. 'What happened in the previous version?'

Olivia leans forward resting her forearms on the table. 'In the original, the murderer was the same but Dominic drowned Rebecca in a bathtub and painted her as a sort of modern Ophelia, surrounded by flowers. Then when he finished the painting, he dumped her body in the sea. In my view it was a better conclusion to the book, but I decided to go along with Avery's wishes. It didn't seem fair to change it when she wasn't around to argue her case.'

'Why didn't she like the original?' I ask.

'There were a few different reasons,' Olivia says vaguely. 'None of them seemed very important to me.'

I feel as though I'm skirting around the edge of something crucial, but I'm not sure what.

'How much do you think she used her real life in her writing?' I ask.

Olivia gives a small, wry smile. 'I don't know. I don't think she was much like Harry Hegarty if that's what you're driving at.'

I chuckle. 'I was thinking more of Rebecca, actually. It's just that the location of the story, the farmhouse, is identical to where Avery actually lived, down to the smallest detail.'

'You've been there?' Olivia seems surprised.

'Yes, I wanted to see it for myself.'

'You really take your job seriously, don't you?' She smiles. 'I don't know much about her life in Cornwall or how far Rebecca's life was based on hers, but she seemed to be happy.' Olivia glances at her phone. 'Oh, my goodness, is that the time?' she exclaims. 'I need to head back to the office soon. But we could continue this conversation as we walk, if you like.'

'Sure.'

I finish my hot chocolate and we stroll together down one of the wide pathways through the park and towards Victoria Gate.

'When you met Avery, did she seem upset about anything apart from Lily?' I ask as we cross the bridge over the Serpentine and look down at the brown-green water. Gabe's expression, tight and secretive, flashes into my mind.

'She was worried about finances. They'd sunk a lot of money into purchasing the farmhouse, and of course she was trying to repay Holden and Pierce. She didn't say in so many words but, reading between the lines, I think they were quite badly in debt.' Olivia frowns. 'She was wondering if she could get more money from her publisher.'

'And what did you say?'

'I said I thought she had a fair deal and she agreed but she said she hoped her next book was a bestseller and that then all their financial problems would be solved. It's strange, now I come to think of it, we got to talking about artists and writers that were only appreciated after they died; Van Gogh, Emily Dickinson, Kafka.'

'Strange why?'

'Well, because she died so soon after.'

Olivia's phone beeps in her pocket and she swipes at the

182

screen, a small frown of concentration on her face. 'I'm sorry but I need to get back to the office ASAP,' she says. 'Have you got all you need?'

'Yes, thank you. I think so.'

'Well, if you think of anything else, just message me.'

'I really appreciate it.'

'My pleasure,' she says. And she turns and walks briskly across the road, her step jaunty, her black hair bobbing on her shoulders.

I walk back the way I came through the park, the conversation with Olivia simmering in my mind. More than ever, I feel the draw of Foxton Farm and the need to get back there. There's something I don't understand yet. Something under the surface. I'm sure of it.

I'm grimy and tired after the tube journey home, so I have a quick shower. Then I get changed and throw a few clothes in a suitcase. Athena's still out, but I need to get going soon. I don't want to be too late arriving in Sancreed.

I scrawl a note for Athena and pin it on the fridge, the one place where she'll be guaranteed to look. Then I toss my suitcase in the boot and hop in the car. It's raining heavily and the traffic out of London on the M25 is abysmal. It takes me over an hour to crawl onto the M4 where everything finally starts to move more freely. My thoughts circle as I drive along in a cocoon of mist and rain, blindly following the red lights of the car in front. The conversations I had this weekend swirl in my head. Could Tom Monroe have had anything to do with Avery's death? Unlikely if he was living in Germany. Is it possible she committed suicide as a way of ensuring the success of her book and to stave off financial disaster for her family? Extremely unlikely. Nobody would do that, surely, unless they were also severely depressed. Everybody seems to agree that she wasn't depressed. But she was clearly emotionally unstable, if what Olivia said is true and she stole money from Holden and Pierce. If she was capable of that, what else might she have done?

Twenty-five

I park up outside the cottage still thinking about Avery and trying to assemble a clear picture of her from all the contradictory accounts I've had. I'm so lost in thought and the rain drumming on the metal car roof is so deafening that I don't hear the farmhouse door opening and the clomp of boots across the yard, and when there's a sharp tap on the glass, I nearly jump out of my skin.

A face appears at the window, an apparition swathed in darkness and distorted by the rivulets of rain. For one crazy, heart-stopping second, I think it's *her* – Avery, conjured up by my imagination and my hand instinctively flies to the lock.

Another knock.

'Alex,' shouts Joe over the clamour of rain. It's not Avery of course. I wind down the window and look at Joe, his face half obscured by a dark, hooded raincoat, like a medieval monk.

'Open the boot,' he bellows. 'I'll take your bags in for you.'

'Are you sure?'

'I don't have time to stand here and argue about it. I'm getting soaked.'

I pull at the lever that unlatches the boot and then climb out into the battering rain as Joe drags my suitcase across to the cottage. Then he runs back with an umbrella and holds it over my head as we make a dash for the cottage.

Inside, in the dry, I push the door firmly closed against the wind and rain and peel off my coat. The rain has soaked through to my sweatshirt in just that short sprint down the path. I take it off and drape it over the radiator. My hands are trembling but, thankfully, Joe doesn't appear to notice my agitation or perhaps, if he does, he puts it down to the cold.

'Welcome back to sunny Cornwall,' he says, pushing his hood back and giving me a wry smile. Despite the hood, his hair is damp. Dark brown curls cling to his head and his eyes are shining with happiness.

I evade his gaze and look around the room. It's clean and there is a fresh smell of pine disinfectant, the cushions are plumped and on the table is a bottle of homebrewed cider and a pink orchid in a pot. Slowly my heart rate returns to normal.

I pick up the cider bottle and examine the handwritten label. 'Thank you,' I say. I'm trying not to think about why he's made all this effort.

'You're very welcome,' he says. 'I'm just glad that you decided to come back.' There's no mistaking the way he says this. He's obviously under the impression that I've returned for him, because I want to explore this thing between us – whatever it is.

I move away and begin emptying my bag.

'I got another week off work. I need some time alone to get my head together,' I say repressively, and I watch his eyes drop, studiously ignoring the sudden flash of disappointment I see in them.

'Yes, of course,' he says bowing his head, as if I'm a queen. There is an awkward silence. 'Well, you must be tired after your journey. I'll leave you to get settled.'

He opens the door and is met by a torrent of rain and wind.

'Jesus!' He slams it shut again. 'I'll just wait for the rain to stop. I don't want to get any wetter. I'm already soaking. Feel this.' He holds out his arm and I touch the hem of his sleeve tentatively. As I do my hand brushes his wrist and a pulse of electricity shoots up my spine. I step back sharply, feeling flustered.

'I am really tired actually,' I say, fake-yawning. 'I should probably go to bed.'

If he's offended or upset, he doesn't show it. 'Okay then, no problem,' he says levelly.

He opens the door again and pokes his head out, holding up his hand. The rain is easing off a little. 'Why don't you come round tomorrow evening?' he says. 'I'd like to take you out to dinner.'

'Alright,' I say, answering automatically before realising I should probably say no.

'Great. Let's say seven o'clock.' He opens the door and steps out into the night.

Twenty-six

The dream starts as it always does. I'm in a sunlit garden at the edge of a swimming pool. I pick up the net that's propped against the wall and drag it through the turquoise water collecting up all the dead insects and leaves. I'm tipping the carcasses out onto the flower bed when I notice a dark shape under the water.

This time it's a girl and she's trapped, weighed down by what looks like an anchor.

Athena, I think, with horror.

I plunge into the pool and power my way through the water towards her. But as I swim, the walls of the pool disappear and suddenly I'm in the sea. Saltwater stings my eyes and underneath me brightly coloured fish dart and weave. Keeping my eyes fixed on Athena who is far out, under a buoy, I battle my way against the current. But when I finally reach the buoy, I dive down and down until I reach her, and I see that it's not Athena. It's a witch with Avery's beautiful, dark, burning eyes and a tangled mane of long white hair. Her face is frightening and deathly pale with anger.

'Slut,' she whispers, digging her sharp nails into my flesh. Then she leans in so that her face, distorted with hatred, is close to mine.

'Leave Joe alone,' she hisses.

I try to escape from her grip, but her long nails hook into my skin and I'm trapped under the water with her. I can't breathe. My lungs are going to burst . . . I'm going to drown . . .

I wake with a lurch, gasping for breath, as if I have really been drowning and I sit up, my heart pounding. The dream is still vivid in my mind. I turn on the bedside lamp and read a little of the book next to my bed until my heart rate slows. I'm just turning off the lamp to go back to sleep when there is a low sound outside.

It's right outside my window.

I sit up and listen, all my senses on high alert.

I stumble across to the window and draw back the curtains.

It's very quiet and still. The rain has stopped, leaving a clear, black dome of sky pierced with tiny glittering stars.

There's no moon and it's very dark but I can just make out the shape of the farmhouse and the hills in the distance. Nothing is moving. There's no one there. I'm about to go back to bed when suddenly an upstairs light in the farmhouse flicks on. I watch mesmerised as shadows shift inside the room. Then, I draw in my breath as someone comes to the window. A silhouette of a woman. Unmistakably a woman. There's something about the way she holds herself. It's not Lily.

The woman opens the window and lights a cigarette. I see the flare of the tip as she lights it and rests her elbows on the windowsill, tapping ash onto the ground below. Then she straightens up and looks out in the direction of the cottage. I draw back further into the room so she can't see me. Then with a sudden, decisive movement, she stubs the cigarette out, drops it out of the window and draws the curtains.

For a moment I stand rooted to the spot, trying to make sense of what I've just seen. Then I climb back into bed and lie in the darkness, brooding. Eventually I give up on trying to get to sleep, so I put on my dressing gown and curl up on the sofa in the living room watching old *Friends* DVDs, numbing my brain until the grey daylight streams in through the window and the crows outside my window start cawing.

Twenty-seven

'We'll have a bottle of Château Latour,' Joe says to the waiter.

We're in an expensive restaurant in St Ives with understated décor and large windows overlooking the inky black sea. I feel scruffy and out of place and wish I'd worn something nicer. My cotton top is straight out of the suitcase and still wrinkled and I've just noticed a small mud stain on the hem of my jeans.

I run my eye down the wine list and wince at the price.

'Are you sure? It's very expensive,' I murmur.

'Don't worry, it's my treat.' Joe sits back and smiles expansively. 'We're celebrating tonight.'

'Celebrating what?'

'I've received planning permission to go ahead with an extension. If things go smoothly, the new cottages and the

B&B will be completed by this time next year.' He reaches into his pocket, pulls out his phone and shows me the architect's plans for the new improved Foxton Farm. He scrolls through explaining the details looking animated and happy.

'That's great,' I say, feeling slightly surprised. His financial situation can't be as bad as Olivia made out.

He takes a sip of the taster wine the waiter has poured, swirling it around the bottom of the glass before lifting it to his lips. Unlike me he seems totally at home in this environment, and I'm made uncomfortably aware of the gulf between us, in both age and experience. Why have I let Joe take me on what he obviously thinks is a date? But then he looks up at me and smiles, holding my eyes with his and deep in my gut I know why I'm here. There's something between us. A pull. A connection that's inexplicable.

The food, when it arrives, is artfully arranged, the sea bass garnished with swirled vegetables and edible flowers surrounded by small dollops of sauce dropped on the plate like jewels.

'It looks too beautiful to eat,' I say, my fork hovering over the food. I take a small bite of fish and the flavour is fresh and delicate.

'Fantastic, isn't it?' Joe grins. 'I used to walk past this restaurant when I was a kid and imagine eating here one day.'

'That's an unusual fantasy for a kid,' I laugh. 'I mean, most small boys dream of being a footballer or a musician, don't they?'

He shrugs. 'We never had much money when we were children.' His lip curls. 'My dad spent it all on booze and gambling, that's when he wasn't beating us up – me and my brother.'

I stare at him. Maybe this is part of the reason for that strange, unspoken connection between us. One child damaged by an abusive father recognises another. 'I know a bit about what that's like,' I say. 'It must have been tough.'

There's a swift flash of anger in his eyes. 'You could say that. Sometimes we didn't even have enough for food. We had to go fishing or get free meals at school. Sometimes we'd even shoplift.'

I'm shocked. It sounds as if his childhood was even worse than mine. At least we always had enough to eat and to be fair to my dad he never laid a finger on me or Athena.

'My older brother, Chris, couldn't handle it. He went off the rails completely. He died of an overdose when he was nineteen.'

'Oh my God. I'm so sorry.'

Joe stares darkly at his food. He's not like anyone I've ever met before. I want to know everything about him and understand what's going on behind those dark, troubled eyes.

'Where's your father now?' I ask.

'Don't know, don't care. He wasn't a good man, Alex.' He draws in his breath and stabs at his food with his fork.

I think about John in Avery's book. Is it possible his character was based on Joe's father?

Joe gives himself a little shake and smiles wryly. 'In some ways, I suppose I have him to thank for the man I am today. I swore I'd never be like him. He's the reason why I worked so hard at school, why I slogged my guts out to get into Cambridge and why, straight out of university, I got a job in sales at a large financial firm.'

Where he met Avery, I think. He must have been mortified when she stole from the company and he must have loved her very much to stick by her.

A smile breaks out on his face. 'Enough about me. What about you, Alex Georgiou?' He says my name slowly, as if he likes the sound of it. I force myself to meet his intense, curious gaze. 'You said you're half Cypriot half English?'

'My mother was English.'

'But she died when you were fourteen?' he says softly.

'Yes . . .' I open my mouth to recount the usual car accident story, but somehow the words stick in my throat. Instead, for the first time ever, I find myself telling the truth. Things I've never told anyone, come spilling out of me.

'She drowned herself in our swimming pool. She tied a diving weight belt round her waist and jumped in at the deep end.'

Joe's eyes scour my face. 'My God, I'm so sorry,' he says simply.

I close my eyes and grit my teeth. 'When I came back from school I found her there. I should have jumped in and tried to untie the belt, but I didn't do anything. I froze. It was my little sister, Athena, who dived in and tried to help her. I just stood there.'

There's a silence. Tears are burning in my eyes. I feel as if I'm underwater, as if it's me trapped, weighed down and helpless.

Joe reaches out across the table and takes my hand. 'It wasn't your fault,' he says.

'You don't understand. Maybe she was still . . .'

I break off because the waiter comes and takes away our plates. Joe asks for the bill. Then, when the waiter has gone, he turns back to me with so much compassion in his eyes it makes me want to howl.

'Why did she decide to take her own life?' he asks gently.

'My father . . . he was similar to your father in some ways. He was violent and abusive. He made her feel like she was a piece of shit.'

Joe shakes his head. 'Well then, she killed herself because of him. Why should you blame yourself for what that bastard did?'

*

I'm not sure I'll ever be able to completely forgive myself for that act of cowardice by the pool that day. But it's a relief to have shared it with someone and Joe's reaction was just perfect. As we walk silently along the seafront back to the car, I feel so close to him. We're the same, him and me. Pain has forged us. Some people lead charmed lives, barely scratching the surface of suffering. They can't understand, even if they mean well. But Joe understands. He knows how the grief, guilt and anger never go away. They stay with you like background noise, a nagging pain that blights your life.

'Cold?' Joe says, breaking the silence and he puts his arm around me, rubbing my shoulder. I let it rest there. The sea shines black and silver in the moonlight and the waves suck gently at the shore.

We're both wounded. Maybe we can heal each other, I think.

When we reach the jetty he stops and leans on the railings, looking down at the boats.

'Chris and I always talked about sailing around the world together one day,' he says. 'When he died, I swore I'd keep my promise to him. Now finally I'm in a position where I might be able to make our dream become a reality.'

He turns to me, his expression hard to read. His face is tanned, windblown and distractingly handsome.

'Would you like to sail around the world with me, Alex?'

It can't be a serious question, but his eyes, fixed on me, are dark and full of feeling and they reach to my core.

'I don't know . . .'

Something is dragging me towards him. An underwater current, impossible to fight. His hand slips to the back of my neck and our lips meet. The wind tugs at my coat, and I lean into him, lost in the moment.

But there's something nagging at the back of my mind. This isn't right. I've been lying to him. With an effort of will, I push him away.

'Wait,' I say. 'There's something you should know.'

Twenty-eight

'What were you going to tell me at the harbour?' Joe asks.

We are halfway to Sancreed on the dark, winding road.

I draw in my breath. There's no way out of this. The longer I leave it, the worse it's going to be. But I'm grateful for the darkness and for the fact that Joe is staring steadily ahead at the small patch of tarmac lit up in the headlights.

'You don't really know much about me,' I say.

He shrugs slightly, his hands gripping the wheel. 'I know enough. And I like what I know.' He glances over and places his hand on my knee.

Heat rushes through me. 'I mean, you don't even know what my job is or the real reason I came here to Sancreed.'

His tone changes slightly. 'Why? Why did you come?'

'It wasn't just for a holiday.'

'I don't understand,' he says warily.

The air in the car is stifling but I plough on regardless. 'I'm a journalist. Avery's publisher sent me *Falling* to review. I thought it would make a good story – I mean the connection between Avery's death and the way her character, Rebecca, dies in the book.' My voice tails off.

There's a long, tense silence. When Joe finally speaks his voice is quiet and hard to read.

'You came to research a story?' he says slowly. His face is swathed in darkness, and I can't see his expression.

'I'm sorry, I should have told you from the start. But I didn't know you then. I didn't know that we would become friends – that I would grow to like you . . .' My voice is pleading. I want him to tell me that he understands. But he doesn't reply, and the silence stretches out as if something is about to snap.

'Say something, please,' I beg.

We're in Sancreed now and Joe takes the turning to Foxton Farm, the wheels skidding slightly on the gravel.

'Are you angry?'

He pulls up outside the farm and switches off the engine, then gives a deep sigh. 'So that's why you decided to get close to me?' he says bitterly. 'I'm research?'

I grab his arm. 'Of course not! I should have told you before. I would have, but I thought you'd tell me to fuck off.'

He laughs grimly. 'Well, you were right about that. I would have.'

'Do you hate me?'

He rounds on me. 'What did you expect? You've used me. You've used *Avery* for what? So that you can further your career? To think I was starting to like you. That I was . . .' He looks at me sideways, a brief glance that expresses not so much anger as something worse – disappointment, maybe even disgust.

'It wasn't like that . . .' I start. But he's not listening.

'I need some time to think.' He climbs out of the car shaking his head.

'Please believe me, I never . . .' I start, following him towards the house.

'Alex,' he cuts me off. 'I don't want to talk to you right now. I'll see you in the morning. Goodnight.'

I watch him stride away towards the farmhouse, a dark, angry silhouette against the light from the window. Then I stumble towards the cottage, tears blurring my eyes.

Inside, I rip off my clothes and leap into bed, burying my head in the pillow. Athena was right, I shouldn't have come back here. All I've been doing is stirring up grief and anger. In the process I've hurt Joe and probably ruined something which could have been great.

Twenty-nine

I wake to a grey, blustery day. The wind is howling around the house, agitating the trees outside my window, so they look like they're doing a frenzied dance. I wriggle down under the duvet. I don't want to get up. I don't want to face the world. My conversation with Joe last night runs repeatedly through my mind. He was so angry. What must he think of me? I don't want to see him and witness his disappointment all over again. Maybe it's best I just pack up and leave before he gets up.

After I've showered, had a coffee and eaten half a piece of toast, which tastes like cardboard, I pull my suitcase from under the bed and drag it into the living room. I draw the curtains and look out at the muddy fields and the small, stunted trees bending in the wind like geriatrics. Then I make myself another cup of coffee and sit and stare at my empty suitcase.

I wish Athena was here. I want so badly to speak to her, but there's no point in calling her now. She won't be up yet. Instead, I pick up my phone and send a message.

Athena, can we talk?

No answer of course.

A tide of misery drags me downwards. If only Mum were still alive. She'd know what to say. At the thought of my mother, tears of self-pity well up in my eyes. Maybe if she'd been around when I was growing up, I would have turned out better. I wouldn't have become the kind of person who lies and uses people to get ahead.

But there's no point in sitting here feeling sorry for myself. I've brought this on myself. I brush my tears away angrily and begin packing.

I'm wrapping my laptop in a long grey sweater when there is a loud rap at the door.

Joe.

I brace myself for a furious tirade. But he doesn't seem angry anymore, only tired and sad. His hair is ruffled as if it hasn't been brushed and his eyes are ringed with shadow.

'Can I come in?' he asks quietly.

'Of course.' I step back and he follows me through into the living room. Maybe now it will come out, all the things he bottled up last night. It's no more than I deserve.

'About last night . . .' he begins. His eyes fall on my suitcase, open on the sofa. 'What's this?'

'I'm leaving. Back to London. I was going to come and tell you, but I wasn't sure you'd be up yet.'

He looks dumbfounded. Jaw slack. Mouth open.

'I thought you were staying for another week.'

'I was. But after last night, what I told you ... I'm so sorry.'

He sinks slowly onto the sofa. 'I don't want you to leave, Alex,' he says quietly.

'You don't?' My voice catches. Hope flares in my chest. 'You aren't angry?'

'No ... well I mean I was a little, last night. I felt ...' He pauses. '... used I suppose.' He gives a gentle, lopsided smile. 'But then I slept on it. And do you know what the first thing I thought of when I woke up was?'

I shake my head.

'You,' he says. 'I thought about you, because you're what I've thought about every morning since I met you. I can't get you out of my head, Alex. I don't want to lose something that could be amazing just because of some stupid little misunderstanding.'

Can it be that simple? I look into his eyes, not daring to believe him. But eyes don't lie. And there's no anger in them. They're soft, sugar-brown, flecked with amber, and there's a hunger in them that makes me catch my breath.

'I'm sorry,' I say again, staring down at the carpet. 'I had no right ...'

'It's okay,' he says. 'You don't have to keep apologising. I understand you. We're more alike than you think.' He stands up and steps towards me and cups my cheek, forcing me to look at him.

His eyes reach inside me to my core, and I can't think straight anymore. Words become irrelevant. The air fizzes between us. I sleepwalk into his arms, and then we kiss. It's a serious kiss this time. A kiss with intent and I'm losing myself in him.

Abruptly, he breaks away, holding me at arm's length.

'Are you sure you want this?' he asks gruffly.

'I'm sure,' I say. Because suddenly, I am sure. I'm sure enough to ignore the small nagging voice at the back of my mind that says this will never work – that it's too complicated.

'Good,' he whispers.

The wind swirls around the cottage and clouds rush past the window, allowing brief, fleeting glimpses of the sun.

His eyes never leave mine as he lifts my T-shirt over my head and traces my collar bone with his lips. I fumble with the buttons on his shirt. Skin meets skin and slowly, hesitantly, I run my hand down over his chest and torso. To one side, below his belly button, my fingers snag on a patch of slightly raised skin. A cruel, jagged-looking scar. I back away to get a proper look and he flinches.

'Not pretty, I know,' he says.

'What happened?'

'It's a keloid from when I had my appendix out.' He shrugs. 'Does it turn you off?'

In answer I kiss the shiny, puckered skin and he groans, pulling me into the bedroom and down onto the bed in a tangle of naked limbs.

The wind has stopped, and the sun has broken out from behind the clouds, a sliver of pure light falling on his muscled shoulder. It feels like a benediction. Joe lies on his side tracing a line from my hip to my thigh.

'What's this part of your body called?' he asks.

I shrug. 'Hip, bum? I don't know.'

'It needs another name.' He frowns in concentration.

I wriggle away. I've just noticed that the curtains are open. Anyone could have seen us. What were we thinking?

'Where are you going?' Joe says as I wrap the sheet around me and clamber out of bed. 'You're not still planning to leave, are you, Alex Georgiou?'

I shake my head and smile. Right now, I feel like I want to stay with him forever. But I know better than to tell him that.

I stand at the window and look out. The fields that seemed so dull a day ago are tinged with a magical light.

Muddy puddles gleam in the sunlight and wind ripples through the grass. In the bare, lichen-covered hawthorn a small bird, a flash of yellow at its throat, balances on a twig. Aside from the bird, nothing stirs.

Thirty

The next few days waft by in a haze of happiness. Joe comes to the cottage every day and we make love in the small four-poster bed under the fairy lights. He takes me sailing again and whisks me out shopping in St Ives where we wander round the crowded streets hand in hand looking in all the quaint and arty shops. He insists on buying me anything I express an interest in – a designer turquoise suede jacket, a beautiful moonstone pendant.

'No more shopping,' I laugh, after he's rushed back to buy a lamp I saw in the window upcycled from old bike parts. 'Or you'll have no money left.'

So, we head down to the harbour and sit on the wall looking out to sea and eating pasties, gulls shrieking and circling overhead.

'Look,' Joe says suddenly, and we watch a surprisingly

tame seal bobbing its head up out of the water close to the shore.

'It's probably from the rescue centre near here. One seal they released had to be taken back because it would chase anyone with a bucket, thinking they were carrying fish.'

I laugh at the image of terrified tourists being chased by a hungry seal and Joe laughs too. His laugh is rich and deep-throated and his hand in mine is warm. I don't think I've ever been so happy.

We have a lot in common aside from an off-beat sense of humour and, despite the difference in our ages, we also share a lot of values. We're both passionate about nature and books and we both love everything to do with the sea. I try not to think about where this is all leading and what will happen at the end of the week when I have to return to London. I'm living in the moment.

I barely think about Avery.

On Friday Joe cooks a meal for the four of us. Me, him, Lily and Lily's boyfriend, Josh.

'I thought you didn't like Josh,' I say, as I help him prepare the cheese sauce for the lasagne in the afternoon.

'Can't stand him,' he agrees cheerfully. 'But it's better that he's here under my roof where I can keep an eye on him. Keep your enemies close, isn't that what they say? At least if they're here, I know where she is and that she's not getting into any trouble.'

'Makes sense, I suppose.' I bring the sauce to the boil, stirring vigorously and then lift the saucepan off the heat.

I feel surprisingly nervous about this evening because, although Lily can't have failed to notice Joe coming and going from the cottage, this is the first time we've officially acknowledged that we're dating. She's obviously not going to approve, given that vicious, little note she wrote the night after Joe and I first kissed, and I'm worried that there will be some kind of scene.

But I don't need to worry. Lily is icily polite at dinner, though she makes a point of bringing Avery into the conversation at every opportunity.

'Mum used to make a top lasagne,' she says as we sit down to eat. 'Do you remember, Joe?'

Joe glances at me and nods.

'Mum and I decorated the Old Barn together.' She interrupts Joe as he discusses his plans for the new holiday cottages. 'Do you like it, Alex?'

And apropos of nothing she adds, 'It's the anniversary of her death in a month's time. We should do something.'

'What sort of thing do you suggest?' Joe asks, taking a slow sip of red wine.

'I don't know. Maybe we could visit her grave. Or maybe

we could go to the Maid of Zennor Festival again. That's where I was the day my mother died, Alex.'

'Lily . . .' Joe's voice holds a warning note. 'Alex doesn't want to hear about that.'

'It's okay,' I say brightly. 'I don't mind. The Maid of Zennor Festival? Where've I heard that before?'

'It's named after the mermaid that supposedly visited the village of Zennor and lured a man away to the bottom of the sea,' Lily informs me. 'I don't remember much else about the story; do you, Josh?'

Josh, who has been pretty quiet up until now, smiles and shrugs. 'No. Wasn't there some bird who was nailed by her husband in a barrel because she'd been unfaithful?'

'No, that was St Senara.'

'Oh, right.'

Josh has an open, guileless face with wide blue eyes and dirty blond hair. I don't understand why Joe dislikes him so much. He seems nice enough to me. He's punching above his weight with Lily, of course, but then who wouldn't be?

I catch her eye, but she looks away quickly.

'I'm going to stay with Josh tonight,' she says coolly, pushing back her chair at the end of the meal. 'Come on, Josh. Let's go.' Josh stands up obediently and Lily gives a twisted little smile to Joe. I understand that the smile means, if you're going to have your fun then I will too. I glance at Joe. His hands are clenched and there's a vein pulsing at his temple, but he keeps his voice level.

'Alright then. But phone me when you get to Penzance. And you're driving, not Josh.'

'Josh seems alright,' I say after they've left and we're sitting on the sofa in the living room.

Joe snorts. 'Yeah, well you don't know him. Appearances can be deceiving. He's been in trouble with the police for using. And he crashed his car a few months ago under the influence. Thank God Lily wasn't with him.'

He looks tired and haggard, and I think how hard it must be for him. He must be worried to death that Lily is so close to a user given the way his brother died. No wonder he disapproves of Josh so strongly. It wasn't what he signed up for, being the single parent of a stroppy teenaged girl, but he seems to take his duty of care very seriously.

'I'm sure Avery would be happy to know that Lily's got you to look after her,' I say.

'I hope so. I do my best.' He shrugs. Then he smiles suddenly and pulls me towards him. 'And now I've got you to look after me.'

Thirty-one

I open my eyes and blink at the grey light seeping through the curtains. Wind rattles the windows, trying to find a way in. A storm is brewing but I'm curled up safe and warm in Joe's large double bed and I feel great. It's the first time I've slept over in the farmhouse. Lily is still at Josh's so there's no awkwardness, and no need to worry about bumping into her in the bathroom.

When I roll over, I see that Joe is already awake, lying next to me on his back, his hands clasped behind his head staring up at the ceiling. His expression, in contrast to my mood, is dark and brooding. Is he thinking about Avery? Whatever's on his mind, it isn't pleasant, and I want to reach inside him and drag him back from whatever bleak place he's in.

'Are you okay?' I murmur and he blinks and looks at me.

His eyes soften and fill with light as they meet mine and happiness floods my veins. I love this power I seem to have to banish the dark, haunted look he has.

'You're awake,' he says, like it's some kind of miracle. Like I'm some kind of miracle. He strokes my hair and kisses my shoulder. 'You look like a siren this morning, like the Maid of Zennor.'

His gaze melts me, and I feel desire tugging at me. I want to pull him close and kiss the stubble on his neck and throat.

But something is holding me back. I have the strange sensation of being watched and when I look over his shoulder, my eye snags on a framed photograph of Avery and Joe on the dressing table. It's a wedding photo, taken in Las Vegas outside the Little White Wedding Chapel. Joe is gazing at her adoringly and she's staring out at the camera, unsmiling. Instead of a dress, she's wearing a white halter neck jumpsuit and she looks slender, elegant and beautiful. From the photo, she stares disapprovingly at me. You're an intruder in my house and in my bed, her gaze clearly says.

'I'm hungry,' I say, untangling myself from Joe's arms. I sit up, my back against the headrest.

He sighs. 'Yeah, me too, I'll make us some breakfast.' He clambers out of bed. Then he looks at his phone on the bedside table. 'Shit. Is that the time? I almost forgot. I've got a meeting with the architect this morning. I should be there in about half an hour.'

I watch him hurriedly pull on his trousers, button up a crisp white shirt and run a comb through his hair.

I search for my knickers and find them tangled up in the sheets at the base of the bed. I wriggle into them and then start trying to find my other clothes scattered around the floor.

'What are you doing?' Joe says. 'You don't have to go. Stay here. Please. I won't be long. When I get back, I'll make us both breakfast. Lily won't be back until late. We can spend the day together.'

It's tempting. I glance over at the photograph of Joe and Avery. *You're not going to scare me away*, I tell her silently.

'Okay,' I say aloud.

'Great.' He kisses me on the shoulder. 'Don't move, alright? I'll be back before you know it.'

Once Joe is gone, I attempt to get back to sleep but I don't feel tired and I'm still uncomfortably aware of Avery's eyes burning into me.

'Stop looking at me like that,' I snap, clambering out of bed, snatching up the photograph, and placing it firmly face down inside the top drawer. I make a mental note to remember to put it back before Joe returns. I feel bad messing with his stuff but really, what was he thinking, leaving it there while we were in bed together?

215

But even with the photograph neutralised, Avery's presence is everywhere in the room; in the hairbrush, which still has white- blonde hairs caught up in it, in the make-up bag on the dresser and in the half-open wardrobe where I glimpse her clothes.

I'm torturing myself, I know that, but I can't help it and I find myself drawn inexorably to the wardrobe. Pushing the door further open, I'm confronted with rows of dresses and tops in expensive-looking materials, mostly in muted shades. I touch them tentatively, my fingers brushing against soft fabric. Then, I take out a silky, silver dress with very thin shoulder straps and hold it up against me in front of the mirror. It's way too long and wouldn't suit me even if it did fit. Feeling short and unattractive, I put the dress back on its hanger and lie down in bed, trying to forget about Avery, trying to think about last night instead. I'm just drifting back to sleep when I hear a noise outside.

A movement on the landing, floorboards creaking.

'Hello?' I call out. My heart is suddenly racing.

No answer. The movement stops. I sit up and grab the lamp. I'm not sure what I'm going to do with it. Maybe smash it over an intruder's head. It probably wouldn't have much impact, but it might buy me some time.

Then there's a scratching at the door and a low whine.

Of course, it's Barney, I think with profound relief.

'What's up, boy?' I say as I open the door and he lollops in. Halfway into the room he pauses, looking puzzled.

He expected Avery, I think. But when I offer him my hand, he walks up to the bed and lets me scratch him behind his ears with an air of polite disappointment.

'Did Joe feed you?' I ask and he sits down gazing at me intently, tail thudding.

I laugh. Who could resist those big, brown eyes? 'Okay boy, I'll get you something to eat.'

I scramble into my clothes and head downstairs to the kitchen where I find a tin of dog food in one of the cupboards. Better to feed him twice than for him to eat nothing, I think, dolloping out the disgusting-smelling meat into his bowl. I place it on the floor, and he snaffles it down eagerly.

'You were hungry,' I say.

I'm hungry too, I realise. I didn't eat much last night. I was too uncomfortable with Lily's hostile gaze on me all the time. Maybe I'll surprise Joe with breakfast when he gets back. I rummage in the fridge and find eggs and bread. In the cupboards, I locate a frying pan. I place it on the hob and start searching for cooking oil.

Then there's a noise. Upstairs. This time it can't be Barney.

I stand for a moment listening, all my senses on high alert. But all I can hear is the hum of the refrigerator and the whine of the wind. My heart hammers against my ribs and fear floods my veins.

There it is again.

The floorboards are groaning as if someone is pacing about above my head. Then there is the sudden sound of a door slamming.

Someone is upstairs.

It's just a draught, I tell myself. But my hands are shaking when I put the eggs back in the fridge. And my chest feels as though it's going to burst as I creep up the stairs.

There's no one in the bathroom or Lily's room so I climb the next flight of stairs to the attic. With my heart in my mouth, I try the handle and to my surprise it opens easily.

'Who's there?' I whisper as I poke my head around the door.

But the room is empty. The wind blows and the apple tree outside casts moving shadows on the wall. I feel strangely detached as if I'm adrift, floating far out at sea.

Of course she's not here. She's dead.

Thirty-two

The front door slams, and I run downstairs and reach the kitchen as Joe comes breezing in.

'You alright?' he says, kissing me on the cheek. 'You look a bit pale. What have you been up to?'

I can't very well say that I've been chasing the ghost of his dead wife about the house. It sounds ridiculous. *It is ridiculous.*

'I'm okay,' I say, trying to smile naturally. 'I was just thinking about making us some breakfast.'

'Don't you worry your cute, little head about that.' He ruffles my hair and ushers me onto a seat at the breakfast bar. 'You sit down. I'm going to make my famous French toast.'

I watch him blankly as he whisks eggs in a bowl. I'm still shaking a little, but thankfully he doesn't seem to notice. I can't hear anything upstairs now. It must have been my imagination or, more likely, the wind. There are lots of draughts in this ramshackle old house. Slowly my heartbeat returns to normal, but my nerves are still frazzled and when Lily raps at the back door I start like a frightened horse.

'Oh, hey Alex.' She looks at me through narrowed lids as I let her in. Her voice is friendly enough, but her expression clearly says, what the fuck are you still doing here?

'Hi.' I feel my face reddening, as if I've been caught cheating or having an affair.

'Alex just popped round to get a new lightbulb for the living room and I invited her to stay for breakfast,' Joe explains glibly, dipping the bread in the egg mixture and then laying it in the sizzling pan. 'I'm just making French toast. Do you want some?'

'Alright.' Lily shrugs and sits down at the breakfast bar next to me.

'Did you have a nice time last night?' I ask.

'It was okay.'

'How come you're back so early? I thought you were going to stay at Josh's,' Joe says as he dishes up fried eggy bread coated in sugar and cinnamon onto our plates.

'He's got a job interview this morning.' Lily presses her lips together in a sullen line. 'Sorry to disturb your little love nest.'

'Nonsense.' Joe is in too good a mood to be baited but there is also a slight warning edge in his voice all the same.

I stare at my plate, feeling embarrassed.

I want to tell Lily that it's okay, I understand that no one can ever replace her mother. But she's scowling at me, and I know now is not the time. Besides, I'm still shaken from earlier and I need to get away from them both and be alone to clear my mind. I wolf down my French toast as quickly as possible, then I drain my coffee.

'Well, I'd better get going,' I say brightly.

'Really? So soon?' Joe looks crestfallen.

'Don't go on my account,' Lily says coldly.

'No, no. I've got some work to do,' I say, retreating to the door. 'I'll see you later. Thanks for the breakfast, Joe.'

Back in the cottage I breathe deeply, trying to regulate my heartrate. The room seems to rock and shift as if I'm on a boat. I stare out of the window at the horizon to steady myself. The fields stretch out to bleak moorland. In the grey sky a couple of distant black crows, wheel in the wind.

What was it I heard upstairs in the attic room? I was so sure I heard someone up there.

Avery is dead and phantoms don't exist, I tell myself. But there's a seed of doubt that stubbornly sprouts in my mind. Maybe, just maybe, if someone had a strong enough spirit or personality in life some of their energy gets left behind, at least in the memories of their loved ones, and maybe that can sometimes manifest itself physically.

No, no, no. I've never been superstitious before. I'm losing my grip on reality. I need a dose of common sense. I need to talk to Athena. I pick up the phone to call her and notice that there are several increasingly irate messages from Lou asking when I'm going to send her my article.

Crap. I was hoping to find out more and make the story more impactful, but I guess I'll just have to work with what I do know.

I try phoning Athena, but she doesn't answer so I sit at the small kitchen table, open my laptop and begin typing from where I left off.

There are many similarities between Avery's life and the book she wrote – from the renovated farmhouse where she lived, to mysterious Carn Euny, a real Neolithic village near Sancreed, and where Rebecca meets her lover, Dom, in Falling.

But that's where the similarity ends, as I discovered when I went to visit Sancreed to see the place where Avery lived.

Sancreed itself is a tiny hamlet in the far west corner of Cornwall. Driving into it feels like a trip into the past, to a gentler, slower-paced time. The old stone farm buildings haven't changed much in decades and there's hardly any traffic to ruin the tranquillity.

On the day I arrived in Sancreed it was drizzling and the farm where Avery lived appeared grey and grim. However, the welcome I received from Avery's husband was warm and unexpectedly hospitable.

I go on to describe my experiences at Foxton Farm, trying

to build a growing sense of mystery and suspense. When I believe I've achieved this, I conclude by saying:

The community in Sancreed is small and tight-knit and I found the villagers to be friendly in a way you rarely find in a big city. It's certainly hard to imagine that any of the people I met during my stay had anything to do with Avery's death. Nevertheless, there are several troubling elements to this story. Pieces that, when added up together, strongly suggest that her fall may have been more than a simple accident.

Firstly, on the evening that Avery died, West Cornwall was ravaged by one of the most ferocious storms of the year, which leads one to wonder what on earth possessed her to go out for a walk along a cliff edge in the middle of such bad weather, especially as, by all accounts, she didn't even like hiking.

Secondly, according to several sources, she received strange messages from an anonymous fan on social media and threatening phone calls in the weeks and months leading up to her death. Could there have been a connection between those messages and her untimely demise? Is it possible a deranged fan decided to make fiction a reality?

Perhaps we will never know for sure. Her death is a mystery. And who doesn't love a mystery with all the threads neatly tied up at the end? But real life isn't like a mystery novel. Real life is messy and complicated. Avery knew that and that's why her books were so good.

I read it through, changing a few words and checking

for grammar and spelling mistakes, then I send it to Lou along with an accompanying note. *Sorry this is late! Hope you like it, Alex.*

Then I stand up and arch my back. I've been writing for hours, and my shoulders are stiff from hunching over the laptop, but my mind feels refreshed. The act of writing has anchored me, and I feel much calmer than before.

The silver sun is peeping out from behind a cloud and there are a few ragged patches of blue in the sky. The weather is about as good as it's going to get. So, I decide to take a drive by myself to visit Mousehole, one of the places recommended in the pamphlets in the cottage. I hop in my car and drive along the winding roads towards the coast. When I arrive, I park near the small harbour and wander around the streets, looking in the quaint galleries and shops. At lunchtime, I grab a quick bite to eat in a pub, then I walk back down again to the tiny beach and the car.

As I'm driving along the road to Sancreed, it hits me that this is my last day in Cornwall before I have to return to London and that I haven't really got any closer to solving the mystery of Avery's death. I'm plagued with doubt that my article isn't good enough. But it's not just that bothering me. I'm also more upset than I'd like to admit at the thought of leaving Joe. Of course, it doesn't necessarily have to end between us, but what are the chances of our relationship surviving long distance? Maybe it's for the best, I think sadly. Maybe he's not ready. His wife's death was so recent and the fact that he's kept all her things just makes me more convinced that he's not really over her yet.

When I get back to Foxton Farm, I'm tempted to pop over to see him and to apologise for leaving so abruptly this morning, but I know that spending more time with him will just make our inevitable separation harder. So, instead I heat up a ready meal and sit alone at the small kitchen table, reading my copy of *Falling* as the sun sinks behind the trees. It's already dark and I've just got to a passage about Rebecca and Dom's love affair . . .

They met in secret every day, while John was away. Spring turned into summer and Rebecca would slip down the path by the well to Dom's house . . .

. . . when there's a sharp rap at the door and Joe enters before I have time to answer. I slide the book under a cushion and pretend to be looking at my phone. I don't really want him to know that I'm still obsessing over his wife. He looks agitated enough as it is.

'Hey, Alex, are you okay?' he says, pacing the room. 'I called round earlier, but you were out. I was worried about you.'

'Yeah, I'm fine. I just took a drive to Mousehole, that's all. Why don't you sit down? You're making me nervous.'

Joe perches on the edge of a seat, then stands up again.

'I could have taken you. Why didn't you ask me?'

'I know you've got work to do and, to be honest, I needed some time to think.'

He sighs. 'I'm sorry Lily was so rude to you this morning. You shouldn't let her get to you. It's just that she misses her mother. She'll come around. It'll just take her a while.'

'It's not that. It's not Lily.'

'What then?' He frowns and paces over to the window. He rests his hands on the windowsill, not looking at me. 'Is it us? This?' He turns and looks suddenly lost and alone. 'You think I'm too old for you.'

'No, you don't understand.' I'd like to kiss him and smooth away the worried creases around his eyes. I want to tell him that I've never been happier in my life than these past few days, but I still can't shake the feeling that someone is watching us, that someone doesn't want us to be together.

'What is it then?' he asks.

'It's just . . . I'm not sure that you're ready for a relationship, that you're really over Avery.' I look away from him because I don't want him to see in my eyes how much I wish that wasn't true.

'Is that what you think?' His voice is husky with relief. He steps towards me and tilts my chin upwards, forcing me to look at him.

'You know that I've never met anyone like you, don't you? Avery was . . . Things with Avery . . . they weren't always perfect . . . She could be difficult . . .'

'What do you mean?' Is he talking about Holden and Pierce, the embezzlement?

Suddenly he grins. 'I don't want to talk about Avery.' He grabs my hand. 'Come on. Let's go out. I want to show you something.'

'What? Now?' I'm still reeling from the emotional roller coaster I've been on for the past few hours.

'Yes. Now. Are you sleepy?'

'No.'

'Me neither. Come with me then.' He picks up my coat and pulls me outside. I shiver in the chill air, and he wraps the coat around me.

'It's a clear night tonight. We need to get right out, as far away from the lights as possible,' he says, taking my hand and leading me across the yard towards the fields.

'Where are we going?' I ask.

'You'll see.'

We clamber over a stile. The grass is soft and wet underfoot. It's very dark and there's a faint smell of manure. I pick my way cautiously, taking out my phone and shaking it so that the light shines on the grass. Nearby something snorts and breaths and I jump.

'Don't worry it's just a cow.' Joe laughs softly.

'Here,' he says when we finally reach the far end of the field. He spreads his coat on the grass and lies down next to it. 'Lie down,' he commands.

I do as he says, feeling the damp from the grass soak through the coat and gazing up at the cloudless, black dome of sky above us and the millions of stars, so bright away from all the light pollution.

'What can you see?' he asks.

'I can see the Milky Way,' I say with wonder in my voice. And for the first time I realise why it's called the Milky Way. Because I can clearly make out the curdled white light smeared across the sky. 'It's beautiful,' I add. I can feel the earth spinning underneath me and I have a giddy feeling of us being all alone in the universe. Just me and him.

'Shh, wait, look. There.'

He points upwards and I catch the tail end of a flash of light.

'Wow, was that a . . .?'

'It's a meteorite. There's a meteor shower tonight.'

I stare up again and see another golden streak of light, so quick and elusive, I wonder if I imagined it. Then another. Definite this time. I feel suddenly very happy. And I can't believe how quickly everything has changed. From being so miserable and scared just this morning to this.

'Wow,' I say. 'You're supposed to make a wish on a shooting star, right?'

Joe rolls onto his side, propping up his head with his hand.

'What would you wish for?' he whispers. 'If you could have anything?'

I can't imagine being happier than I am right now, in this moment. 'I don't know. Just to stay here with you, I suppose.' The words are out of my mouth before I have time to censor myself. Joe is silent and I feel embarrassed and worried that I've said too much. Way to scare a man off, Alex, I think.

But then his hand creeps into mine and his thumb rubs gently against my palm. 'Well why don't you?' he says.

'What?'

'Why don't you stay here with me?'

He sits up and gazes into my eyes. 'I know this is a bit soon,' he says. 'But I know that I love you, Alex, and I want you to move in with me.'

Thirty-three

I'm speechless. I can't quite believe this is happening. Did he just ask me to live with him?

My thoughts are in turmoil. I've known Joe less than two weeks and it seems crazy to make such a big change on the basis of such a short relationship. On the other hand, I already feel close to him and at the back of my mind there's always Isaac and the way he left me because I was too scared to commit. I don't want to make the same mistake twice.

I think Joe senses my hesitation, because he says, 'I know this must all seem a bit sudden. I know it would be a big upheaval for you.' He sounds diffident, unsure of himself which just makes him more attractive to me. 'I'll understand if you need time to think about it . . .'

'No.'

'No?'

'No,' I say, 'I don't need time to think about it. Yes, I want to move in with you.' Because suddenly everything seems very clear and simple. I love him too. This feeling can't be anything else. And why shouldn't we take it a step further? That's what people do when they love each other, isn't it?

'Really?' The disbelief and happiness in his voice is palpable.

'Yes, really.'

He turns onto his side, propping his head up on his elbow and gazing down at me.

'Well, what do you know? We're going to live together,' he says.

And we're both laughing as if the air around us is drugged and then we're kissing, and I don't think I've ever felt as happy in my life.

Thirty-four

'You're what?!'

Athena takes her earbuds out, closes her laptop and gawps at me as if I've just told her I'm going to the moon. It's a couple of days after Joe's proposal and I've returned to London to sort a few things out before I go back to Foxton Farm. I haven't even had time to unpack yet, but I couldn't wait to share my news with my sister.

'I'm moving down to Cornwall.'

Athena's jaw drops open even wider. 'Wait, what? Do you mean you're moving in with Joe Lewis?'

'Yes, of course. Who else?'

There's a long pause. She selects her words carefully. 'When are you planning to go?' she asks finally.

'Next month. I'm going to hand in my notice at work and then I'm moving down to Cornwall.'

'But you've only known him, what? Less than three weeks.'

'So . . .?' I say defensively. 'When you meet the right one you just know.'

'And Joe is the right one?' She raises her eyebrows so high they disappear under her fringe.

'Yes,' I say emphatically. I'm starting to feel frustrated. Athena's never been in love before. Not really in love, the way I am with Joe. She doesn't understand.

'What about your career? You finally have the job of your dreams and you're going to throw it all away for a man.'

'It won't mean giving up my career. I'll still be able to work freelance and it will give me the chance to develop my blog.'

She frowns. There's another silence. I chew the skin around my thumb nail and pull off a little too much skin, so it starts bleeding. I'm annoyed and disappointed by her reaction. I thought she'd be happy for me.

'His wife died recently,' she adds. 'Do you think he's ready for a committed relationship?'

'She died nearly a year ago actually. And I honestly don't know if he's ready. All I know is I've got to try. I love him, Athena.'

She snorts. 'He's years older than you. His stepdaughter is closer to your age.'

'Age is just a number.'

'Oh, don't give me that crap.'

I glare at her. 'You don't understand.'

'You're damn right I don't. I mean, what about the whole thing with his wife? How do you know you can trust him?'

'You can't live your life doubting everyone, just because of Dad. At some point you need to take a leap of faith. Besides, you don't know Joe like I do. He's the sweetest person.'

Athena purses her lips. 'He's all charming now but what if he changes when you move in?'

I stand up. I've had enough of this conversation. Athena's really annoying me. If I stay in the room any longer, I'll say something I regret.

'Anyway, I don't really see that it's any of your business.' I stalk towards the door.

'What about the flat? How am I going to pay the rent?' Athena calls after me.

So *that's* what she's worried about. I might have known it was money.

I pause in the doorway. 'You'll have to find another flatmate. I'm sorry. I'll help you out with the rent until you do.'

Athena is so selfish, I think, unpacking and shoving my dirty clothes into the washing basket. Why can't she just be happy for me? I'd support her if the situation was reversed. I *have* been happy for her every time she's met a new guy.

234

It's not my fault her relationships never last longer than a few months and that she finds it impossible to trust men.

I'm even more convinced that Athena is just bitter and jealous when I tell the people at work because their reaction couldn't be more different from hers. Everyone is really excited for me and even Lou doesn't seem put out when I go to her office to tell her the news.

'That's great, Alex! Congratulations.' She smiles warmly, patting the chair next to her desk.

I perch awkwardly on the edge. I'm not used to her being so friendly and it's slightly unsettling. 'I'm sorry for the inconvenience. I can work until the end of the month . . .'

She flaps her hand. 'Don't worry about it. I don't see why you can't continue to write for us remotely from Cornwall.'

She smiles conspiratorially and taps at her computer, turning the screen around, so I can see she's been reading my article. *The Mysterious Death of the Thriller Writer*. It's been a few days since I sent it to her, and she hasn't mentioned it until now. I'd assumed that she didn't like it.

'This is great work,' she says. 'Really intriguing. I've decided to make it the lead article of the Arts and Culture Section.'

'You have?' I feel an instinctive thrill of excitement, immediately tempered with anxiety when I remember Joe and Lily.

'Could you hold off on publishing for a while, please? I need to check with my partner. He hasn't read it yet and I want to make sure he's okay with it.'

Lou arches an eyebrow and closes the document. 'Alright, I suppose there's no rush. But try and persuade him, Alex. You know this could be a big story. It could be the making of your career.'

I'm stunned and elated by Lou's reaction to my feature. It seems as though all my dreams are finally about to come true. This is what I've been working towards for so long, after all. After work, I go out with a couple of colleagues to celebrate, but while I'm ordering shots at the bar, Joe nudges his way into my mind. What will he make of what I've written? I wonder. True, I left out a lot of things I could have put in, out of respect for him and Lily, but I guess he might not see it that way. If it comes down to a choice between Joe and my career, I'm not sure what I'll choose. But to my relief, no life-defining decision is required because when I send Joe the article that evening, he calls back almost immediately.

'You're a good writer and it's a great piece,' he tells me. 'You should go ahead and print it.'

I hesitate, hardly daring to believe it can be that easy. 'Are you sure? What about Lily?'

'Don't worry. Lily won't read it. She never reads the news.

She's always on Instagram or TikTok or God only knows what sites.'

As it turns out Joe is wrong about Lily seeing the story because it takes off in a way none of us expected. The week after publication, it gets picked up by several national newspapers and even makes it onto the TV news. Over the next month the story gradually gains traction. Pretty soon #WhathappenedtoAveryLewis becomes a thing on social media, and all over Twitter, Instagram and Facebook people are sharing theories about her death.

Before long it seems every time I turn on the TV, I'm confronted with a windswept newscaster standing on the edge of the cliffs at Bosigran, speculating about her fate. Several journalists contact me asking me to do an interview and I even get a call from a prestigious news outlet asking if I'd like to apply for a job. As if she somehow psychically knows, Lou phones me minutes later offering to increase my salary.

'You've really hit the mark this time, Alex. I always knew you could do it,' she coos, all sweetness and light.

The next day Olivia messages me to tell me that, thanks to my article, Avery's book has skyrocketed to the top of the Kindle chart. *It's in the top twenty bestselling paperbacks*, she writes. *It's even outselling Gemma K's new autobiography.* She attaches a screen shot of the book in first place.

Avery would be thrilled, she adds.

I'm not so sure that's true and I can't help a nagging feeling of guilt and anxiety about how all this is affecting the Lewis family.

'I had no idea this would become such a big thing. I'm sorry,' I tell Joe during one of our late-night phone conversations. I rest the phone on my pillow, lie down and gaze into his brown eyes. We've taken to leaving the call on all night, so it feels as though we're sleeping together. I feel closer than ever to him but I'm worried that this new development will cause a rift between us.

To my relief his mood seems buoyant.

'Don't worry. Lily has taken it surprisingly well,' he says. 'And the extra money will come in handy. If sales continue the way they are, the book will make thousands this month alone.'

'It's a shame Avery isn't alive to see this,' I say tentatively.

'Yes, I think she'd have been glad to see how popular her book has become.' He reaches out and touches the screen. 'But I don't want to talk about the book. I want to talk about you. When are you coming back here? I miss you.'

I feel warmth flood my body as if he has actually touched me.

'I miss you too. I just have a couple more days at work and I'll be there. I can't wait to see you.'

The next few days are busy with final preparations.

Athena and I have interviewed several potential flatmates and eventually settled on a recently divorced care-worker called Mindy who likes snakes. She wants to move in as soon as possible, so I spend my last few days in London emptying my bedroom and packing up all my things. I haven't got much. All my belongings fit into a couple of suitcases and three large boxes. And when I put the back seat down it all fits fairly easily into my Nissan Micra.

The night before I leave, Athena and I have another big row because I discover that she's gone ahead and accepted financial help from our father behind my back. We're still upset with each other the next morning, but she grudgingly comes out to wave me off.

'Just take care of yourself,' she says coolly, through the open window.

'I will, you too,' I reply. 'I'll message you to let you know when I arrive.' And, with that, I set off for Cornwall ready to start a new chapter in my life.

Thirty-five

I didn't know that life could be like this. I don't think I've ever been happier. I'm falling more in love with Joe each day. I wish Athena could see the way he treats me. She'd have to eat her words. He's so kind and thoughtful and he does such sweet, romantic things. As for the age gap I really can't say I notice it. Joe is still young at heart and when we're together, we're like giddy teenagers high on love. Only a few days ago, for example, he dared me to swim with him in the freezing cold sea in St Ives. All I can say is thank God for the Gulf Stream, but even with its warming effects the water was like ice! Afterwards we were so cold, we couldn't stop shivering. We drove back to Sancreed and huddled in blankets next to the open fire, with mugs of steaming hot chocolate, trying to get warm. Then, when we finally stopped shivering, we made love on the rug in front of the fire.

I suppose the only blot on our happiness is Lily. She makes it blatantly obvious at every opportunity that she's not thrilled that I've moved in with them. She hasn't said it, in so many words, but I can tell from the way she avoids me and from the accusatory looks she throws Joe's way every now and then. Of course, I don't blame her. I know exactly how she feels. I haven't forgotten how much I resented it when Olena moved in with our father and I must admit I gave her a hard time. But then Olena was different. She tried to take over from our mother and to get involved in the discipline of me and my sister. I'm not like that. I don't want to interfere in Lily's life, after all she's nearly a grown-up. I only want to be her friend.

I try to explain this to her after a particularly frosty evening meal when I find her in the conservatory, lying on the sofa, scrolling through her phone.

She sighs loudly as I enter the room.

'Hey, Lily, can we talk?' I ask, trying to sound authoritative and friendly.

She rolls her eyes and sits up slowly, folding her arms across her chest. 'What about?'

I perch opposite her on the edge of the small armchair, choosing my words carefully. 'I know it's a big change, me moving in with your dad, and it can't be easy for you. I just wanted you to know, I appreciate you welcoming me into your home.'

She raises her shoulders. 'I didn't really have a choice, did I?'

I bite my lip and try again. 'No, I understand. I know you're used to having your stepfather to yourself and it can't be easy for you what with losing your mum . . .' Her face goes dark at the mention of her mother, but I plough on regardless, determined to find a way to get through to her. 'I just want you to know that I lost my mother too when I was about your age, and I understand what it's like.' Her face grows even darker. 'Also, that I'm here if you need me or if you ever want to talk,' I finish lamely.

Silence.

'There's no way I want to come between you and your father and I'm certainly not trying to replace your mother.'

Lily snorts and stands up. 'You couldn't replace her anyway. You aren't even in the same league as her. Not even close.'

'I know,' I say, desperately, as she stalks towards the door.

'I've got to go out,' she says coldly. 'I'm meeting Josh.'

Hopefully, with time, Lily will come around. Once she gets to know me properly, she'll see that my intentions are good – that I'm not trying to usurp her mother or take her father away. But I do understand her resentment and I wonder if Joe and I are partly to blame. We've been so wrapped up in each other the past week or so and it occurs to me, after my conversation with Lily, that maybe I have been a bit insensitive, keeping him all to myself. So, that evening, I suggest to Joe that he spends some quality father–daughter time with her. He agrees that it's a good idea and so, the next day – good father that he is – even though I know he hates musicals, he takes her to see *The Book of Mormon* in Bristol.

I decide to take advantage of the time alone to catch up with some work. There are a couple of reviews I need to complete. But it's hard to settle to anything. I feel uneasy in the house on my own. I'm hyper-aware of all the strange noises it makes: the rattling of the doors, the grumble of the boiler. It feels hostile – almost as if it's trying to tell me I'm not welcome. Avery is all around, from the pictures on the wall to the curtains and cushions. Her photo on the mantlepiece seems to sneer at me:

You really think you can make Joe and Lily happy? You'll never make them happy like I did. You'll never be as talented and beautiful as I am.

I move the laptop into the kitchen away from her critical eyes, but I still can't concentrate. After typing and retyping the same paragraph several times, I close the laptop with a snap, put on my coat and trainers and head out with Barney for a walk.

*

It's a beautiful, crisp, cold day and as I wander into the village, breathing the pure, unpolluted air, my anxiety dissipates. It's all in my mind, of course.

I'm near the village centre when I bump into Charlie with his dog, Marshall, heading in the opposite direction. Charlie's face is half hidden by a scarf wrapped over his nose and I don't recognise him until he greets me.

'Alex! I thought it was you. Good to see you!' he exclaims. 'I heard on the grapevine that you'd moved down here – someone told me that you'd married Joe Lewis, but I wasn't sure if it was true . . .'

'We're not married,' I say, 'but I've moved in with him.'

'Wow.' He stares at me, then shakes his head slowly. 'Well, congratulations, but I thought . . .'

'Who told you?' I interrupt quickly. I wonder if everyone is talking about us in the village and what they make of us shacking up together less than a year after Avery died.

'You can't keep anything secret in this place,' he says lightly. Then he laughs at Marshall who is sniffing Barney's bum. Barney growls at him gently and he backs away. 'Sorry about his terrible manners. Anyhow, you're a local now. How are you settling in?'

'Very well thanks. It's such a lovely part of the world.'

He smiles. 'I told you, this place gets under your skin.'

'You were right.'

There's a slightly awkward pause. Charlie rocks back on

his heels, smiling broadly. 'Well, I was just going to head back. I don't suppose you've got time for a drink?'

The invitation seems very natural, and I find myself accepting before I have time to think. But as we walk into the village together it occurs to me that Joe might not like me spending time on my own with a young, attractive man. But it's too late now. Besides, I'm pretty sure that Charlie's just being friendly.

'I read your article about Avery, by the way,' he says as we pass the turning to Foxton Farm. 'It was good.'

'Thank you,' I murmur. I'm trying to remember what I said about Charlie in the article and hoping that it was nice.

'It was all over the TV and the internet. The village was inundated with press. You couldn't move for news crews.'

'I'm sorry,' I say. 'I had no idea it would turn into such a big thing.'

'Why apologise? You've really put Sancreed on the map. Tourists have been flocking here to see the place where Avery Lewis lived.' He grins. 'It's been great for business.'

We've all benefitted from Avery's death, I think guiltily, apart from Avery herself. We're like parasites feeding off her carcass.

At the far end of the village, Charlie stops outside the Crown.

'Here we are,' he says.

And we duck into the warm interior, blowing on our hands to warm them up. The pub is empty apart from a red-faced man in a hat and muddy wellington boots, who couldn't look any more like a farmer if he tried. The same red-haired barmaid that was here when Athena and I came on our first night here is serving behind the bar.

'Hiya, Andrea,' Charlie greets her cheerfully. 'I'll have a pint of Stella and . . . what'll you have, Alex? You've met Alex, haven't you? She's just moved in at Foxton Farm.'

'Yes, I know.' Andrea smiles faintly. 'What will you have, then?' she asks me coldly, pouring a pint and handing it to Charlie.

'I'll have a Coke please,' I say, a little disconcerted by her frosty manner. She seemed friendlier the last time we met.

'Where's Joe today, then?' she asks, her eyes glittering with curiosity, as she plonks the glass on the counter.

'He's gone for a day out in Bristol with Lily.'

'Oh, I see.'

Charlie and I take our drinks and sit by the window, looking out at the empty, grey road.

'So how are you finding it? It must seem a bit quiet here after London,' Charlie says, sipping his beer and leaving a moustache of foam on his upper lip.

'I like it. I miss my sister though.'

'Mm.' Charlie nods. 'That was the girl you came in here with before.'

'That's right.'

'She made quite an impression on Liam – that's the guy I was with. You both did. It's not often we see such a couple of stunners in these parts.'

I blush, embarrassed and tear the corner of my beer mat.

'Sorry, that probably wasn't appropriate,' he says. 'But I meant it as a compliment.'

'I know, it's alright. Thank you.'

'I'm not trying to come on to you or anything.' He smiles and lowers his voice. 'It's just the company here gets really dull sometimes and it's nice to talk to someone new.'

'I understand.' I like talking to Charlie too and I realise I haven't really spoken to anyone apart from Joe or Lily since I've been here.

I'm about to ask him what he does for entertainment but at that moment Andrea sidles over, clearing up glasses and wiping down tables on her way.

'So, how are you settling in?' she asks when she reaches our table.

'Fine, thank you,' I say warily.

She hovers. 'And everything's going okay with you and Joe?'

'Fine,' I bristle. It's an impertinent question. After all, she barely knows me and there's something malicious in her expression that I don't like.

But she doesn't appear to notice my tone and takes my curt reply as an invitation to sit down.

'I wouldn't rush into anything, if I were you,' she says, resting her arms on the table. 'I'm not sure that he's really over his wife, bless him. It's only been about eleven months since she died.'

'I know that,' I say coldly. I shift my chair slightly, hoping Andrea will get the hint that I don't want to talk to her.

'It's really none of your business, Andrea,' Charlie says, coming to my defence.

Andrea sniffs and glares at Charlie. 'I'm only trying to help. It's just that they were so in love and she died so suddenly. It was such a shock to him.' She leans in close. 'I was talking to my friend, Gerry, about Avery the other day. Gerry lives in a house at Bosigran, right opposite the cliffs where she died. She was there that night. She saw Avery drive up and park.'

'She did?' In spite of my feelings towards Andrea at this moment, I'm interested. If she's telling the truth, then her friend must be the witness Metcalfe mentioned.

The journalist in me wants to ask Andrea more about her friend. But I stop myself. I've put Joe through enough already and there's no point in looking into Avery's death anymore. The article is published, and I don't want to hurt our relationship by dredging up Joe's past again.

'Excuse me, I need the bathroom,' Charlie says abruptly.

Andrea watches him balefully as he weaves his way through the tables to the toilets.

'A word of advice,' she says, when he's out of earshot. 'You want to be careful.'

'About what?'

She purses her lips. 'About the company you keep. Don't worry. Joe won't hear anything from me. But this is a small place and word gets about.'

I'm about to lose my cool. She really is out of order now. 'What do you mean?' I ask through gritted teeth.

'Well . . . Joe and Charlie aren't exactly friends.' She lowers her voice and leans close. 'Charlie and Avery were . . . well, you know . . .'

It's not hard to grasp her meaning. My face grows hot. How dare she spread rumours about Avery, who is dead and can't defend herself? I'm taken aback by my own reaction, but I feel strangely defensive of Avery. Then I remember *Falling*, how Rebecca becomes Dominic's lover and how Joe said his relationship with Avery was far from perfect. She may have a point.

'Charlie said he didn't know Avery all that well,' I say uncertainly.

She shrugs and gives a worldly smile. 'Yeah, well, he would say that, wouldn't he? Listen, just . . .'

But she breaks off because just then Charlie returns from the toilet and gives Andrea a quizzical smile.

'You poisoning Alex's mind with all your conspiracy theories?' he says.

'Course not,' she sniffs. 'Just watch yourself,' she says to me and, with a withering look at Charlie, flounces off.

'What was that all about?' he asks when she's out of earshot.

'Oh, nothing much,' I say, reddening. I'm aware of the elderly woman in the corner staring at us curiously and I wonder how quickly it will get back to Joe that I was in the pub with Charlie.

'I wouldn't pay too much attention to what she says, if I were you.' He grins. 'She's a gossip queen.'

'I see,' I say, nodding and smiling. It's hard not to like Charlie, he's so affable, but it's also difficult to know who or what to believe and I feel uncomfortable for the remainder of our conversation, and as soon as I politely can, I make my excuses and leave.

Back at the farm I try to get on with some work again, but Andrea's words have left a sour taste in my mouth. I can't get them out of my head. Is there any truth to them? Is that what Joe was referring to when he said things weren't always perfect between him and Avery? There's only one way to find out and although I'm scared of how he might react, I resolve to broach the subject with Joe when he returns.

But Joe and Lily don't get back from Bristol until late, and it's even later before Lily goes to bed.

'You have a nice day without us?' he asks, kissing me on the mouth as he comes into the bedroom and throws his jacket over the back of a chair. I'm propped up against a pillow, scrolling through Instagram, my eye snagging on a photo Olena has posted of Chris in his football kit. He looks happy, I think. Maybe he is happy. I hope Dad treats Olena better than he treated Mum.

'It was okay.' I shrug. 'How about you? Was the show good?'

He grimaces and flings himself down on the bed next to me. 'Lily enjoyed herself, which is the main thing. What did you get up to?'

I open my mouth to tell him about bumping into Charlie and having a drink in the Crown, but somehow the words don't come out. If what Andrea said is true, then mentioning Charlie will only upset him.

'I did some work, and I went for a walk. That's about it,' I yawn. I'll ask him tomorrow, I think.

Thirty-six

Communication is the key to a good relationship; I know that.

But somehow, I never do find the right moment to ask Joe about Charlie and it's impossible for me to talk about Avery. I certainly can't tell him about the strange notions I've been having or the disconcerting sensation that Avery's still here – that somehow her essence has permeated the walls and the foundations of the house itself. Even saying it to myself sounds crazy, and logically, in the plain light of day, while Joe is around, I know it's all in my head. But at night she haunts my dreams and I wake in a cold sweat. And when the house is empty, I hear strange noises and wonder if I'm losing my mind.

All these secrets begin to create a distance between us and even if I wanted to speak to Joe, it would be hard because he's always busy lately with the renovations to the house. Although the money is rolling in from Avery's book now, he still chooses to do as much of the work as he can himself. And he spends his days manically sawing, plastering and sanding in the old stables only emerging to grab a quick sandwich at lunchtime and sometimes working late into the night.

I suppose there's a part of me that misses my life in London. I wish there was someone, other than Joe, that I could confide in. And I miss Athena more than anything. We haven't talked properly since our argument in London. We've had a couple of short video calls, but Joe was there, and we kept the conversation polite and superficial so I'm not even sure if she's forgiven me. So, when she phones in the middle of March and asks if she can come and visit for the week, I'm overjoyed.

'Of course!' I exclaim without a second's thought. 'That'd be great!'

'Fab. I can't wait. Can you meet me at the train station?' she says. 'I'll message you when I know what time.'

'Sure, sure.'

There's a pause.

'So, how's it going?'

'It's good. I love it here with Joe.'

It's true. It *is* good. So why do I feel as though I'm lying?

*

I'm counting the days until Athena's visit, planning all the fun things we can do together.

But Joe doesn't seem to share my enthusiasm when I tell him. I've made us some sandwiches and brought him a beer out to the old stables and we're sitting outside in the weak winter sun on sacks of cement.

'You could have consulted me before you invited her,' he says.

'I didn't invite her. She invited herself,' I protest. 'Besides, she's my sister. I couldn't exactly tell her not to come, could I?'

He sighs and rakes his fingers through his hair. 'I know. It's not that I don't want her to come. I like Athena. It's just that with all the renovation work, where is she going to stay? The spare bedroom is completely gutted, and I don't want to kick Lily out of her room.'

I don't want that either. I can just imagine Lily's reaction. Things between Lily and me are just beginning to improve and I don't want to jeopardise the tentative progress I've made. 'She could stay in the cottage?' I suggest.

'You're kidding, right? That's booked up for the next six months.'

'How about the attic room?'

There's a silence. I mean Avery's old study, of course. We never use the room and although he hasn't said anything directly, I know that Joe wouldn't like me using it. For a

254

moment I think he's going to object. But then he just shrugs and smiles. 'Alright then. Why not? You might need to give it a clean, though. I haven't been up there since Avery died.'

In the afternoon, while Joe is in Penzance buying tiles for the new kitchen, I go up to the attic room to make a bed for Athena. It's strange but, I feel nervous as I climb the stairs, as if I'm intruding somehow. As I shove the door open, a breath of cold, stale air drifts out and wraps itself around me. The simple, pragmatic explanation for the cold air, of course, is that the room is unused, and the radiators are never switched on, but I can't escape the familiar sensation that Avery is here, watching and resenting me.

'This is my house now,' I say out loud, feeling faintly ridiculous, as I march inside.

Of course, there is no answer. Just the patter of the rain outside and a strange ticking noise from the floorboards. Some kind of wood worm? The wallpaper is old and peeling from the wall.

I stand there amongst the detritus of her life; postcards of famous female authors above her writing desk, a Russian pen stand that looks like a rocket and a photo of Gabe and Lily, aged about eight and six respectively, in their school uniforms. I tear down the postcards and a bit of paint comes off with the Blu Tack. It doesn't matter. We're going to repaint anyway. Then, rubbing my hands to keep them warm, I turn on the radiator and make up the bed, smoothing down the covers until they look perfectly flat. I want to make everything as comfortable as possible for Athena.

In the wardrobe there are more of Avery's clothes. I push them aside, making room for Athena's, and at the bottom of the wardrobe I discover a lamp and plug it in. It's still working but there is no bedside table to put it on, so I remove all Avery's things from the desk and push it over to the bed, setting the lamp on it. Satisfied that everything is perfect, I am about to leave when I notice the pile of dust and junk in the space where the desk has been. Amongst all the other random objects that have fallen behind the desk there are a couple of pens, a red ring-binder folder full of papers, a piece of paper and an old card. On the piece of paper there are some typed-up notes. For a book?

John Stonehouse, born in 1925. Joined the Labour party aged 16. 1969 allegations of spying.

Who is John Stonehouse, I wonder vaguely. I fold up the paper and put it in my jeans pocket. Then I pick up the card, pulling off clumps of dust and white-blonde hair.

It's a Valentine's card.

Inside in thick felt pen it says:

To Joe, with all my love forever A xxx.

On the front of the card there's a picture of a puppy resting its head on a heart-shaped cushion with the words

'To My Valentine' embroidered on it. It's a surprisingly cutesy choice for the sophisticated woman I imagine Avery to be. But it's not that, or even the reminder that their love was still strong after years of marriage, that troubles me.

It's the handwriting.

Heart hammering, I dash downstairs and snatch up my handbag from where it's hanging in the porch. Then, taking the stairs two at a time, I rush back up to the attic. Sitting on the newly made bed, my breath coming in ragged gasps, I unzip the pocket inside my bag. There it is. Along with tampons and Paracetamol, there's the note I received that morning in the cottage – the vicious, little message warning me to stay away from Joe.

I unfold the paper, slightly ragged around the edges now, and lay it on the bed next to the open card. My heart kicks against my ribs. For a moment I stop breathing. Because, when laid side by side like that, there can be no doubt.

The writing is identical.

Thirty-seven

Blood roars in my ears. The whole room sways and I lean back against the pillows, trying to catch my breath. I think of the woman I saw smoking at the bedroom window. I must be going mad.

It can't be true.

But it is true. The evidence is right here, in front of me.

The Valentine and the note were written by the same person. I received the note nearly two months ago. It can only mean one thing:

Avery was here on the farm. Avery is alive.

Hands shaking, I thrust the note into my pocket and slide the Valentine behind the bookcase. I'm thinking hard, stacking up the evidence in my mind. It *is* possible. Her body has never been found and she could have planted her bag and her phone on the cliff side to make people think she was dead. But why? Why would she do that?

I look out of the window at the yard, the pile of sand and the cement mixer. The sky behind the cottage is dark, threatening rain, and the sun disappears in a flash of silver. My gaze falls on the door, and I remember the figure in the red coat outside the cottage that night – the night I received the note. When I first saw her, I imagined she was Avery's ghost, an idea I dismissed as fanciful. But what if my instinct was right after all? What if it *was* Avery outside the cottage that night? What if Avery wrote that note? Not her ghost of course, but the real live flesh and blood woman. She came to claim what is rightfully hers, I think with a shiver. Her farm. Her man.

Where is she now? And where has she been hiding all this time? I look over my shoulder with sudden dread as if she might materialise in the room behind me. But of course, there's no one there.

Fingers trembling, I open Avery's laptop and switch it on. I'm not sure exactly why or what it is I'm looking for but if there's a clue to what Avery was thinking just before she disappeared, it will be in this slim, silver box. I'll check her search history, I think vaguely. But the laptop is password-protected, of course. I try a couple of obvious guesses. But with no luck. Perhaps if I take it to the police, they'll be able to open it . . . but what are the chances that they'll believe me? They'll think I'm crazy. I mean, I would. The whole idea does seem incredible.

'What the fuck are you doing in my mother's room?'

The words jolt me out of my thoughts, and I start guiltily, swivelling round.

Lily is standing in the doorway, looking at me as if she'd like to kill me. 'And what makes you think you have the right to use her laptop?'

I switch off the laptop and close it, wondering if Lily can see that I'm shaking. I turn to her with a smile that I hope conveys calm and confidence. I have every right to be here, I tell myself. I'm not about to be intimidated by a teenaged girl.

'Athena's coming to visit,' I say calmly. 'She's going to stay in this room. I was just getting it ready for her. Didn't Joe tell you?'

Her mouth twists. 'Oh, and you need to nose into my mother's private stuff to get it ready, do you?'

'Well, no. It's just my laptop is playing up,' I improvise. 'I'm trying to write an article and I thought I'd use this one instead. Not that I really need to explain myself to you,' I add.

'You're a liar,' she hisses. 'And you're stupid as well. Stupid if you think I'll believe your lies.'

'That's enough, Lily.' My voice rises. The frustration of the past few weeks bubbles to the surface – all the little digs that Lily has made and the snide remarks. I grow hot with anger. 'I don't think your stepdad would like it if he knew how you're speaking to me, do you?'

Then to my astonishment, she strides over and pulls me up by my hair to my feet.

'Get out!' she shrieks. 'Get out of my mother's room!'

'Lily, calm down,' I splutter, trying to fend her off. But she's not listening. She shoves me towards the door, and I tumble backwards, hitting my head against the sharp edge.

'You bitch!' I exclaim, pain shooting through my neck and down my shoulder.

'What the hell is going on?' Joe calls up from the bottom of the stairs. 'Are you okay, Alex?'

'She was looking through Mum's stuff, snooping around. She's a sneaky cow,' Lily shouts.

'Don't talk about Alex like that,' Joe says wearily as he climbs the stairs.

He stops abruptly when he sees me slumped on the floor.

'Jesus, Alex. What's she done to you?'

'It's okay, it was an accident,' I say. But Joe rounds on Lily, his eyes blazing with anger.

'Go to your room. I mean it . . . Now.'

I wonder if Lily is too old to be sent to her room but maybe it's the look in Joe's eyes or maybe she realises she's gone too far because, to my surprise, she flounces off without another word.

'Alex, are you okay?' Joe kneels beside me, parting my hair to see if I'm injured.

'I'm alright,' I say, standing up shakily. There may be a small cut on my head, but that barely registers, and Lily's outburst is unimportant compared to the huge discovery I've just made.

'Do you know of someone called John Stonehouse?' I ask as I follow him downstairs.

'What? No, I don't think so. Come into the kitchen, I'll get you cleaned up.'

If Avery is still alive, does Joe know?

He can't, otherwise what would he be doing with me? But what kind of person would let their husband and their own children think they were dead?

'Sit here,' Joe commands and he rummages in one of the kitchen cabinets, pulling out a bottle of antiseptic spray. 'I can't believe it. I thought she'd grown out of this behaviour,' he mutters, as he tilts my head to one side attempting to spray the cut.

'I'm okay,' I say, pushing him away and standing up. I have a sudden, urgent need to get out of this house, away from Lily, away from him. 'I'm going to go out for a walk. I think I need some fresh air to clear my head.'

'It's going to rain soon,' Joe protests. 'It's not a good idea.'

But I'm already halfway to the door. Grabbing my coat, I step outside into the cold and damp.

I head out across the fields. Directionless and heedless, I find myself stumbling up the hill along a waterlogged path towards Sancreed Beacon. I've never been this way before and I'm vaguely aware of various ominous signs, warning of danger from old mineshafts. I don't take much notice. I can see the old mines – just a few square, water-filled holes. Sure, it wouldn't be good if you fell into one but I'm not about to stray from the path and I have other things on my mind. The wind is whipping itself up into a frenzy, ripping through the reddish-brown bracken and bending the few threadbare trees. I pull my jacket close around my shoulders and trudge on to the top.

I'm thinking about the conversation I had with Olivia about artists that were only appreciated after their deaths. What if she meant it literally? What if Avery planted the evidence to make it look as if she'd died the same way as the victim in her book? It could have been a publicity stunt. I think about the financial difficulties they were in. I already know that she was willing to break the law – to lie and to cheat. She must have been disappointed that no one picked up on the similarity . . . until I came along.

By the time I reach the beacon the wind is even wilder, pummelling me until I almost lose my footing. I shelter against the large, stone slab and look out over the landscape.

From here, even in the twilight, there's a good view of Sancreed. Where are you, Avery? I wonder. Are you somewhere nearby? What have I got myself into?

'My God, you'll catch your death! What were you doing, you crazy girl?' Joe says, tapping my nose affectionately when I finally return, drenched to the skin.

'I climbed to Sancreed Beacon,' I tell him, as I slip past him to the bedroom to change my clothes.

Joe follows me. 'What the hell for?'

'I don't know.' I shrug. 'I've never been there before, and I needed to think. There are a few things on my mind.' I strip off my jeans and my jumper which are soaked through and pull on a pair of leggings and a T-shirt, shivering.

He sighs. 'I'm sorry about Lily, I'll speak to her tomorrow when she's calmed down.' He comes up behind me and wraps his arms around me, kissing my neck. I wriggle away.

'It's not Lily,' I say.

'Then what?' Joe frowns and slumps on the bed. He looks suddenly old and tired. 'You're not happy, are you? Do you regret moving here?'

'No, you don't understand,' I say. When I look at him, I'm torn. I want to kiss the corner of his lips and smooth away the worried creases around his eyes. I want to tell him that I've never felt closer to anyone, apart from Athena. But Avery is everywhere between us, like a force field holding me back and there's the nagging suspicion that if Avery is alive then he must have been complicit.

'I've just got a headache, that's all,' I murmur. As I speak, I realise it's true. The tension of the day has finally caught up with me and there's a sharp pulse behind my temple that could turn into a migraine. I can't think about Avery anymore. It's making me ill. *She's* making me ill.

'Poor baby.' Joe brings me a couple of painkillers and I crawl into bed and lie there trying to empty my mind.

But my headache grows more intense and a wave of nausea washes over me. I dash to the toilet and throw up. I throw up a couple of times before I finally crawl back into bed and doze off.

When I wake up my headache has subsided. I can hear Joe watching TV downstairs and Lily chatting and laughing with someone on her phone. I clamber out of bed, feeling a little shaky and change my clothes. As I take off my jeans a piece of paper flutters out. It's the paper I found on Avery's desk with the name John Stonehouse written on it. I pick up my phone and Google him and find that there's a whole Wikipedia page devoted to him. Apparently, he was a Labour politician famous for being a Czechoslovakian spy and for faking his own death, leaving a pile of clothes on a beach in Miami so that people would presume he'd drowned.

I read the article twice with growing conviction. It can't

be a coincidence. Is that where Avery got the idea? Was she trying to think of ways to fake her own death?

I pick up my phone and send an email to Olivia.

Dear Olivia,

Thank you for taking the time to meet me the other day. You were very helpful. I hope you enjoyed the article I wrote about Avery Lewis. I'm thinking of writing a follow-up about other books she's written, and I have a couple of questions for you about her work. Do you know what she was planning to write after Falling? *I found some references to John Stonehouse in her notes the other day. Do you have any idea why she would have been researching him?*

After I've pressed send, I notice buried amongst all the spam in my inbox that Avery's editor, Lucy Rivers, finally sent me a message a few days ago.

Dear Alexandra,

I'm so sorry I didn't get back to you sooner. I've been in hospital recuperating after major surgery, and I am only now just beginning to clear the backlog of emails that's built up.

I must admit I was initially a little puzzled by your query. No one here ever sent you a copy of Falling *to review but it turns out to have been a serendipitous mix-up because your article has been instrumental in increasing sales of the Inspector Hegarty mysteries. We all loved your piece on Avery Lewis here at Phoenix Publications and are thrilled by the success of* Falling.

I realise it's a little late now as your article has already been published. I'm just writing to let you know that I'd be more than happy to answer any further questions you may have in the future.

Warm regards,

Lucy

I read the email again, my eye snagging on one sentence: *No one here ever sent you a copy of* Falling *to review.*

So, who did? Was it Avery herself in the hopes that I would do exactly what I have?

Have I been unwittingly working for her all along?

Have I been played?

I climb back under the covers and turn off the lamp. I'm exhausted and drained by the events of the day but it's hard to switch off with all the thoughts swirling around in my head and when Joe comes to bed much later, I'm still awake, fretting. I listen to him fumbling with his belt buckle and pretend to be asleep.

Thirty-eight

Athena is waiting on the platform, leaning on her suitcase and scrolling through her phone. There's a worried frown furrowing her brow. Her hair is tied back but a curl has escaped and is falling over her cheek. This is the first time I've seen her in over a month. My little sister. My heart pulls tight with love.

'Sorry we're late. Joe had to stop off and pick some stuff up and it took longer than we thought,' I say, as I hug her.

It's not the truth. In fact, we were delayed by an argument with Lily. She wanted to go for a weekend away with Josh, but Joe said no. It escalated into a furious row with Lily threatening to go anyway and Joe threatening to ground her.

'Here, let me.' Joe takes Athena's case and kisses her lightly on both cheeks. He chats and laughs easily with her on the way back to the car and I watch him, amazed at how quickly he's recovered from the argument. He seems relaxed, happy even. It's hard to believe that just minutes ago he and Lily were screaming at each other. For Athena's sake, I try to pretend everything's okay too, but I'm still shaken by some of the things Lily said and Athena senses that something is off.

'You alright, Alex? You seem . . . a bit quiet,' she says in the car as we speed along the narrow road to Sancreed.

Out of the corner of my eyes I catch Joe's eye.

'I'm tired, that's all,' I say smiling wanly. 'I didn't get much sleep last night.'

That much is true. I woke at four o'clock in the morning after a nightmare in which Avery fell over a cliff edge, pulling me with her. I couldn't get back to sleep and slipped out of bed, trying not to wake Joe. Then I prowled the house and read *Falling* again until I finally dropped off at about seven, only to be woken by Joe and Lily arguing half an hour later.

I turn round, draping my arm over the back of the seat and try to smile. 'What about you, Athena? How are you?'

'I'm alright.'

'How's Mindy settling in?'

'She's good. She keeps herself to herself.'

'And Albert? How's he?'

She looks sheepish. 'Actually, I met someone else. His name's Ben.'

I raise my eyebrows.

She rummages in her bag and finds a photo on her phone then passes it forward to me. I enlarge a slightly blurry photo of a handsome young man with dark, curly hair.

'He's good-looking, I'll give you that.'

'He's gorgeous, isn't he?' she enthuses. 'And he's nice and clever. He's studying physics at Trinity College, Cambridge.'

'No kidding.' I glance over at Joe. 'Joe went to Cambridge too.'

'Really?' Athena says. 'Is that right? It's such a beautiful college, isn't it? I went to stay with Ben last weekend. I wonder if it's changed much since you were there. Where did you stay in your first year?'

But Joe doesn't answer because he's just seen a fox and he brakes suddenly.

'That was close,' he says as we drive on. 'I probably should have hit him. He's probably the same bloody fox that's been trying to get into my hen coop.'

'Oh, I think I saw that fox,' Athena exclaims. 'That night it was snowing I went out and I saw a fox. It was really cute.'

'Not so cute when it's after your chickens,' Joe mutters.

'I saw it too,' I add. 'It was making a weird screeching noise, but I didn't know you were wandering around by yourself in the middle of the night, Athena.'

I'm thinking about the footprints I saw that morning in the snow. They must have been Athena's. At least I know now that they probably weren't Avery's.

Back at the farm, while Athena is settling herself into the attic room, I check my phone and see that Olivia has replied to my email.

Dear Alex,

It was nice to meet you too!

In answer to your query, I believe that the John Stonehouse notes you refer to were probably linked to Avery's next book. She had sent me a synopsis, which involved someone faking their own death and the notes were probably related to that.

I hope this helps and don't hesitate to contact me if you have any further queries.

Best wishes,

Olivia

I close the email, thinking hard. It doesn't really prove anything either way, I conclude. On the one hand it provides a possibly innocent explanation for the John Stonehouse notes, but on the other there's no reason why Avery couldn't have been inspired by her own research.

'So, what's the plan?' Athena interrupts my thoughts as she comes breezing into the living room.

'Whatever you like,' I say smiling. I'm glad to have her

here to distract me from my suspicions, which I know are becoming obsessive and unhealthy.

The next few days pass all too quickly. It's great having Athena around. Her vibrant presence about the house cheers us all up and even Lily seems to get on well with her. Most nights we stay up late, the four of us, drinking Joe's homemade cider, discussing everything under the sun and during the day while Joe is working on the house, Athena and I go for long tramps along the beach in the rain and the sun. But even though I try hard not to think about Avery, she's still always there, at the back of my mind, and I'm constantly plagued by the fear that she is somewhere nearby, watching my every move.

'What's bothering you?' Athena asks near the end of the week. We're walking along the blustery beach just beyond Penzance, our feet sinking in the soft, wet sand, the tidal island of St Michael's Mount ahead of us, lit by the sinking sun.

'What do you mean?' I ask.

She glances sideways at me and brushes away a strand of hair that's blown into her face. 'There's something upsetting you, I can tell. Don't try to deny it. You're not yourself. Is everything okay with Joe?'

I stare at my elongated shadow in the sand.

'Yes, Joe's great and Lily . . .' I sigh. 'Well, Lily is Lily, but I'm working on it. Nothing I can't handle.'

'So, what is it then?'

We stop at a river too wide to jump across and head upstream to a small bridge. By the side of the river small black and white birds hop in the sand and flutter out of our way when we approach. Athena's going to think I'm insane if I tell her what's really on my mind. But it's true that it's been weighing on me and maybe it will help to share my thoughts. 'Okay,' I say. 'But please hear me out before you make a judgement.'

'Alright,' she agrees warily.

We sit together on the low sea wall, staring out at the silver blue sea and I tell her everything. My suspicions about Avery. The Valentine with the matching handwriting. The woman in the red coat.

'What do you think?' I ask when I've finished because Athena is silently digging a hole in the sand with her toe, a tense, thoughtful expression on her face.

'I don't know what to think.' She stands up abruptly and we walk on in silence for a while, turning up the causeway towards St Michael's Mount. Finally, she says, 'I mean, are you sure about the handwriting?'

My heart sinks. I knew she wouldn't believe me. 'Yes, I'm sure. I can show you the Valentine when I get back to the house.'

We walk as far as we can along the causeway, until it's swallowed up by water. Then we stop, the black water lapping at our feet. 'It'll be dark before we can go all the way,' says Athena. 'Let's go back. We can come again another time.'

'Okay.' I turn, feeling strangely reluctant to return home.

As we walk back along the causeway, I catch sight of someone on the beach. A woman walking briskly towards the car park.

Slim. Straight back. Ash-blonde hair. Bobbed. *Wearing a red coat.*

My breath catches in my throat. *It can't be.* But it is. It's the same red coat, the one in the photo in the living room. I'm sure.

'My God,' I whisper. 'I think that's *her*. Avery.'

'What?'

There's no time to explain. I start running, my feet sinking in the sand, my heart pounding. Athena races up behind me.

'Wait, Alex. What are you doing?' she asks breathlessly but I ignore her. Avery's walking fast. I can't afford to slacken my pace. I keep running, nearly slipping on a pile of bladderwrack. I'm getting close as she climbs the steps to the car park from the beach. But then I lose her for a moment in the crowd of people strolling along the promenade. I push my way through them and catch a flash of red. She crosses the road and I dash after her, ignoring the cars hooting and screeching to a halt and finally catch up with her just outside a large hotel.

'Avery,' I say, grabbing her roughly by the shoulder.

She turns.

I blink. The sinking sun is shining in my eyes, blinding me and for a moment I see *her*. Avery – ringed with fire, lit from behind like an avenging angel.

'Ouch. Jesus, get off me, Alex. What the hell are you doing here?'

I stagger backwards, confused. A cloud passes over the sun and her features morph and resolve themselves.

'Lily . . .' I stammer. Heat rises in my cheeks. I was so sure it was Avery. Did Lily hear me say her name?

If she did, she doesn't mention it. Her eyes narrow and she crosses her arms. 'Yeah?' she says defensively. 'What do you want? Joe knows I'm here, by the way.'

Athena has caught up with us and she's hovering awkwardly, looking from me to Lily. 'Small place, Cornwall.' She smiles.

We both ignore her.

'Your hair,' I say accusingly. 'What have you done to your hair?'

'Well, thanks very much, Alex,' Lily says sarcastically. 'I've had it cut and dyed, haven't I? I'm going to a party tonight. Don't you like it?'

'It's very nice,' Athena says soothingly, pulling me away. 'Come on, Alex. Let's leave Lily alone. Unless you need a lift? Do you need a lift back to Sancreed, Lily?'

'I'm alright thanks,' Lily says politely. 'Josh is going to drive me home.'

'I don't get it,' I say in the car on the way back. I clutch the wheel and brake suddenly as a tractor pulls out.

'Do you want me to drive?' Athena says. 'You seem a bit distracted . . .'

'She's done her hair exactly like Avery's. Same colour. Same cut. Same everything. She must have done it deliberately. She's taunting me.'

Athena sighs. 'Taunting you? Why would she do that?'

'I don't know.' I shake my head. 'Maybe she knows that Avery's still alive and she knows I know. She wants to throw me off.'

'Would you just listen to yourself, Alex? Do you know how crazy that sounds?'

I bite my lip. There's no point in arguing. She doesn't know Lily. She's only seen Lily's sweet side. But she'll believe me when I show her the Valentine.

When we arrive back at Foxton Farm, I can hear the chainsaw buzzing from the old stables where Joe is working. I can talk to Athena without him overhearing.

'Come with me,' I say, flinging off my coat and shoes and hurrying up the stairs to the attic room.

'I hid it here.' I kneel on the wooden floorboards and

slide my fingers behind the bookcase. But I can't feel the card.

'What the . . .'

'It's cold up here,' Athena grumbles. 'Is this going to take long?'

'It must have slipped further behind. Here, help me move this.'

It's heavy, but together, Athena and I manage to shift the bookcase, widening the gap between it and the wall. But there's nothing there but dust.

The Valentine has gone.

Thirty-nine

'Someone's taken it!' I exclaim.

I scrabble frantically in the desk drawer. Maybe I moved it and then forgot? But no. I'm sure I hid it behind the bookcase; I remember distinctly putting it there. My head is spinning. I feel as if I could be losing my mind.

Athena glances behind the bookcase. 'Well, it's not here now.' She shrugs. 'Joe probably cleaned up and threw it away. Come on. I could do with a coffee; I don't know about you.'

I'm close to tears. This is so frustrating. Athena doesn't believe me about the handwriting and now I've got no way of proving it to her. Reluctantly, I follow her downstairs to the kitchen. Is she right? Could Joe or Lily have been tidying up and thrown it away? I doubt it. Neither of them does much cleaning that I can tell, and it certainly wouldn't have occurred to them to dust or sweep behind the bookcase. I pause in the kitchen doorway, gripped by a sudden, chilling conviction.

'Avery's been in the house. She must've moved it.'

Athena gives a short snort of laughter. 'Now you're being ridiculous, Alex. Avery's dead. You know that, don't you?' She fills the kettle at the tap and turns it on. 'Sit yourself down. You'll feel better after a coffee.'

'You don't believe me.'

'I mean . . . I don't know what to think. Maybe someone else sent the Valentine. You should speak to Joe about it.'

I plough onwards, following my own train of thought. 'Avery wrote down the name John Stonehouse on a piece of paper. It was on her desk. Do you know who he was?'

Athena sighs wearily. 'No.'

'He was a politician who faked his own death in the seventies. He left a towel on a beach in Miami and flew on a false passport to Australia.'

'So? There could be a lot of reasons why she was interested in him. Maybe she was doing research for her next book. It doesn't mean she was planning her own disappearance.'

'Think about it though. Her body's never been found. And she was in financial difficulty. Her agent told me.'

Athena pours the coffee and sits down opposite me.

'Alex . . .' she says gently, looking directly into my eyes. 'Do you remember that time you went to the police in Cyprus?'

279

I wince because of course I remember. It was the lowest point in my life. A few weeks after Mum's death I became convinced that she'd been murdered, and I pestered the local police every day. I even sat in the police station and refused to move, until eventually a kindly officer sat me down and outlined to me patiently and clearly the reasons why they knew my mother had committed suicide.

'This is different.'

'Is it?' Athena stands up abruptly and goes to the window. When she turns again, I see that her eyes are shining with tears. 'I think you want Avery to be alive.'

'Why would I want that?'

'I don't know. Maybe you associate her with Mum in a way.'

'God. Please spare me the amateur psychology,' I say. But in my heart, I wonder if she's right. Is this what this is? Am I just playing out a childhood trauma?

'You should speak to Joe about the Valentine. I'm sure he'll be able to explain it.'

'He'll think I'm insane.'

Athena gives me a lopsided smile. 'Maybe, but I think you should give him a chance. I think he would forgive you anything.'

Since when has Athena been Joe's champion?

'I thought you didn't like him,' I say.

'Well, I've changed my mind. I've got to know him

properly over the past few days and you were right. He's a great guy, Alex, and he's obviously crazy about you.'

Athena's got a point. I should give Joe more credit. After all, I already ruined one relationship because I couldn't bring myself to open up. I don't want to make the same mistake with Joe. If we're going to have a future together, I need to trust him. So, the first opportunity I get, the evening after Athena goes back to London, I broach the subject.

We're up in the attic room. I'm stripping the bed and Joe is measuring the floor with a view to replacing the old wooden boards.

'All done,' he says, standing up and letting the measuring tape retract with a snap. 'We've got to replace them soon. The wood is riddled with death watch beetles. See those little piles of sawdust? That's them.'

'My God,' I say. 'I've only heard of death watch beetles in the Edgar Allan Poe short story, you know, *The Tell-Tale Heart*. I had no idea they were a real thing.'

'They're real alright,' Joe says grimly. Then he rifles through the wardrobe.

'We should get rid of these clothes too,' he says. 'I mean, Avery doesn't have any use for them anymore. Unless you want anything . . .'

'No thanks,' I say.

Just a few days ago I'd have been so happy with the

matter-of-fact way that he says this, and I'd have taken it as evidence that he's getting over Avery, but now I'm not so sure.

'Are you certain she won't need them?' I say before I lose my nerve.

'What?' He swivels round and stares at me.

I speak slowly and deliberately. 'I mean, are you sure she's dead?'

There's a long silence. His mouth opens and closes like a fish out of water. His expression would be comical if this wasn't so serious. 'What do you mean?'

'I mean her body's never been found, has it?'

As what I've said sinks in, his expression changes from shock and disbelief to anger. Raw, painful anger. 'What the fuck are you talking about, Alex?'

For a second, he looks so furious, I wish I could swallow my words. What was I thinking? But it's said now. There's no going back.

'I think she faked her own death,' I say.

He makes a strange noise in his throat and steps towards me.

'You . . .' he begins. His fists are clenched by his sides. A vein is throbbing in his temple. For a moment I think he's going to hit me. Then he sighs. 'Never mind.' And he sweeps past me and down the stairs.

'I know that sounds crazy . . .' I say following him, tears starting in my eyes.

He wheels round on the landing. 'You're right, it does sound crazy.' His eyes are blazing. 'Why the hell would Avery pretend to be dead?'

I tell him what Olivia told me about what Avery said and I outline some of the reasons that made me think she could still be alive, reasons that seemed so convincing in my head just a minute ago but that, now, out loud, seem like the plot of one of Avery's more outlandish mystery novels.

'Just think about it,' I continue desperately. 'Nobody actually saw her jump. She could've placed her phone and her jacket there and hidden down in the cove until night-time, then made her way back in the dark.'

'Back to where? Where exactly do you think she is?'

'I don't know but she's obviously somewhere near because I've seen her here outside the cottage.'

'You've seen her, really?' His tone is scathing.

I nod.

He's visibly shaking with anger. 'Well, you've got a good imagination,' he says coldly. 'But it doesn't make any sense. How would Avery get the money from her book? The money from her books goes to me now that she's dead. Unless you think I helped her fake her death and that we plotted it together?'

I shake my head mutely, feeling miserable.

'No. But I found a Valentine from her to you in her room.

And the handwriting was the same as this.' I thrust the note into his hand.

'What's this?'

'Someone put this under the cottage door the morning after we went sailing. I thought it was Lily, but then this morning I found the Valentine card Avery sent you. 'It was the same handwriting.'

'A Valentine?' he frowns. 'Where is it?'

'I don't know, I lost it.'

Joe looks down at the note, with a puzzled expression. Then, suddenly, to my astonishment, he throws his head back and laughs. 'Oh my God,' he says. 'Poor Alex.'

I can't see what there is to laugh about. 'The writing was identical,' I say.

'This isn't Avery's handwriting,' he says.

I stare at him bewildered. 'It's not? But I don't understand.'

'Avery didn't write this note and she didn't send the Valentine.'

'She didn't? But then, who?'

He walks over to the window, leans on the sill, and looks out at the darkening sky. 'Andrea.'

'Andrea?' My mind is scrambling.

'Andrea. You know – the barmaid at the Crown.'

'Andrea,' I repeat slowly. 'With red hair?'

'That's her.' Joe nods grimly. 'She's a bit of a psycho but I didn't think she'd stoop to this.'

My mind is reeling. I sink onto the bottom stair, trying to make sense of what he's telling me. The Valentine wasn't from Avery and if it wasn't written by Avery, then the note wasn't either.

That means she isn't alive. Relief flushes through me. Of course, it makes sense. The card was only signed A. A for Andrea not A for Avery.

'And all this time I've been thinking . . .' I clap my hand to my mouth. I'm mortified that I've made such a colossal blunder.

'I'm so sorry,' I say slowly. 'I've been an idiot.'

Joe laughs and ruffles my hair. 'You're forgiven. My God, how long have you been thinking these things? You must have been driving yourself crazy.'

'A while,' I admit shame-facedly, following him down to the living room.

'Why did Andrea write you a Valentine, though?' I ask, thinking about the rumours she spread about Charlie and Avery and the strangely bitter way she talked about Avery. 'Did you two have a thing?'

Joe grimaces. 'Not exactly. I slept with her one night after Avery died, in a moment of weakness. But it was a mistake.'

'Why was it a mistake?'

He gives a short laugh. 'Well, clearly you can see for your-self from the note she wrote you. She's nuts. We only slept together once, and I told her I couldn't get involved with her, that I wasn't over Avery, but she was obsessed with me. She wouldn't leave me alone.' He picks up the note. 'Even so, I can't believe the crazy bitch sent you this. I'll go and speak to her – tell her she's way out of line.'

'No, please don't, it's okay,' I say hurriedly. 'Maybe it's best just to leave it.' Andrea hasn't bothered me since our last conversation in the pub, and I don't want to stir up more trouble.

'Well, if you're sure . . .' He takes the note gently from my hand. 'You should get rid of this, though. It'll only upset you if you carry this bit of poison around with you.' And he rips it up and flings the pieces into the fire.

Forty

Over the next few days, we don't mention the note or the Valentine. I think Joe realises that I'm embarrassed by the whole episode and tactfully avoids the subject and I'm only too happy not to talk about it. All my suspicions and fears were groundless. Avery is dead. She's finally been put to rest (at least in my mind) and I no longer have nightmares about her at night or feel her presence when I'm alone in the house. It feels as though a huge weight has been lifted and I can now move on with my life with Joe. Everything is going to be okay, I think. We begin to talk about our future together and even Lily seems to be coming round to the idea that I'm here to stay in her own grudging way.

It's about a week after Athena's visit and I'm all alone in the house. Joe is in Truro visiting his mother and, as far as

I'm aware, Lily is in Penzance visiting Josh. So, I decide to clean her room. I know that she probably won't appreciate me invading her space but really the place is a pigsty, it's been bothering me for a while, and I can't help myself.

I lug the vacuum cleaner up the stairs and hoover the landing then I open Lily's bedroom door and freeze in the doorway because she's inside, sitting on the bed.

'Oh, sorry, I didn't realise you were . . .' The words die on my lips.

Something isn't right.

She's wearing a T-shirt, the words *just chillin'* scrawled across it, and her jeans are pooled round her ankles. There's an expression of intense concentration on her face and she doesn't seem to have registered that I'm there. For a moment I can't make sense of what I'm seeing. Then, with a sharp intake of breath, I absorb the whole picture: the thin red line etched on her inner thigh, the tiny beads of blood bubbling out of her skin, the nail scissors in her hand.

'Lily! What are you doing?' I gasp, steadying myself on the door frame as understanding jolts through me.

She looks up at me and I flinch. Her eyes are so full of grief and anger.

'Get out!' she shrieks, flinging the scissors away and scrabbling into her jeans.

I take a cautious step towards her and pick the scissors up from the floor. The tips are stained with blood. 'Lily . . .'

She snatches them out of my hands. 'What the fuck? Why didn't you knock?' she hisses.

'I'm sorry, I thought you were out.'

She hunches over, pressing her knees to her chest, and I hover by the end of her bed, trying to think what to say.

'Why are you still here, Alex?' she spits. 'Why don't you just fuck off and leave me alone?'

I want to do as she says. More than anything I don't want to have to deal with this, but I'm scared to leave her alone. I'm worried what she might do. I wish Joe were here. Or even Avery. I'm sure Avery would know what to do. She wouldn't be so helpless in this situation.

'I'm sorry, I don't think I can. I'm worried about you.'

She makes a sound – something between a laugh and a howl. 'Don't worry, I'm not about to top myself if that's what you think.'

I sit down on the bed next to her. Maybe I can keep her talking until Joe gets home. 'Why though, Lily?' I ask.

She gives me a macabre, little smile. 'I like the blood. It looks good, don't you think? It feels good too.' She picks up the scissors. 'Do you want to try? It's quite therapeutic.'

I shift away, feeling repulsed. I'm scared and totally out of my depth and my first instinct is to run away and leave her to it. But I tell myself firmly that she's just a young girl in pain and that she needs my help.

'I don't understand. Help me understand.'

She winces. 'I just miss my mother so much. It hurts so much. You know when you have a headache, and you press your temple?'

I nod.

'It concentrates all the pain in one area and it's better somehow.'

'I see.' Because I do see, and I remember something. 'After my mother died,' I say quietly, 'I used to sit under water at the deep end of the swimming pool and hold my breath for as long as I could . . . until my lungs felt as though they were going to burst.'

For those few minutes under the water the world was far away, and the physical pain in my chest was pure and simple. It was the only time I could forget.

Lily looks at me, something softening in her eyes, and I can sense I'm getting through to her. I glance down at her thighs and notice that, as well as the fresh cuts, there are old scars, faint pink lines scored into her flesh.

'How long have you been doing this, Lily?' I ask.

Her shoulders slump. All her anger vanishes, and she looks suddenly like a little girl. 'It's only what I deserve,' she whispers.

I'm not sure I've heard her correctly.

'What you deserve? Why do you think you deserve to be hurt, Lily?'

She picks at the turquoise nail varnish on her toes. 'Because I'm a bad person.'

'You're not a bad person,' I say with what I hope sounds like conviction. 'Why would you think that?'

'You don't know me,' she spits, and the anger flashes in her eyes again. 'If you knew all the things I've done, you'd agree.'

'Why don't you try me?'

She stares at me for a moment, weighing me up, like a wild creature deciding whether to run or to fight. Then something opens in her face and for a moment I think I'm really getting through to her. She's starting to trust me.

But then the doorbell rings.

'You'd better answer that,' Lily says.

'Okay, but first give me the scissors please.' I open my palm like a teacher, and she hands them over reluctantly. 'You'd better wash those scratches and put some antiseptic on,' I say briskly. 'You don't want them getting infected.'

I turn to go but she catches my arm. 'Don't tell Joe, please,' she says. 'I don't want him to worry.'

'Okay,' I agree, surprised. Right now, I'll say anything to placate her. But I already know I'll have to break my promise as I run downstairs. What choice do I have? It wouldn't be responsible of me to keep this to myself. Perhaps it's Joe now. Maybe he's forgotten his keys. As I open the door, I open my mouth, ready to tell him everything.

But it's not Joe. It's Josh clutching a bunch of flowers in one hand and a four-pack of beer in the other and looking so normal it takes my breath away.

'Hey, is Lily about?' he asks.

'Um, well . . . She's not feeling too . . .'

'I'd really like to talk to her. We had an argument earlier . . .' He breaks off and grins over my shoulder.

'Oh, hey Lily.'

I turn to see Lily gliding down the stairs. She's brushed her hair, applied eyeliner, and is smiling brightly. You'd never guess that just a moment ago she was gouging a hole in her thigh with a pair of scissors. The only thing that betrays her real state of mind is the fact that she's clutching and unclutching her hands – something I've noticed that she does when she's upset or agitated.

'I'm sorry, babe,' Josh says, holding out the flowers sheepishly. 'Can we talk?'

'Sure,' she says, picking up her coat. 'Let's go. I need to get out of here anyway.'

'Shall I put the flowers in water for you?' I ask, as Josh doesn't seem to know what to do with them.

'Yes please,' Josh says politely. 'See you later, Alex.'

'Yeah bye, Alex.' Lily swans past, looking so happy and carefree that it's hard to believe she is the same broken person I spoke to just a few moments ago.

Forty-one

'I'm worried about Lily.'

It's late in the evening and Joe and I are curled up by the fire watching TV. Lily's still out with Josh, and I take the opportunity to talk about what I witnessed earlier in the day.

'Oh?' He pauses the show and sighs. 'I know she's been the bitch from hell the past few weeks and you've been really patient. God, you deserve a medal for all you've had to put up with . . .' He leans over and kisses my cheek.

'It's not that . . .'

'She'll be off to uni in a few months and out of your hair.'

'You don't understand. I mean, yes, she has been difficult. But that's not what I'm talking about. I'm seriously concerned about her mental health.'

He stares at me. 'What do you mean?'

I sit up, taking a deep breath, and tell him what I walked in on this morning and that I suspect she's been cutting herself for a while.

He turns off the TV and rubs his forehead repeatedly as if there's a mark there he needs to clean. 'Are you sure?'

I nod. 'I'm afraid so.'

'Jesus.'

'You didn't know then?'

'Of course I didn't know,' he says, shaking his head and staring darkly at the fire. 'She's been a mess ever since Avery died, but I had no idea things were this bad. I should've known.'

'She puts on a pretty good show of being really tough.'

'Mm.' He picks up the poker and jabs at the fire, sending sparks flying. 'What the hell are we going to do with her?'

'Maybe she should see a doctor or a therapist,' I suggest. 'This is too serious for us to deal with on our own.'

He nods thoughtfully. 'You're right.' He puts down the poker and rakes his fingers through his hair. 'My God. That girl is nothing but trouble.' He looks at me. 'Why do you think she does it? Did she say?'

I try to blot out the image of her sitting on the bed – those grey eyes, full of fathomless anger.

'Obviously she's still not over Avery's death. But I don't know if it's just that. She said that she was a bad person – that she had done bad things.'

'Bad things?' he repeats blankly. 'What kind of bad things?'

'She didn't say. I think she was about to tell me then Josh arrived to pick her up.'

Joe stands up and paces the room. His agitation is palpable. 'I can't believe I didn't know about this,' he says at last. 'I should have known.'

'You can't blame yourself.'

'I'll arrange for her to see someone as soon as possible.' He mutters almost as if he's talking to himself, and he scrolls through his phone. 'The doctor gave us the number of a bereavement counsellor just after Avery died. Now, where is it? Ah, here it is.'

He takes the phone through into the kitchen and I can hear him talking in a low voice.

Then he comes back in looking at his watch.

'Where the hell is she? She should be back by now.' He rounds on me. 'Why did you let her go out alone in such a vulnerable state – with Josh of all people – for Christ's sake? What were you thinking?'

I know he's just lashing out because he's so worried about Lily, but I can't help being upset. Joe has never spoken to me like this before and he's looking at me the same way he looks at the patch of mould on the ceiling in the stables.

'I couldn't exactly stop her,' I say defensively. 'Since when has she done anything that I've said?'

He exhales heavily and sits down. 'You're right. I'm sorry. I'm just . . . Fuck. This has come as a shock, that's all.'

'I know. But it's only eleven o'clock and she's with Josh. He'll look after her.'

Joe snorts derisively. 'You know what I think of him.'

'Yes, I know you said he'd been in trouble with the police but that was just for smoking grass, right?'

Joe shakes his head. 'That wasn't all. There were some incidents last summer . . .'

But I don't get to hear what the incidents were because just then the front door slams and we hear Lily stumbling in the hallway, tripping over something, and cursing loudly.

'Lily?' Joe calls as she passes by the door to the living room.

'Hi, bye,' she says popping her head round the door and smiling at us, glassy-eyed.

'Have you been drinking?' Joe asks. 'Are you drunk?'

But she's already clattering up the stairs.

'I'd better go and speak to her . . .' Joe mutters. 'I'll be right back.'

I turn the TV back on and try to concentrate on a panel show. I don't want to think about how that conversation will go. Lily's bound to be angry when she finds out I've betrayed her confidence and I half expect her to come storming downstairs to confront me. But all is quiet and after just a few minutes Joe comes back looking deep in thought.

'How did that go?' I ask.

'I can't get any sense out of her at the moment,' he says. 'I'll talk to her in the morning.'

Forty-two

I'm dreading the inevitable confrontation with Lily. It's the first time she's ever confided in me and I'm guessing that she'll interpret the fact I told Joe as a betrayal. She's going to hate me more than ever now, I think. But what choice did I have? Eventually she'll understand that it was for her own good.

As it turns out, I don't have to face her until the next evening because Joe takes her to the therapist in Penzance before I'm awake and when they return, she storms straight up to her bedroom and doesn't emerge for the rest of the day.

'How did it go this morning?' I ask them tentatively over the evening meal.

Lily glowers at her plate and picks at her food. Joe shrugs wearily.

'Time will tell,' he says.

'Excuse me,' Lily says, cold as ice. She pushes the rest of her food to the edge of her plate and stands up. 'I'm not hungry.' And she stalks off upstairs again.

Over the next few days, she barely speaks to me. In fact, she seems to be doing everything she can to avoid me. Whenever she sees me, she turns in the opposite direction and once when I come into the room she even says pointedly, 'There's a bad smell in here,' and stalks out.

Her consistent hostility is wearing me down, poisoning the atmosphere in the house, as if there is something festering away in the walls. It even starts to infect my relationship with Joe. Lately, he's distracted and irritable and even though I try to be understanding because I know he's got a lot to deal with, what with Lily and the renovations, a couple of times we argue over small, petty things – a mix-up over supplies for the cottage or the way I save documents to my laptop.

Lily is Joe's stepdaughter. He loves her and we all need to live together, at least until she goes to university. So, it's up to me to clear the air and get things out in the open. I corner her one morning in the bathroom when she's brushing her teeth.

'Lily, we need to talk,' I say.

She turns her grey eyes on me and looks at me,

emotionless as a cat. Then she rinses her mouth and spits in the sink.

'I'm sorry, I know that I promised I wouldn't tell Joe. It's just I didn't know what else to do . . .'

No answer. Just that unnerving silence.

'How was the therapist?'

She wipes her mouth on the towel. 'Excuse me,' she says coldly, trying to push past me.

I grab her arm and she twists towards me, a look of such bitter hatred on her face that for a moment I imagine she might hiss at me. 'I just want you to know I'm here for you . . .' I say falteringly.

'Sure,' she says in a voice laced with sarcasm and barges past me to her room, slamming the door behind her. A couple of seconds later I hear the key clicking in the lock and the swell of loud music invading the hallway.

I wish she would shout at me or even shove and push me like she did before. This cold disdain is worse somehow. It's unsettling. I'm worried about Lily's safety and her emotional well-being, but I must admit I'm also a little scared of her. A few times over the next couple of days I catch her watching me, a sly, speculative look in her eyes, as if she's planning something.

It's very hard to like someone when they so obviously don't like you. But Lily is young, she's been through a lot and for Joe's sake I'm willing to try everything I can to make things work between us. In a couple of weeks, it's her eighteenth birthday and I want to make it special. I want to do something to show how much I genuinely care.

I know that Joe is going to surprise her with a new car, a brand-spanking-new, red and white mini, still sitting in the showroom. But I want to get her something that's just from me, and I rack my brains for the perfect gift. But it's not easy. I know that if I buy clothes or jewellery, they'll probably be the wrong style and since the money has been rolling in from Avery's book, Joe has lavished Lily with so many presents, I can't think of anything she might need or want.

It's a Monday morning and I'm walking Barney round Carn Euny and I'm just passing Charlie's workshop when inspiration strikes. Lily's birthday is in the same week as the anniversary of Avery's death. What could be better and more meaningful than a portrait of her mother?

I tie Barney to a post outside and push open the door to the workshop.

Charlie is inside whittling away at a piece of pine wood, small woodchips flying, scratchy jazz music, saxophone-heavy, playing loudly on his computer.

'Alex, long time no see,' he says, pausing the track and pushing his straggling hair back from his eyes. 'How are you doing?'

It's the first time anyone's asked me how I am in a while, and I fend off a sudden and ridiculous urge to cry. Maybe Lily's attitude is finally getting to me, or the way a distance seems to have been growing up between me and Joe, because I realise in that moment that I'm far from fine.

'I'm okay,' I manage brightly. 'You?'

'Can't complain.' He smiles, weighing the chisel in his hands. 'Business is good. Is this a social call or . . .?'

'Not really. I can't stop long. I was just wondering . . . do you take commissions?'

He puts down his chisel, giving me his full attention. 'Sure, I do, why?'

'Do you think you could do a portrait of Avery?'

'Avery?' He looks startled. 'Um . . . maybe,' he says.

'It's for her daughter's – for Lily's birthday,' I say. 'I want to get her something special.'

Charlie scratches his head. 'Are you sure that's what she wants?'

'I think so, why?'

He laughs. 'Well, it's not exactly every teenaged girl's dream, is it – a portrait of their mother?'

'For some it might be,' I say, feeling a sudden surge of anger at his flippancy. I dig in my pocket and show him the photo of my mother in my wallet. 'I carry this with me always. It's my most treasured possession. If your mother dies when you're young, maybe you learn to appreciate them as you should.'

'I'm sorry,' Charlie says softly. 'I didn't know.' He gazes at the picture then hands it back to me. 'Your mother was beautiful.'

'Thank you.' I feel slightly mollified and a bit embarrassed at my outburst.

'But are you sure Lily felt the same way?' he asks. 'As far as I know, she didn't get on well with Avery.'

I'm shocked. 'What do you mean? She worshipped her.'

Charlie frowns and purses his lips. 'I don't think so. Avery told me herself that they were always fighting. That week before she went to London for example, they'd had a huge argument.'

My scalp prickles. 'What about?'

'I don't really know the details. But I know it was bad, and that before that, Lily had tried to run away. Their fights were physical sometimes. Lily could be . . . difficult.'

I touch the back of my head where I still have a slight bump from when Lily pushed me. It's not too hard to picture her being violent. Even so . . .

'Whatever problems they had, I'm sure she must have loved her mother,' I say stubbornly.

'I suppose so.' He shrugs. 'Well, whatever you think – if you're sure. I'm a bit busy right now. I've got a couple of festivals coming up, but I guess I can fit it in. I'll need a photo though, or preferably a couple of photos. Do you have any?'

'Not on me but I can email you some later today.'

'Okey doke.' He smiles and glances at his watch. 'I was going to take a break now anyway. Do you fancy a drink? A coffee or tea?' That lopsided grin – a twinkle in his green eyes. 'Something stronger maybe?'

I'm tempted. Charlie is good company and it's a relief to be away from Foxton Farm – from Lily's oppressive silence and Joe's irritability, but I need to get home. I don't want to risk someone seeing me here and reporting it back to Joe.

'No thanks,' I say airily. 'I've got some errands to run. I'll send you those photos though.'

'Okay then.' He looks disappointed.

As I'm leaving, he pushes a flier into my hand. 'It's next week. I'm going to have a stall there,' he says. 'You should come. It'll be good. They're trying to make it really special this year. It had to be cancelled last year because of the bad weather.'

I look down at the paper in my hand. It's a pale blue sheet with a line drawing of a mermaid on the front and *The Maid of Zennor Music Festival* printed in bold letters underneath. Below that there's a list of obscure bands that will be playing.

The Maid of Zennor Festival, I think vaguely. I remember

Lily saying something to me about it over dinner one night but for the moment I can't recall the details.

'Thanks, sounds good,' I say. 'I'll see if Joe wants to go.' I fold up the paper and slot it into my back pocket. Then I turn to leave. Charlie has already gone back to chiselling his sculpture and he waves distractedly.

'Bye,' he says, not looking up.

I close the door, walk up the garden path and continue down the muddy lane looping back towards Foxton Farm. But there's something scratching away at the back of my mind. Something Charlie said that doesn't make sense ... and about halfway back, just before the spring and the cloughtie-covered tree, I stop suddenly, my heart pounding against my ribs.

Can that be right?

I turn and run back to Charlie's, nearly slipping on the mud in my haste.

'What's up?' he says, looking up from his work in surprise, as I barge in, panting for breath.

'You said the festival was cancelled last year?' I say. 'Are you sure?'

He raises his eyebrows and nods. 'Yeah, I'm sure. I'd paid for a stall and didn't get a refund. I remember I was fuming.'

I stand in the doorway. The earth seems to rush under my feet, and I feel dizzy and faint.

'Why? Is anything wrong?' Charlie asks. His voice comes from far away – a place of reason and sanity.

I give myself a shake and manage to smile. 'No, everything's fine. Thank you. I'll see you later.'

Outside I breathe the chill, damp air and unfold the flier again, my hands shaking. The Maid of Zennor Festival. 15th of April – the anniversary of Avery's death.

I remember now where I heard of it. Lily said she was there with Josh that night. I'm sure it was that festival because I remember her telling me the story of the mermaid, the Maid of Zennor. But she couldn't have been there, could she?

Because the festival didn't happen.

Forty-three

I retrace my steps as quickly as I can. But when I reach the turning to Foxton Farm, I'm seized by a paralysing fear. I can't go back there. Not yet. I need to get my thoughts in order first, work out if my growing suspicions are real. Instead, I walk straight past the turning, through the village and along the narrow road towards Sancreed.

I step onto the grass verge as a car speeds by, spattering me with muddy water. The festival didn't happen; so, Lily either lied or she was confused. But I don't think she could've been confused. How could she have muddled up the dates? You don't forget where you were the night your mother died. I remember every detail of the day my own mother died and the way it neatly bisected my life in two. Before and After. The blessed normalcy of the morning at school before and the endless horror of the night after shut in my bedroom, crying my guts out.

Lily lied then. But why? The question drums in my head all the way to Sancreed and, as I'm entering the village, an image of Lily on the beach at St Ives flashes into my mind. I mistook her for Avery that day. That wasn't a coincidence, was it? Because from a distance they look very alike. They have the same thin, straight-backed silhouette – and Lily could have easily covered her hair or dyed it like she did that day in St Ives.

Struck by a sudden conviction, I rush across the road to the Crown and find it empty of customers. Andrea is sitting at a table alone, eating a sandwich and flicking through a magazine.

'What can I do for you?' she asks coldly, after she's finished chewing and rising reluctantly to her feet.

'Um, nothing. Don't get up. Actually, I just wanted to talk.' I am out of breath and the wind has raked up my hair into a wild nest. I probably look like a mad woman. I pat it down, feeling self-conscious under her disdainful scrutiny.

She eyes me warily. 'What about?'

'Do you remember the day I came here with Charlie?'

She nods slowly.

'We talked about Avery Lewis. You told us then that one

of your friends saw her on the cliffs at Bosigran, the night she fell. Was that true?'

She looks affronted. 'Of course it's true,' she says stiffly. 'Why would I make something like that up?'

'You wouldn't, of course,' I say hurriedly. 'I was wondering, could you tell me how I can contact your friend? I need to speak to her.'

She takes another bite of her sandwich and chews slowly. 'What about?'

'It's really important. Could you give me her contact details? *Please*.'

She hesitates. Then sighs and scrawls a rudimentary map on a paper napkin. 'She lives on the road between St Just and St Ives, near to Zennor. And her name is Geraldine Blake,' she says grudgingly. 'I'll let her know you're coming.'

'Thank you so much,' I say, snatching up the napkin and making my exit before she changes her mind.

I head back to Foxton Farm to collect my car, armed with a new sense of purpose, but as I make my way up the driveway my confidence deserts me. My feet become heavy and slow as if they're weighed down and my heart strikes against my ribs. The house looks foreboding, the stonework stained with wet patches and the grey slate roof slick and dark with recently fallen rain. The windows gape out balefully as though they're waiting for something. Or someone.

I shudder. Why have I never noticed how menacing it is before?

I get in my car, sit in the driver's seat and ring Joe.

'Alex?' he answers abruptly. 'Where are you?'

'I'm just on my way to Penzance. I'll be a couple of hours probably.'

'Alright then.' To my relief, he doesn't even ask me why I'm going to Penzance. 'See you later,' he says, sounding preoccupied. 'Take care.'

About an hour later I'm outside a small, whitewashed house. It's on the end of a row of three houses opposite the old tin mine.

When I ring the doorbell, a plump, elderly lady opens the door.

'Hi, you must be Geraldine,' I say.

'I'm Gerry, yes.' She smiles quizzically and pats her curly grey hair. Her cheeks are rosy and her eyes bright blue.

'I'm Alex Georgiou. I'm a friend of Andrea's.'

'Ah yes, she called me and told me you might be coming. Come in, come in. Would you like a cup of tea?'

Gerry keeps up a steady stream of chatter as she leads me into her small, cluttered living room.

'Sit yourself down, now,' she says, removing a grey cat and plumping a cushion for me. I sit in an armchair facing the large bay window. The window overlooks a small car park, and the crumbling ruins of the mine chimney across the road are stark against the fading light. I must admit Gerry would have had a perfect view of any cars that pulled up there, though the cliff edge itself is obscured by low, stunted trees.

Gerry clatters around in the kitchen then returns, fussing with a nest of tables, finally extracting the smallest and placing a mug of tea on it. Then she opens a tin of short-bread biscuits.

'How can I help you?' she asks, offering me one.

'Er, thank you.' I take a biscuit and nibble the corner. 'I'm here to ask about Avery Lewis – the woman that fell off the cliff about a year ago. Andrea says you saw her that day?'

Her eyes widen. 'Gosh yes. Wasn't it terrible? I told the police everything I saw. Poor woman.' She shivers. 'Why do you want to know about her?'

'I'm writing a book about crime authors. Avery Lewis is one of the writers that features in the book.'

'Oh, I see.' She sits on the sofa folding her hands in her lap and looks out across the road. 'Well, let's see now. She parked right over there.' She points at the car park. 'I noticed her because her driving was quite erratic and, when she got out, she wasn't wearing a coat, just a thin, blue fleece. It was very windy, and it started raining a few minutes after she set off walking. I said to Bill – that's my husband – I said, that young woman is going to get drenched.'

'She was on her own?'

'Oh yes.'

'There wasn't anybody with her? A young girl maybe?'

Gerry frowns and shakes her head. 'Definitely not.'

'And there were no other cars in the car park?'

'No. You know, this place doesn't get that many visitors at the best of times and the weather was bad. I mean the sky was dark and it was really brewing up a storm. That's why it was so strange her going for a walk.'

I gaze out across the road. Gerry's house is set back from the road, and it must be about fifty metres away from the car park. It would be difficult to see someone clearly, especially if it was getting dark. 'Did you get a good look at her face?' I ask.

'Not really.' She shrugs. 'I only caught a glimpse. She had her hood up.'

'So, how could you be sure it was her – Avery Lewis?'

She stares at me. 'Well, it had to be, didn't it?' I mean the police showed me the photos and it definitely looked like her. She was carrying the rucksack the police found later at the scene. And I believe they found her phone there too.'

'You didn't see her return?'

'No. I was in the living room all evening watching TV. Anyway, her car was still here in the morning.'

312

'But she could have returned on foot. You weren't watching the window all the time?'

Gerry flushes faintly. 'No, of course not. But where would she have gone on foot in the rain? Why would she have left her car?'

'I don't know,' I say. Good question, I think.

'If you ask me,' she says. 'It was probably suicide. I mean why go for a walk in that weather? And I could tell she was distressed by the way she was driving and when she got out of the car. You know how you can just tell sometimes from a person's body language? I wish I'd listened to my intuition and called someone.'

I lean forward. 'Can you pinpoint what it was about her body language that made you think she was upset?'

She looks vague. 'Oh, I'm not sure.' She scrunches up her face. 'It was something about her hands, I think. She kept doing this.' Gerry holds out her arms and clenches and unclenches her fists.

And my heart strikes in my chest like a gong.

'Thank you so much for taking the time to talk to me,' I say, wrapping the conversation up as quickly as I can and gulping down my cup of tea.

'Oh, is that it?' she says. 'Well, you're very welcome and let me know when your book comes out. I'd be interested to read it,' she calls after me as I let myself out.

*

Relatives often have similar mannerisms I tell myself as I get back in my car and drive towards Foxton Farm. It doesn't prove anything.

But the more I think about it, the more convinced I am that it wasn't Avery who Gerry saw in the car park that day. It was Lily.

Forty-four

I speed back to Sancreed along the narrow, country roads, swerving round bends, oblivious to the other traffic, oblivious to the gathering rain clouds. Questions buzz in my mind like a horde of angry wasps. Why did Lily put Avery's bag and phone on the cliff edge? Was it to make it appear as though she'd fallen?

The sky is heavy and grey on the horizon, threatening rain. I'm driving headlong towards it, into a storm, but what choice do I have? I suppose I could follow the signs towards the A30 back to London, back to Athena and safety, but I can't run away from this now. I'm in too deep. I owe it to Joe and weirdly I feel as if I owe it to Lily too. Even now, suspecting what she's done, I feel strangely protective towards her.

Did Lily kill Avery? I grip the wheel tightly. The thought

is repugnant, but right now it's the only thing that makes sense and I can imagine how it might have happened. According to Charlie, Lily and Avery were always fighting. One of their arguments could have gotten out of hand. Lily's surprisingly strong and I've experienced her violent temper for myself. It would have been an accident, though. I can't, even now, believe that Lily would have killed her own mother in cold blood. But if she did kill Avery, what did she do with the body? Surely she wouldn't have been able to dispose of it by herself. Someone must have helped her . . .

Joe?

No, he couldn't have, I realise with relief. He wasn't even in Cornwall at the time.

Josh then . . .?

I need to talk to her, to tell her that we can sort this out together, and that even though she's done a terrible thing, there's still hope, if she will only confess and face up to it.

I reach Sancreed and turn up the driveway to Foxton Farm, my heart thudding in my chest as I pull up outside the house. I kill the engine and sit in the car for a moment trying to steady my breathing.

A flash of lightning cracks the sky and rain starts pouring down as I approach the house. There are no lights on inside and the hallway gapes cold, dark and empty. I stand at the foot of the stairs and call up.

'Joe? Lily?'

No one answers. The only sounds are the clock ticking in the kitchen and the rain outside, pummelling the roof and windows.

Heart hammering out of my chest, I climb the stairs slowly to Lily's room. I'm pretty sure she's not there, but I tap on the door just in case.

'Lily?'

The window is open, and rainwater is gusting in, soaking into the carpet. I close the window and look around. Her bed is a tangle of sheets. Clothes litter the floor. The perfume she wears lingers in the air, a sickly sweet smell like overripe fruit. She must have been here recently but there's no sign of her now.

Why did you lie, Lily? I think, looking nervously around her bedroom. I'm torn between the desire to help her and the fear of what she might do, if she knows that I know.

In contrast to the rest of the room her desk is strangely tidy. All her schoolbooks are piled neatly to one side and in the middle of the desk there is a single sheet of paper weighed down with a Japanese Good Luck cat, its paw swinging up and down in response to some draft or vibration I am unaware of.

That paper . . .

My mouth is dry. My breathing is so loud. It's the loudest thing in the room.

This can't be what I think it is. Please God, no.

I move the cat, pick up the paper and read the simple, scrawled message.

I can't go on like this. I'm sorry. It was an accident. I didn't mean to kill her. Please tell Josh I love him.

The writing is shaky and barely legible. I read it again, desperately telling myself that I'm jumping to conclusions, but her meaning is clear.

Where is she? Am I too late?

For a few seconds I stand there, frozen in shock, and then adrenaline courses through my body spurring me to action. I need to act quickly. I fumble with my phone and ring Lily.

No answer.

Then I tap on Joe's number. But my call goes straight to his voicemail.

Fuck. Joe. Where are you?

Next, I try Lily again, with no luck.

Shoving the phone into my back pocket, I rush out onto the landing.

'Lily!' I call frantically. I slam open all the doors, scouring every room. I even run up the stairs to the attic room. There's no sign of her.

Stay calm, I tell myself. Breathe.

Hopefully this is just Lily being dramatic – trying to frighten us. Most likely she's safe and well somewhere. Maybe she's even with Joe.

Feeling a little more composed, I search methodically downstairs.

No Lily.

I'm in the kitchen and try phoning her again when I hear something, a barely audible tune.

I put down the phone and listen intently. I'm not imagining it. It's a Stormzy song Lily likes. 'Heavy is the Head'. Her ringtone. And it's coming from the garage.

I push open the door. Inside, the song becomes louder and is joined by the steady thrum of the engine and the rain on the roof.

It takes a few seconds for me to take in the scene and absorb the full horror of what I'm seeing.

A vacuum hose is snaking its way from the exhaust pipe, along the concrete floor and in through a small slit in the rear-seat window. Poisonous, grey smoke is filling the SUV cabin.

'Lily, no!' I scream.

Then I'm by the car, trying to wrench open doors, but they're all locked. Through the smoke I can just make out Lily lying on the back seat.

'Lily!' I shout. 'Hang in there. I'm going to get you out.'

No response.

Tears sting my eyes and my breath is coming in ragged gasps. Praying that I'm not too late, I wrench open Joe's tool cupboard and pick up the heaviest-looking hammer. Using as much force as I can, I swing it at the rear-seat window.

On the second attempt the glass smashes and I shove my arm through the jagged hole I've created. Ignoring the sharp glass shards, I reach down and pull at the lock. Then I fling open the door, hook my elbows under Lily's armpits and drag her out of the car.

She slumps onto the ground, limp and lifeless. Is she breathing? I kneel on the concrete beside her, tears rolling down my face, choking in my throat, and I lift her head, giving her a short, sharp slap on the cheek.

'Lily, Lily. Please, wake up. Lily . . . please.' I shake her and suddenly to my intense relief, she gives a small gasp and coughs.

'Lily, can you hear me?'

'Wha . . .?' she murmurs, and she looks up at me with glazed, grey eyes. 'Alex?'

'I'm going to get help,' I say. She's alive at least, but she needs medical attention. I stand up and am heading back to the kitchen to get my phone when the garage door rolls open, and Joe appears with Barney by his side. Barney runs up, sniffing Lily and whimpering.

'Joe, thank God you're here! We need to call an ambulance. Lily . . . Lily tried to kill herself.' I burst into tears of relief. Now he's here my self-control deserts me. He'll know what to do. He can sort this.

320

But he just stands there in the doorway, his hands hanging by his sides, a silhouette against the bright light outside.

'Call an ambulance, quickly,' I say again. He must be in shock because he doesn't seem to hear me.

'Joe! She needs to get to the hospital. Where's your phone?'

Finally, he gives a deep sigh and strides towards me, stepping over Lily.

'You've cut yourself,' he says slowly, taking my arm in his hand. And I glance down at my arm which is dripping with blood.

'That doesn't matter now. We need to call an ambulance.'

He grips my arm more tightly. 'I'm sorry, Alex, but I can't let you do that.'

There's something strange, almost offbeat, in his tone and I stare at him in surprise. What's wrong with him?

'Why not?' I say. 'Jesus, let go. You're hurting me.'

I wrench my arm free and open the kitchen door. I pick up my phone and I'm just about to call emergency services when there's a heavy thwack at the back of my head. A sharp pain. Something explodes inside my skull. Bright stripes of light streak across my vision.

Then nothing.

Forty-five

'Alex.'

Somewhere from far away someone is saying my name.

'Please, Alex, wake up.'

I open my eyes and stare up at a sloping, white ceiling. My vision is blurred but I can make out a thin thread from a spider's web strung across the dark wooden beams. I blink at it in confusion. My head is throbbing, there's a ringing in my ears and my gut twists with a fear I don't yet comprehend.

'Alex. You gave me quite a fright. I thought I'd lost you for a moment.' Joe's face appears above me, looming in and out of focus. My thoughts are slow and hazy. What the hell just happened?

Lily. Lily tried to kill herself, I remember with a jolt.

'Where's Lily?' I say, raising my head and looking around.

I'm in the attic room, lying on the sofa bed. But how did I get here?

Joe must have carried me up here I think as my mind sluggishly tries to fashion my disjointed thoughts into something coherent.

'Shh,' he says, pushing me gently back down onto the pillows. 'You need to rest.'

'But Lily . . . Is she alright?'

'Yes, she's fine. Everything's going to be okay.'

Then it comes back to me with a lurch of horror.

You hit me.

I touch the back of my head gingerly and my fingers come away sticky with blood. I try to get up and away from him, fear coursing through me. But Joe pushes me back down, less gently this time, and pins me to the bed.

'Calm down, Alex. I'm not going to hurt you. I'm sorry I had to use force. I needed to stop you . . .'

'You didn't want me to call an ambulance. Why?'

But I already know the answer. I reach into the darkness to grasp it. It's an ugly, misshapen answer, grotesque and slippery, but I grab it and hold it up to the light.

The answer is that he couldn't risk them finding out the truth. The truth that Lily didn't try to kill herself.

'You tried to kill her. You wanted it to look like suicide,' I say. My voice is hoarse, scraped out. Is he going to kill me too?

He doesn't answer. He just sighs and sits on the bed, stroking my shoulder. I shudder and move away. 'Why?' I whisper.

'I didn't want to hurt her, but she was planning to go to the police. She threatened to tell them everything.'

'About Avery's death?'

He nods and I look at his face – his handsome face – the face I fell in love with, and I feel physically sick. Bile rises in my throat. Horror is a huge black wave engulfing me, dragging me under. The truth burns through me. I'm just starting to understand who he really is and what he's done. Because of course it wasn't Lily who killed Avery.

It was him.

'You killed Avery.'

He nods sadly. 'It was an accident,' he says. 'We had an argument, she fell and hit her head on the fireplace.' His eyes fill with tears and, for a second, I believe him. I want to believe him. An accident is understandable. I could forgive him if it was an accident.

But there's what he did to Lily. When she threatened to talk, he tried to dispose of her with a callousness I can't wrap my head around.

She's still in danger.

'Lily?' I say. 'Where is she?'

He opens his mouth to answer but at that moment

there's a sound from downstairs, a muffled thumping. The sound of someone banging against the garage doors.

He looks over his shoulder. 'Stay here,' he says. Then he stands up swiftly and leaves the room. I stagger to my feet, trying to follow him. But he's too quick for me. He slams the door in my face and when I rattle the handle, it won't budge. He's jammed it somehow. I'm trapped.

A wave of dizziness washes over me.

Bastard.

I trusted and loved him. How could I have fallen in love with him? How could I have been so blind?

Thoughts swarm in my mind. Adrenaline courses through my body.

If he's tried to kill Lily once, he'll try again, I think, anger and fear bubbling up inside me.

Well, I'm not going to let him.

I rush over to the window, slide it open and look down at the ground below, assessing my options. There's an apple tree but it's too far away to reach. There's also a heap of builder's sand almost directly underneath me. It could break my fall, but what if I miss it? The drop must be at least twenty feet, if not thirty. If I try to jump, I'll certainly break a leg, maybe even worse.

But I must do something. I can't just stay in this room while Lily's fighting for her life. Every second counts.

Desperately, I search the room for something . . .

anything to use. I wrench open drawers and scrabble in the cupboards. At the top of the wardrobe, I find a pile of old bedding. Reaching up, I drag it out and it tumbles to the floor, an avalanche of sheets and blankets.

I've never seen it done, but how hard can it be? Fumbling with the knots, I tie the corners of the sheets together, using a double fisherman's knot, a really secure link that my father taught me. Then I loop the end round the wooden bed post and check that it will take my weight. Next, I feed the rope through the window. It doesn't quite reach the ground but it's enough. It'll have to be.

I climb up and out onto the window ledge and look down, feeling giddy.

And suddenly I'm back there, by the side of the swimming pool in Cyprus, frozen with fear.

What if the knots don't hold? What if I lose my grip? What if Joe hears me?

I failed my mother. What if I fail Lily too?

You have no choice. You can do it, Alex. You're not that hopeless, terrified child anymore. History will not repeat itself. The voice is kind and firm and comes from somewhere deep inside me.

Taking a deep breath and ignoring the dizzy, sick fear I feel when I look down, I lower myself out of the window. My arms strain with the weight and my feet scrabble to get a grip on the wall as I inch downwards. I should've spent more time in the gym, I think, because my palms are burning, and my arms feel as if they're going to rip out of their sockets. But somehow, through sheer willpower, I manage to hold on. I'm more than halfway down when finally, I lose my grip. The sheets slide out of my grasp, and I tumble to the ground.

I land heavily. But thankfully my fall is mostly broken by the pile of sand against the wall. After a couple of disoriented seconds, I stretch my limbs experimentally. Nothing seems to be broken. Somewhere nearby Barney has started barking.

Shit. He's going to alert Joe.

Shakily, I stand up and, staying close to the wall, I creep around to the front of the house. Barney is tied to the fence post. When he sees me, he barks more, straining at the rope and wagging his tail eagerly.

'Quiet, please, Barney,' I beg silently.

Too late. A door slams somewhere inside the house and then, a few heart-stopping seconds later, the front door flies open and Joe strolls out, stretching languidly.

I dive down behind the skip, hardly daring to breathe.

Jesus. Has he seen me? Please God no.

Squeezing myself into the smallest space possible, I pray he doesn't notice me, and I wait, listening intently, my heart in my throat.

'What's all the fuss, eh, Barney?' I hear him say in his deep Cornish burr. His tone is gently amused.

Heavy feet crunch closer on the gravel, and I freeze. My

heart is beating so loudly inside my chest I think he'll be able to hear it. But then he sighs and turns back into the house. There's the sound of his footsteps receding and then silence.

After a few moments, I raise my head above the skip and, dusting myself off, I move quietly along the side of the house. Ahead of me the gate beckons, the path to the village, to freedom and safety. It's very tempting to make a dash for it, to escape. I could fetch help.

But no. By the time I got to the village it might be too late.

I'm terrified, but it's up to me. There's no one else who can help Lily. Heart beating out of my chest, I make my way to the front door. It's still ajar. Slowly I nudge it further open and peer in. The hallway is empty. I slip in, soundless as a snake, and creep along the corridor. In the kitchen I can hear loud music from the garage. Slowly, I slide open the cutlery drawer. Inside a blade glints. I pull it out and run my finger along its cruel, sharp edge.

Forty-six

I can feel cold sweat all over me. Radio 6 is playing, the deep, gravelly voice of Iggy Pop introducing a song over the growl of the engine. I clutch the knife tightly in my hand. The door to the garage is ajar, and from the kitchen I can just make out Joe. He's feeding the vacuum tube back through the window of the car. Lily is slumped on the back seat.

I sway a little, fighting off a wave of nausea. It's one thing thinking in the abstract about the terrible things he's done. It's quite another to witness them with my own eyes. How can I reconcile the gentle Joe I loved – the Joe I slept next to, who I let into my heart – with this Joe? This monster.

I lean on the kitchen counter and try to breathe. The nearest police station is miles away. If I phone the police, it will take them too long to get here. I could call Charlie but what if Joe hears me?

No, that's not an option.

I know what I have to do.

The next few seconds are a blur.

I have no time to think. He hasn't seen me. He's facing away scrolling through his phone. I open the door and step quickly into the garage. The knife slips in my sweating hands and my heart races. And suddenly I am right behind him, close enough to touch. My breath hitches in my throat. He swings round, a look of surprise and slight annoyance in his eyes.

'Alex . . .' he says wearily as if I'm a minor problem that keeps cropping up. He glances down at the knife in my hand and laughs – a gentle, teasing laugh. 'What are you doing with that?'

My hand shakes. I clench my teeth. 'Take out the hose pipe. Let her go.'

'You don't understand, Alex. I can't. She would go to the police. My life would be over. But I won't hurt you. I couldn't hurt you.' He reaches out and touches my cheek with his knuckles. 'I love you, Alex. You love me too, don't you? You can't deny it. What we have is a once in a lifetime connection. You wouldn't turn me in. We're in this together Alex. You and me against the world.'

He's lying, I think. He never loved me. He never loved

anyone but himself. If I don't do something soon, Lily is going to die.

There's a roaring in my ears. The knife handle seems to throb. Rage and anger pulse through it into my arm, making me strong. The blade is sharp. It slides deep into his chest and a fountain of blood spurts out. I stare in shock and disbelief as he staggers backwards.

'Fucking hell, Alex,' he says mildly, as if I've accidentally trodden on his toe. He looks down at the cascading blood and his eyes widen. 'What have you done?' Then his knees buckle, and he collapses to the floor.

Is he dead? Have I killed him?

I don't stop to check. There's no time to waste. I yank the vacuum pipe out of the car, open all the windows and the garage doors. Then I scramble into the driver's seat and, hands shaking, I release the hand brake. Veering out of the garage in a screech of tyres, I drive at the gates and down the gravel driveway.

In the back Lily stirs and sighs. I drive and drive down the winding tunnel of trees away from Sancreed, away from Joe until we hit the big Sainsbury's and the main road.

I don't look back.

Forty-seven

A month later

In her hand Lily clutches a bunch of delphiniums, Avery's favourite flower, and we walk slowly together across the field.

I was reluctant to return to Sancreed. I still get headaches sometimes and sudden waves of panic that can be overwhelming. But Lily wanted me to come with her to pay our respects and to help her collect some of her belongings from the house. I couldn't let her do it alone. Besides, she'll be moving to Germany to live with her dad soon, so this is my last chance to see her before she goes.

When we reach the hawthorne tree, newly in bud, she stops abruptly. 'It was here,' she says quietly.

There's nothing now but a patch of disturbed black earth.

Avery's body has been exhumed and cremated. Around the edges of that open wound, soft, green grass sprouts and, further in the woods at the edge of the field, a pool of bluebells shivers in the breeze.

Lily places the flowers on the ground and says a little prayer but then her self-control deserts her and she falls to her knees in the mud, sobbing as if her small body can't contain all the grief inside.

'It was my fault,' she wails.

I squat beside her and put my arm around her shoulders. 'You weren't to blame.'

'You don't understand. I helped him. It was because of me . . .' She sobs, wiping snot away with her sleeve and looking at me, her big, grey eyes shining with tears.

'Shh.' I take her hands and pull her to her feet. 'You don't have to explain.'

'But I want to,' she protests. 'We came here together, Joe and me, and we buried her. He said he would kill me if I didn't do as he said or if I told anyone. He said that if he didn't kill me, I would go to prison for aiding and abetting a murderer.'

'You must have been so scared,' I say.

I think guiltily of all the weeks I lived with Lily without noticing how terrified she was of Joe. I thought she was just a damaged and bolshy teenager. I was so wrapped up in Joe. I thought I was in love with him. When I think about it now, I feel sick.

'I can't believe I fell for his lies,' I say bitterly, as we walk on towards Carn Euny past the horses in the field. Sunlight falls gently on the grass in pools and a blackbird flaps past with a twig in its beak.

'Yeah, well, you weren't the only one,' she says.

Something in her voice sends a shiver of alarm up my spine. An idea that's been at the back of my mind for a while now leaps to the fore.

'You don't just mean Avery, do you?'

Her head drops. 'No, not my mother,' she whispers.

'Lily, do you mean . . .?' I take a deep ragged breath. 'I found a Valentine in the attic. Joe said it was from the barmaid at the Crown – Andrea. But it wasn't from her, was it?'

'No.' She shakes her head, and her voice is so quiet, it's almost lost in the rustle of the leaves in the wind.

'It was from you.'

'Yes.'

'How come you signed it A not L?'

'A was for Ariel. It was his nickname for me,' she says bitterly. 'You know, like Ariel in *The Little Mermaid*. Because I was such a good swimmer.'

'Oh.' My belly twists with nausea. I remember how Lily clammed up in the Admiral Benbow after Joe mentioned that they called her their little mermaid. I'd assumed it was because of simple grief for her mother's death but it turns out she was in the grip of a much darker and more complicated emotion. 'How long . . .?' I ask.

'It started just after my sixteenth birthday. My mother was in bed with flu, and he took me out alone on his boat. We stopped off at that cove we took you to. I knew it was wrong, but I was in love with him, and I thought he loved me.' She wipes her nose and stares savagely at the ground. 'But he doesn't love anyone. Only himself.'

She's right about that, I think. 'You can't blame yourself,' I say. 'You were just a child. You still are a child. You're a victim too.'

She looks stricken. 'But it was my fault. I'm the reason she died.'

'What do you mean?'

'My mother found the Valentine and confronted him. They fought. I heard them upstairs in the bedroom screaming at each other. She threatened to go to the police.'

'But I don't understand. You were sixteen. What he did with you was repulsive, but it wasn't illegal. The police couldn't have done anything.'

'She wasn't talking about my relationship with Joe. She was talking about the money that went missing at Holden and Pierce – the place where they used to work. She said something like, "I can't believe I covered for you. But I'm not going to anymore, not now I know what a piece of shit you are."'

'I see,' I say slowly.

Of course, it makes sense that it was Joe who embezzled the money, not Avery. But why did she agree to take the blame? How could an intelligent woman be so dumb? She must have been blindly in love with him. Like me.

'After she said that, everything went quiet,' Lily continues. 'I ran upstairs. But by the time I got there she was lying on the floor, and he was on top of her . . . strangling her. I tried to pull him off, but I wasn't strong enough.'

Joe lied about how Avery had died, I think bitterly – the same way he lied about so much else.

'Then he made you help him dispose of the body.'

She nods, wiping her nose. 'It was his idea to make it look as if she'd fallen from the cliffs. He thought if the police believed she'd been swept away in the storm, then they wouldn't search for her.'

I think about Joe's alibi. The sailing event in Southampton.

'And he made sure he was far away when you planted the evidence,' I say. It was his backup plan all along – to make sure Lily was implicated if anything went wrong.

'I should've gone to the police straight away,' she says, 'I should have . . .'

I put my arm round her. 'It's not your fault. You didn't kill her.'

She shrugs my hand away impatiently. 'I might as well have.'

We walk on and skirt the edge of Carn Euny.

'Your mother would have forgiven you,' I say, as we make our way across the field, through the stone remains.

'I don't think so.' Lily shakes her head. 'She must have hated me. I deserve to be hated.'

'She would have forgiven you, I'm sure.' I rummage in my bag and pull out the copy of *Falling* that I've brought. There's a passage in it that I wanted Lily to hear. 'Listen,' I say, 'I want to read you something. Let's stop here for a minute.'

We sit side by side on a low stone wall, and I turn to the final chapter. On the last page, Harry Hegarty is sitting in his caravan alone and watching a video that his ex-wife has sent him of his daughter. I clear my throat and read aloud.

'He lost count of the number of times he watched the video. She was a miracle. The way the light fell on her hair, the way she turned and laughed at something her boyfriend had said. It didn't matter that she wasn't speaking to him right now. It wouldn't matter if she never spoke to him again. His love for her was bone-deep and everlasting. It was enough to know that she was alive in this world and happy.'

'You see?' I say, 'That's about you. That's how your mother felt about you.'

'Do you think so?' Lily asks tremulously. A large tear rolls down her cheek.

'I'm sure,' I say firmly.

*

We walk on and reach the cloughtie-covered tree. Lily has brought a small photo of Avery, which she ties to one of the branches.

'She believed in stuff like that,' she says. 'You know, the magic of nature and the old Celtic spirits.'

On the back of the photo, Lily's written 'I love you forever', in black felt tip.

I look at the writing, remembering the message Joe burnt.

'It was you who put that note through my door, wasn't it?' I say.

She grimaces. 'Yes. But it wasn't because I was jealous – well, maybe I was a little. But by that time, I knew what he was, who he was, and I hated him too. I sent the note as a warning. I was trying to protect you.'

I nod. 'But I didn't listen.'

'No.'

Perhaps Lily wasn't the only one who was jealous, I think, remembering Joe's inexplicable animosity towards Josh with a twist of nausea.

'He's locked up now. He can't hurt us,' I say.

It's true. Joe has been charged with first degree murder and attempted murder. He was discharged from hospital a few days ago and is now in Long Lartin prison awaiting trial. With Avery's body and our testimony, there should be enough evidence to put him away for a long time.

Last night, one of the warders phoned and told me Joe had asked for me to be on his list of people he could phone. I refused, of course. I don't want to speak to him ever again in my life.

'How's your brother?' I ask Lily as we make our way back to the house.

'He's okay. He just feels guilty he didn't do or say anything.'

I remember the sense I had that Gabe was holding something back when I spoke to him in London.

'How much did he know?' I ask.

She grimaces. 'He didn't know about the murder, but he knew about Joe and me. Mum told him when she went to visit him just before she died. It's not his fault. He wanted to tell the police, but I persuaded him not to.'

When Lily and I get back to the house there's a small, white van parked outside, and the front door is flung wide open. Music is playing, Tom Jones's deep voice blaring out into the quiet, spring sunshine.

Joe, I think, a pulse of alarm shooting up my spine.

Next to me Lily stiffens, and I guess she's had the same thought. But it can't be Joe. He's safely locked up. I clasp her hand for reassurance. Hers or mine, I'm not sure which.

'We can do this,' I murmur.

In the hallway we squeeze past a couple of large cardboard

339

boxes and find the source of the music, a transistor radio on top of the dresser. And in the living room there's an old lady. She's kneeling on the floor, sealing a box labelled 'books' with duct tape.

'Oh, hi,' she greets us cheerily, snipping the tape with a large pair of scissors and scrambling nimbly to her feet. She's a small, birdlike woman with skinny legs and a barrel body.

'You must be Lily,' she says. 'I must say, you're even prettier than your pictures.'

Lily looks as startled as I feel.

The woman gives a tinkling little laugh. 'I'm sorry, I should explain. You don't know who I am. I'm Joe's mother, Donna.'

She tilts her head to one side and examines me. 'And I suppose you're Alex. Joe's told me all about you.'

I'm lost for words, completely nonplussed by her conversational friendliness. You would never guess from her tone that her son had recently been arrested for murder.

'I'm just collecting a few of his things,' she explains. 'I wasn't expecting anyone to be here. I've packed away the kettle, but I've got a Thermos of tea. Would you like some?'

We sit at the kitchen table and sip tea out of plastic mugs, while she keeps up a steady stream of chatter. I try to reconcile the woman in front of me with the woman who created and nurtured a monster like Joe, but I can't.

She seems like a very ordinary, pleasant sort of person. The only thing that she has in common with Joe seems to be a total lack of shame. It's jarring. I don't expect her to take responsibility for her son's actions, but some acknowledgement of what he's done would be nice. So, I find myself saying pointedly:

'We were just visiting the place where he buried Avery's body before we came here.'

She turns to Lily. 'Yes, your poor mother.' She shakes her head sadly. 'I don't know how it came to that. Joe was such a sweet little boy. He always did have a bit of a temper mind you.'

I swallow an angry retort and glance anxiously at Lily who is staring steadily into her tea.

Lily stands up abruptly. 'I'm just going up to my room,' she says tightly, heading to the door.

I wonder if I should follow her, but Donna is continuing obliviously and has produced a small photo album from her bag. She thrusts it under my nose.

'This is Joe when he was a baby, and this –' she turns a page – 'is Joe on his sixth birthday. He was always a good boy.'

I stare blankly at an image of a plump, brown-haired boy grinning in front of a large birthday cake decorated as a football pitch. I don't think I would have recognised him if she hadn't told me it was him. Donna flicks through more photos: Joe on his bike, Joe at the beach with a bucket and spade, Joe on a seesaw. I'm struck by the fact that he always seems to be on his own.

'Have you got any photos of Chris?' I ask.

'Chris?' She looks bewildered.

'His brother, Chris.'

'Joe didn't have a brother. He was an only child.'

'But he told me . . .' I break off, sighing. What's the point? Of course, he lied. Why should I be surprised?

Donna frowns. 'He did have a friend called Christopher at secondary school. They were very close – maybe he thought of him as a brother.'

'Did Christopher die of an overdose?'

'Not to my knowledge. He was a very clever boy. He went to Cambridge to study physics I think.'

'So, he was there at the same time as Joe?'

She blinks at me. 'At Cambridge? Bless you, no. Joe studied at Southampton. But as far as I know he'd dropped out after a couple of months.'

'As far as you know?'

'Yes, he'd broken off all contact by then. I think he went travelling in Australia and South East Asia. But I didn't hear from him for years after. Not until a few months ago in fact.'

I think about what Joe told me about his dad – how much he hated him.

'I suppose he broke off contact because of his dad,' I say tentatively, because by now I'm starting to doubt everything he ever told me.

She laughs, surprised. 'Well, he didn't really know his dad. He left when Joe was still a baby.'

I absorb this information in silence, sipping cold tea that tastes of plastic and rancid milk. Of all Joe's lies I think this is the one that hurts the most. He used his dad's fictional abuse as a way to create a bond between us. And it worked. I remember feeling so close to him that evening in the restaurant when he told me all about his childhood. And now it turns out to be just more of his bullshit. He was manipulating me all along. Was anything he ever told me real?

Forty-eight

Before we leave for London, I stop by at Charlie's house to pick up the portrait of Avery and to see Barney.

The two dogs bound up to me. Marshall dances round me yapping excitedly and Barney puts his large paws on my shoulders and licks my face enthusiastically as I crouch down to greet him.

'Thank you so much for taking him in,' I say to Charlie. 'I don't think he would have been happy stuck in our tiny London flat with me and my sister out all day.'

'It's my pleasure. He's a lovely dog. The only problem is that Marshall is madly jealous of him, aren't you, you daft bugger?' he says, scratching Marshall's neck.

'I'm sorry it's taken me so long to get around to collecting the painting,' I say.

'No problem. It's round the back here.' He leads me to a

small space at the far end of his studio. 'To be honest, I didn't think you'd come, what with all that went on. Are you okay?'

I nod. 'I still get headaches sometimes but I'm okay.'

He shakes his head. 'I had no idea. What a bastard. I wish Avery had told me what was going on. I might have been able to help.'

'I'm sorry,' I say. 'Andrea told me you were . . . close.'

He stares at me. Then laughs. 'You think . . .? No, Andrea has a vivid imagination. We were friends, that's all.'

He pulls his phone out of his back pocket and shows me a photo. It's of a handsome man with grey hair and a tanned face. 'This is my boyfriend, Simon,' he tells me. 'He lives in London, but he's been talking about moving down here.'

'Oh.' Not for the first time, I feel pretty foolish.

'Avery and I were just friends. Not even all that close. But I liked her. She was a nice woman, funny and self-deprecating. Some people thought she was stand-offish, but I think she was just shy.'

He turns a canvas round. 'Here you are. Hope you like it.'

'I love it.'

I'm not lying. The portrait is very good. Avery is instantly recognisable. He's captured her cool beauty well, the ash-blonde hair, the slightly imperious curve of her neck. But there's something in her eyes that I never noticed in her photos – a warmth and humour, and behind the warmth a shadow of uncertainty – of fear.

Forty-nine

Over the next few days in London, I gradually slot back into my old routine. Fortunately for me, Mindy has landed a new job in Manchester so I'm able to move back in with Athena and carry on with my old job at the *Post*. I try hard to throw myself into my work and put everything that happened in Sancreed behind me. But it's not easy. Every night I'm plagued by nightmares and sometimes when I'm walking down the street or on the tube, I'll see someone who resembles Joe and I'll stop in my tracks, overwhelmed by panic, unable to move or breathe.

Eventually, a couple of weeks after my return to London, I realise that I'm never going to find peace, or get the closure I need unless I confront Joe directly. The thought of seeing him again is terrifying, but when I phone the Prison Visitor Booking Office, they suggest arranging a non-contact meeting and assure me that there will always be an officer present. I figure I can probably handle seeing him if there's a strong pane of glass separating us.

In the event though, when I arrive at the visitor centre and sit down opposite him, it's still a shock, though not exactly in the way I expected.

His smile is so familiar and natural, and he looks at me in that disarming way he always has, with those melting sugar-brown eyes, as if I'm the only person in the world. And for one dizzy and disorientating moment, it's not horror I feel, but the ghost of love.

'I've missed you, Alex,' he says in his soft Cornish burr. And, God help me, for just a split second I want him to wrap me in his arms and tell me that the last month was nothing but a bad dream. But then he begins to talk about his case, about how he thinks his lawyer is letting him down by making him plead guilty, and I remember it was him, *he* was the bad dream, and any residue of love I feel is rapidly replaced by anger and disgust.

'So, you're giving the lawyer the same old bullshit you fed me,' I say. 'Why don't you tell me what really happened with Avery? Why did you kill her?'

'What do you mean?' His smile freezes, his eyes suddenly hard and watchful.

'You told me her death was an accident.'

'It was.'

'You said she hit her head on the fireplace, but Lily saw you strangle her.'

He sighs and then speaks slowly as if he's explaining something to somebody very simple. 'Alex, you must see that Lily's lying.'

'Why would she lie?'

'Isn't it obvious? Poor kid. It's not really her fault. She had this hopeless crush on me. I thought it was harmless at first and I tried to ignore it as much as I could, but she wouldn't leave me alone and when I rejected her advances, she became vindictive.' He shakes his head, warming to his theme. 'She lied to Avery about us and managed to turn her against me. That's the reason Avery and I argued. I didn't mean to hurt her, but the fight got physical. She pushed me and I pushed her back and she fell and hit her head.'

So, he's sticking to that story.

'And then when you and I got together,' he adds, 'Lily was so jealous. You remember how hostile she was towards you?'

I nod mutely. I can't speak. Rage is boiling up inside me, but I want to wait and hear him out. There's a cold hard part of me that is curious to see how far he'll go with his lies.

'I didn't want to say anything to you at the time,' he continues, 'but she was acting up because she was so jealous of you. And she's lying now because she'd say anything to get

348

revenge on me. Hell hath no fury like a woman scorned, as they say.'

Bile rises in my throat. I'm pretty sure that when we hear the pathologist's evidence in court it will confirm Lily's version of events. But there's no point in pursuing this conversation any longer. He's obviously never going to tell the truth about Avery's death or the real nature of his relationship with Lily. So, instead, I ask him about the copy of *Falling* and the note I received at the beginning of all this. The question of who sent it has been bothering me ever since I got that message from Avery's publisher saying it wasn't them.

'It was you who sent me Avery's book, wasn't it?' I hazard.

And to my surprise he doesn't even try to deny it. He just nods and smiles. 'Yeah. That was me.'

I think about the slight difference in style and writing quality between the parts that dealt with Rebecca's death and the rest of the book.

'You changed the way that Rebecca died.'

He grins and leans back, putting his hands behind his head and looking pleased with himself. 'Yeah, that's right. In the original she drowned in the bath and the painter dumped her body in the sea. I altered it so that Rebecca's death would match Avery's. It didn't take long. I knocked it up over that weekend in Southampton. Then I emailed Avery's agent with the changes, pretending to be Avery.

I needed money and her books weren't selling very well. I hoped that people would take notice of the similarities between the book and real life and that it would help to stimulate sales. But no one paid any attention, so I decided to send it to you.'

And I fell right in with his plans like a gullible idiot, I think.

'Why did you choose me in particular?' I ask.

'I don't know. Maybe it was fate. I found your details online. You worked for a prestigious newspaper and, well . . .' He leans forward and smiles. 'I liked your picture.'

I ignore the flirtatious way he says this. I'm revolted by him, and I can't believe he seems to think that he still has a chance of winning me over. 'Weren't you worried about drawing attention to her death?' I say coldly. 'Weren't you concerned that the police would open an investigation?'

'Not really. I had a watertight alibi thanks to Lily, and I was confident I could make the police think she'd been killed by a deranged fan if they did suspect foul play.'

'So, all that stuff about a stalker. You made that up?'

'Well no, not entirely. She did receive some pretty weird messages. But the phone calls never happened.'

How easy I was to manipulate, I think ruefully, and I remember the article I wrote – the article that has made him a rich man. I'm not sure what will happen to the royalties from Avery's book now. But I know I'm going to do everything in my power to make sure that money goes to Gabe and Lily and not to him.

'You look angry.' He puts his head on one side and gives me a lopsided smile. 'You get a little crease in your forehead when you're angry. It's really cute, do you know that?'

I resist the urge to punch the glass. Instead, I clench my fists by my sides and say carefully, 'The day after I came back from London, the first time, I saw someone smoking in the window. A woman. Was it Andrea?'

'Andrea?' His eyes widen – all innocence. 'No, that must have been Lily.'

'It wasn't Lily. I'm sure. Don't lie to me. I know it was Andrea.'

He lifts his hands up as if he's surrendering and his smile broadens. 'Okay, you got me. Andrea came round that night. But you and I weren't an item at that point and anyway she never meant anything to me. You're the only person I've ever truly loved. You're my girl, Alex.'

He leans forward and gazes at me with a pretty good facsimile of love. 'I think we could forgive each other anything,' he says. 'I've already forgiven you for this.' He lifts his prison issue grey sweatshirt, showing me a long straight scar above the other, older scar.

I wince and draw in my breath.

'I was lucky. It could have been a lot worse.' He grins. 'You only punctured my liver. The doctor said you missed my heart by a few millimetres. I don't think it was an accident that you missed. I don't think you could have killed me. Not really. You love me. We're meant to be together.'

I take a deep breath, my heart hammering in my chest.

'I don't love you. And you certainly don't love me,' I say loudly and clearly. 'I don't think you know the meaning of the word and I never want to see or speak to you again.'

I watch his face darken with anger and then before he has the chance to reply I hang up my phone, stand up and leave the room.

Fifty

Ruby winds her way over the sofa and up onto my leg. I sit very still.

'Go on, you can do it,' says Athena.

Cautiously, I touch the snake's skin and feel the muscles moving underneath. It's a strange feeling but not totally unpleasant.

'See. There's nothing to be scared of. She's quite sweet really.'

'I wouldn't go that far,' I laugh. I think I'll always be scared of snakes. But recently I've learned that my fear doesn't need to define my actions. After facing up to Joe, I feel that I can face anything. Even the past. Even the mistakes I have made.

'I'm sorry,' I say to Athena as she slides Ruby back into her cage. 'Do you think you'll ever forgive me?'

'What for?'

'I think you know.'

Her face puckers in confusion. 'No, I really don't. Do you mean for ignoring my advice and leaving me alone in London? Because . . . it was fine really . . .'

'No, I don't mean that.' I suck in my breath. The words are sharp as knives in my throat, but they need to be said. 'I'm sorry I was a coward. I'm sorry for just standing there when you tried to save Mum.'

Athena stares at me in surprise. 'It wasn't your fault. Lexie. She was already dead. You knew that.'

'I thought you blamed me.'

'Of course I didn't.' Her face twists with an old pain. 'I thought you blamed *me*.'

'What? Why?'

'Don't you remember? That Christmas we came to England. It was me who made her go back.'

I do remember.

That Christmas, Athena cried every day. Our apartment in London was small and cramped compared to the spacious, light-filled rooms we were used to, and every day was cold and dark as if someone had sucked away the sun. We were both homesick, but Athena was more vocal about it than me and after one day when Athena begged Mum to take us home, she finally agreed. Not long after, we packed up our bags and flew back to Cyprus. Dad was at the airport to greet us with a bag of pick and mix sweets each for me and Athena and a diamond necklace for my mother.

'Everything will be different from now on,' he said.

And for a while it was. Until it wasn't. Then three months later we found Mum in the swimming pool along with all the dead cockroaches and ants.

'It was her decision to return,' I say. 'You weren't the reason she went back. I think she would have gone anyway. She loved him. She was obsessed with him. She couldn't keep away.'

Athena looks at me with something like hope in her eyes. 'Do you really think so?'

'I do,' I say firmly. 'We've both been blaming ourselves. But it wasn't our fault. It was him. He abused her verbally and physically until her self-esteem was so low, she couldn't take it anymore. She didn't even think about us because she thought we'd be better off without her.'

'It wasn't all Dad's fault,' says Athena. 'He was no saint, that's for sure. He was definitely partly to blame, and he certainly didn't handle the whole situation very well, but it wasn't easy for him. She was mentally ill.'

'That's what he wants us to believe.'

Athena shakes her head. 'No, it was true,' she insists. 'Don't you remember? She used to bash her head against the wall sometimes and scream and throw things at him.'

I stare at Athena, astonished. Is it possible that I've

blanked this out of my memory? I think of that stormy night I came downstairs and saw my parents struggling, I assumed he hit her head against the wall. But perhaps he was actually trying to stop her hurting herself. I've been wrong about so much. Could I have been wrong about that too?

'You might be right,' I say slowly. 'God, it's amazing we've both turned out as sane as we have, with the upbringing we had.'

Athena laughs. 'You speak for yourself,' she says. 'I don't know that I'm all that sane.' Then she stops laughing and fixes earnest, brown eyes on mine. 'But seriously though, Alex. I think I only made it through my childhood because of you.'

I'm deeply touched. At this moment I feel closer than ever to her.

'I feel the same way,' I say. 'I love you, little sis.'

'Aw, stop it. You're going to make me cry and I don't want to ruin my make-up. I'm going out with Ben in a minute.' She glances at her phone. 'Jesus. That reminds me, I'll be late if I don't get a move on. See you later, Alex.' She kisses me on the cheek. Then she picks up her bag and breezes out of the house, slamming the door behind her.

Once she's gone, I go to the kitchen and pour myself a lemonade. Then I pad out into the garden on bare feet.

It's a beautiful, warm day. The grass is soft and dry under-foot. A bird is trilling in the neighbour's tree and there's a low background hum of traffic. I feel happy and light. I sit on one of the garden chairs and lift my face to the sun. Everything's going to be okay, I think.

I've been sitting here just a few minutes when the blissful peace is broken by the sound of the phone buzzing in my pocket and an instinctive pulse of alarm shoots up my spine. But I'm learning how to deal with the panic. I inhale slowly, telling myself to stay calm. I've changed my number; it can't be Joe.

It's not. It's a message from Lou. I shield the phone from the glare of the sun with my hand and squint at the screen.

Have you had any more thoughts about writing the true story of Avery Lewis? she's written. *I know that it must all still be quite raw for you, but I do think we should strike while the iron is hot and interest in the case is high. You never know, you may find that it's cathartic getting it all down on paper.*

I smile to myself at Lou's clumsy attempt at sensitivity. But she might have a point. Perhaps it would help to write about everything that happened. Besides, I know that it'll make a great feature and I never could resist a good story. I slot the phone back in my pocket and wander into the house. Then I sit at the desk in my bedroom, looking out at the red brick wall and the green shoots sprouting in its crevices. Life finds a way, even in such a barren environment, I think, and I open a new document on my laptop and begin to type.